I0770855

AT THE
Heart
OF THE
Game

ALSO BY PAULA BENGE

A Neapolitan Fairy Tale at Lake Okoboji

PAULA BENGE

Published by Walking Hill Press

ISBN: 979-8-9913320-0-2
Ebook: B0DCCZ5KWR

Cover design by Annemieke Beemster Leverenz
Cover photo by Dawn Muncy

Printed in the United States of America

Chapter 1

Outside the batter's box, the college recruit swings her bat like a storm gathering strength. Number Eleven is a double threat—fast and powerful. And, after three at-bats, facing her for a fourth time sets my fingers drumming on my thigh.

"Come on," I breathe as her gaze darts to my sweaty fingers. "Let's play."

She swings again, thumping her back with the bat. Cheers mixed with jeers spill onto the field. Dads enthusiastically ump from the side, feeding off each other as if the high school state championship is personally on the line for them.

It's not annoyance that keeps me from glancing over, but a stab of grief. If my dad were here, I *know* he'd be smack in the middle of them, so full of nervous energy he couldn't sit, and memorizing each play. Instead, he's missing and doesn't even know we're here.

Maddie appears, striding up on my right in that fearless way third basemen have.

"We've got all day, River." She pitches her voice to carry as she punches her glove. Her sly gaze slides from me to Eleven. "It's not your fault you're intimidating."

Eleven ignores her.

I should turn away, hold up two fingers for the outfield, smooth my braid, swipe the dirt with my hand—anything to stay loose. But I've done all of that already. Behind home plate, Jaiden frowns at Eleven, her catcher's helmet dangling from her fingers.

The umpire steps back. "Time." He points to Eleven's coach.

I groan, ripping off my glove and smacking my leg. Eleven's coach is calm as he pulls her close by the shoulder. Which is all... nice, but it isn't how my dad taught me to play. And I didn't practice my tail off over the last year for my looks. I need Eleven's coach to march her to the batter's box and shove her over the line so we can get this done.

A gritty country song blasts across the Oklahoma City stadium as my infielders join me in the pitching circle. Even here, where the Women's College World Series is played, I duck my head to see their faces rather than the tops of their heads. The tallest barely reaches my chin, but at six-feet tall, I'm used to this view.

Maddie leans close. "Eleven is officially a rain-delay human." Her mischief is underlined by broken wings of eye-black across her cheeks.

Shortstop Katelynn snorts.

Second baseman Meagan raises her hand. "Can I be one too?"

"No." Katelynn laughs, and Jaiden gives me a wry grin. But my attention wanders to Eleven nodding solemnly at her coach.

Jaiden turns to the first baseman. "Brooke, hurry and tag Eleven out, will ya? Let's wrap this up and go eat."

"I'm in," Maddie says and fist bumps Brooke, fire replacing her humor. "It's sacrifice-your-body time. Make good throws. We're getting this out."

Brooke smirks and nods to the stands. "That'll show Coach O'Daniel what we think about him recruiting Eleven for her bat."

Judging by the hush, that missed the mark. Maddie and Jaiden are college recruits, too. And earning a scholarship to keep playing? That's all I've ever wanted, especially if it was a chance to play for someone like O'Daniel. It's true that Eleven's reputation for home runs paved the way for a great coach to believe in her. Still, she's lucky. We all want to impress him.

One by one, they shift, peering at Eleven as the silence between us grows. I slide my glove on and tug the laces. *College recruit.* We can't screw up. Eleven is too good.

Jaiden re-tucks the back of her jersey. Meagan fixes her ponytail. No one makes eye contact. Our school has never brought home a state softball trophy. Although, the way they avoid my eyes is a sharp reminder of how close we were last year.

Katelynn clears her throat. "I don't know where Coach is taking us for dinner." She smirks. "But dessert is on me for whoever gets this out."

Our attention shifts as fast as trout to a minnow.

"Are you serious?" Jaiden's blue eyes narrow as she leans past my oversized shadow.

"Yup." Katelynn grins. "But who says I won't be keeping it myself?"

Brooke snickers, and Meagan rolls her eyes, but Eleven nods. Maybe her coach is telling her to watch my curveball in case I leave it hanging like last year. Heat rises, prickling my cheeks. It's okay, we'll get them this year.

That's what my teammates say to my face. But they're so agonizingly careful not to mention what happened that it seems to grow between us.

I glance at Mom and Grandma in the stands. If only Dad were here. He'd know what to do about that hanging curveball. I scuff the dirt with my cleat. The thing that haunts my days and nights is not knowing where he is. If those holding him against his will knew how much I needed him… Well, let's just say if he were here, everything would be different. But, as it is, not even my brothers have time for me.

Then Eleven's coach taps her helmet, and Jaiden straightens. "Here we go."

"You've got this, Seven." Maddie pins me with her gaze.

"Let's do it." I force a wicked grin as the others bump gloves and leave the mound.

Jaiden lingers, covering her mouth. "Keep it low, okay?"

My grin disappears. "If she tries to bunt, I'll put it way out in the black. She's super-fast."

"She won't bunt with two outs," Jaiden scoffs. "And she won't surprise us. Work the count, Harte." She holds my gaze as she slides her catcher's helmet on and swaggers back to home plate, leaving me alone.

"You've got this," I tell myself. "You know what to do." And I do, but…

I pick up the resin bag, bouncing it in my hand as my chest tightens. In a small, dark way, I wish there was someone else. Someone to finish this and not let my team down—again. Because, although there's more to me than softball, it's the shiny part. And people think they have the right to judge me by what my performance means to them, rather than to me. I fling the resin aside and swallow.

Jaiden's waiting, staring as if she can read my mind. And, best friend that she is, she deliberately uncurls her middle finger in the shade of her thigh. I choke back a grin as Eleven steps back in the box.

But after all that stalling, Eleven watches my change-up strike and swings at my rise ball. That fast, it's a zero-two count—no balls and two strikes. I punch the air triumphantly—on the inside. She's right where I want her. Let's get this done... *except...*

Her steely gaze meets mine and certainty settles like a plunging elevator. She hasn't struck out once today. She's not worried... she's ready.

And, as if testing me, Coach Rogers calls a curveball.

My stomach tightens. I give Jaiden a slight shake of my head. *Help me out here, Jaid.* But she nods, as if it's just a curve, and I can do it, no problem.

She's wrong. As soon as it snaps, I know. Eleven drops her hands and swings.

It's an awkward arc, but the crack of her bat sends lightning skittering down my spine. The ball soars overhead, and I refuse to admire the power that hit took. Or the heat that sends it rocketing like a stupid home run. Again.

Eleven is almost to first base before her bat hits the ground. Brooke can only watch as she flies past. The ball nicks the top of the outfield fence and ricochets. Relief that it's not a home run evaporates as Eleven cranks up her speed.

Our right fielder and center fielder barrel toward each other, focused on the ball. Eleven rips through second.

The center fielder scoops the ball and fires, but Eleven pounds third and heads home. It's up to me to cut the throw and give us a last chance at an out. My body tenses as hours of practice take over—cut the throw, send it home, get the out. Cut the throw. Send it home...

Without warning, Jaiden yells, "Four! Four!"

I duck immediately, the ball crossing where I'd stood. But my breath catches. A long throw from center to home? If we miss, she has a sure in-the-park home run.

I turn as Eleven launches herself, hands-first, into a dive at home. Jaiden lunges for the ball, then swivels forward, glove slicing Eleven's path like a sword and—

They crash in a violent heap of color.

I freeze, unable to look away. Even the breeze dies. A sheer cloud of dust drifts above their tangled limbs. Then Jaiden, smeared in dirt, her chest protector pushed off center, thrusts her glove high. At the sight of the ball, the ump ninja-punches the air.

Eleven's. Out. Game over.

In slow motion, my gaze shifts to Jaiden. There's a roar that's not all in my head as she surges to her feet beside a dazed Eleven and whips off her helmet, slinging it behind her with a grin.

Fans spring from their seats. My teammates pour onto the field. Then Jaiden leaps on me at full speed, and I squeeze, chest protector and all, staggering under her weight. Someone yells, "We won! State Champs!" I'm not sure if it's her or me.

The tidal wave of girls swamps us, pulling us under, then pushing us up again. I lean on them, not sure if I can stand by myself. When we break apart, salty and wet, I'm ready for the pomp and circumstance of victory. I want it all. Since it has cost me so much to get here, I want it to be a freaking big deal.

But the aftermath of winning is a blur—fast streaks of color and sound. No matter how much I try to hold on to the moments, they slip past, leaving a cocoon of happiness surrounding my heart that all the sweat and dirt and cold rivulets from the ice bag wrapped to my shoulder can't dim.

Finally, Mom appears and wraps me in a hug. Her ribs are solid under my arms.

My smile falters.

"He'd be proud, honey," she whispers, warm against my ear as I lower my head to her shoulder. "When he comes back, you'll tell him all about this."

I close my eyes at the familiar tightening around my chest. Here's another thing I'll add to the list to tell him, but it'll be too late. Dad won't *see* what he helped me accomplish. He won't feel lung-jarring claps on the back. Or pose in pictures. He won't taste victory or share triumph.

My chin wobbles. Why did he have to go? Why didn't we take him and run away while we could? Then we wouldn't live in this agony of wishing he was back.

Grandma, being Grandma, taps my back. She isn't having any of this watery-eyed stuff. She pulls me into a brisk hug, then pushes me to arm's length to peer into my wet face. "You ready for the trip tonight? You're not too tired for baseball tomorrow, are you?"

"Game seven?" I smile for her, wiping my cheek with my palm. "There's no such thing as too tired for the World Series. Are you kidding?"

Jaiden and Maddie thread through the crowd and head straight for us. I gesture to Grandma. "She asked if we're ready to go."

"There's more." Grandma presses something into my hand. "Congratulations, girls."

For a second, I stare at the tickets. Then I look into her smug eyes. "Behind the scenes tour of the stadium? How?" But Jaiden and Maddie bounce with excitement, and my jaw drops. "You knew?"

"My dad's letting me drive." Jaiden's practically vibrating.

As I watch her, another terrible truth twists my heart. Jaiden and I have played our last game together after all of these years side-by-side, T-ball to varsity. Next August, she'll leave for Oklahoma State, and I'll stay at the junior college. We'll never be the same.

To keep from falling apart, I surge and catch Jaiden and Maddie in a desperate hug. They giggle as we nearly topple over, then tug me into a silly dance I can't refuse. Grandma claps, laughing delightedly, and the sight brightens my heart.

We'd have kept going, celebrating and simply living, except, out of nowhere, Coach Rogers appears.

I stop mid-twirl at the sight of him, and my mind short-circuits, finally overwhelmed. I barely feel Maddie bounce off me with a grunt. Jaiden sputters to a stop, laughter dying in her throat as Coach gestures with an unusually formal air to the older man beside him. Parents and players pause to whisper on the landing.

But I only have eyes for Coach O'Daniel. And he stares right back.

Chapter 2

Everyone knows Coach O'Daniel is one of the best college softball coaches around. But for me, it's more than that. He looks exactly as he had when I was thirteen, even though he'd seemed old then with his snowy mustache and white hair. At his Northbridge University softball camp, I'd thought he'd looked like Teddy Roosevelt with a softball bat. Later, I realized that was too simple. He's much more intimidating than that.

"River," Coach Rogers says. "I'd like you to meet Coach O'Daniel."

I recall all the years I spent trying to get recruited for college, dreaming of a moment like this. Instead, I had one setback after another until the Division I rosters—even Coach O'Daniel's—had filled for my class. Next month, I'll sign with the junior college, so why meet now? He isn't here to talk about playing for him. I mean, it's too late, isn't it? No. It must be something else.

Then O'Daniel smiles, his great mustache spread like bird wings, and the world tilts. Does he remember that bench at Northbridge's softball camp? And the crying camper with tie-dyed socks? My face heats as I remember the way I'd fallen apart that day, yet when Jaiden and Maddie let go, I'm drawn to him, searching for hints of the compassionate person I'd known.

"Congratulations, River," O'Daniel says. "Nice job today. Now, I hear you haven't committed to a college..."

I drop my gaze before he can see how much that hurt. I'd yearned to have somewhere to commit to, worked for it year after year. Prayed for it. No one would have me except the junior college.

"... we've had a pitching position that's opened unexpectedly," he says, and, finally, his words register. My gaze flies to his. "An athlete who'd committed to us has changed her mind."

I frown at this bizarre statement.

He gestures to the field. "We came to watch Andy, number eleven. She's our top recruit."

I blink. Eleven's name is Andy?

"But you two battled it out." He nods once. "Like I said, excellent job."

Coach Rogers murmurs, "I can't believe they sent Eleven home at the end. I mean, I'm not complaining, but you never want a third out at home..."

Coach O'Daniel blinks politely, but turns to me. "As you know, Andy's got a big bat and lots of speed, but your pitches were moving. You have good instincts."

His eyes twinkle, and it's so familiar. Like the look Dad had when we'd rehash each play on the way home from a game. A warmth sparks in my chest where cold has reigned for so long.

He studies me. "We'd love to recruit an athlete of your caliber to Northbridge. Would you be interested in seeing what we have to offer?"

"Yes." I feel the smile on my face, but... is he for real? "Absolutely."

He hesitates. "This is such an unusual situation that I'll just ask. Do you have plans tomorrow?"

My smile fades. My brows pucker. I turn from him to Mom as sympathy fills her face. Over her shoulder, Jaiden pales, and Maddie looks like she's been sucker-punched.

"I know we're four hours away," Coach O'Daniel says. "But if you can make it to our recruited training camp tomorrow, you'll meet varsity players. I think you'll fit right in."

And just that quick, every disappointment over softball, every heartbreak in life, rips me anew. I avoid the others' gazes, but sense their restlessness. We've planned this trip forever, saved our cash, and made a playlist for the drive. This is our untouchable weekend.

"Um, I... have plans tomorrow." I twist my hands. "Is there another time?"

Coach O'Daniel tugs the edges of his windbreaker. "Of course. We'll make another day work closer to Christmas. We'll be busy with pre-season training over the winter break and start our season in February instead of the fall, like your high school."

Christmas? And it's October now. I'm not the only senior waiting for her break. Other pitchers will learn about this opening, if they haven't already. What if someone more qualified snatches this opportunity from me?

"Luck happens when preparation meets opportunity." Dad's favorite saying pops into my head, just as inconvenient now as the first time he'd said it.

But the Series doesn't always have a game seven, and I've *never* had tickets before. Tickets and friends and plans. Coach O'Daniel loves sports. He wouldn't want me to miss this, right? Just this once, can't I have both? Is the first of December so bad?

Shafts of early evening sunlight shine on the coach's white hair and make his blue eyes glow. He tucks his hands in his windbreaker pockets, just as he'd done at camp, and something twists inside me.

Playing for O'Daniel is my dream, a once-in-a-lifetime opportunity. Giving up a weekend of fun to play ball is nothing new. I've done it for years. I swallow past the lump in my throat.

"Tomorrow is fine," I say, then wince as the sound of Grandma's gasp probably reaches the parking lot.

Chapter 3

The barn is dark when I get home, and the house feels as cheerful as a funeral home. I'd expected to be happily tucked in a car with my best friends by now, watching miles roll by. Instead, I start my old farm truck and bump over rutted tracks to the back pasture.

My brothers' truck lights grow as I near the troublesome spot where the creek crosses under our fence. Always vulnerable to a gulley-washer rain—and slick as muddy snot when wet—it *had* to be fixed today before more calves escaped. Of course. No one can say my twin brothers aren't diligent about their work. They've attacked it with the same gusto they threw at college, and sports, and... finding Dad.

I get out and nearly trip over the four boots littered on the grass by the pickups. Zeph squints against the headlights to nod hello. He turns back to the creek, and my eyebrows rise at the annoyance on his face. At least he's *wearing* his boots along with his frown. On the far side, our best friend Fletch, also wearing boots, sports a similar expression. Their clothes are dark and damp, smeared in red mud.

From below the bank, there's a sudden yelp and splash. Zeph and Fletch burst into laughter.

I rush over, afraid of what I'll see. But Kody, Zeph's identical twin, is fine. He's thigh deep in the dark water with the newly repaired fence bobbing securely behind him, although he isn't looking at it. He reaches into the swirling water and rescues a drenched baseball hat, then bends again, and hauls a spluttering stranger upright in a muddy gush.

"I told you it was slick, Ty," Kody says testily.

The new guy straightens, a few inches shy of Kody's six-foot-eight height. He spits into the creek, shaking his short, dark hair like a wet dog. He takes his hat, beating water from it against his leg, and turns to glare at Fletcher, who's still sputtering chuckles.

"Nope." Zeph smirks, all signs of displeasure gone. "No free steak dinners, after all, Kody. Your lucky hat has let you down."

"Leave my hat out of this. It's still dry," Kody snaps. "And we were finished."

"The bet was for neither of you to go under." Zeph crosses his arms.

Kody spits downstream and shakes his head. Ty turns gingerly, wiping a wet arm across his forehead. But as he lowers his water-logged hat to his head, he spots me leaning against the pickup. His lips part, and his dark eyes widen. Uncertain, I manage a casual two-fingered wave, and he blinks.

Kody follows his gaze. "Riv? What're you doing here?"

With a fortifying breath, I straighten. "New plans. Jaiden's scalping my ticket."

"What?" Kody rears back. "You're the biggest baseball fan I've ever seen."

"Cardinals' fan." I hunch my shoulders. "And the others went without me."

Zeph tugs off his gloves. Across the creek, Fletch studies me as he picks up tools. He's always wanted me to join him at Northbridge University. Next year, as a sophomore, will he still want to play big brother? Do I want him to? His protectiveness can rival my actual brothers. Still, I love I can count on the 152-pound wrestler in him to always have my back.

It's just... too painful to think about, though, while the ache from watching my friends leave is so fresh.

"What happened?" Kody scowls. And it's that tone of his.

Freaking predictable. Actually, I should probably thank him. It's much more gratifying to glare at him. Worlds better than feeling sad.

"You should congratulate me, Kod. I'm going on a recruitment visit tomorrow."

"The junior college already wants you." He grabs a sapling for leverage as he climbs the slick bank of the creek, Ty behind him. "You're nuts to miss the World Series."

"Who is it?" Zeph lowers his voice. "Is it Division I? Dad would be so excited."

Dad would be ecstatic. And *he* might've figured out how to do both the recruitment and the baseball game. Who knows what might've happened if he'd been here.

"It's Northbridge."

Kody's surprise is gratifying.

"No way." Fletch grins as he cautiously crosses the creek, boots under his arm. "Hey, we'll show you around." He gestures toward Ty, whose dark eyes land on each of us in turn.

"But it's four hours away." As usual, Kody's aim is merciless. He knows I've always been a homebody.

I wipe damp palms on my jeans. "I haven't decided yet. Mom said

I need to check my transcript to be sure I've met the requirements for Division I."

Kody winces. "How are your math grades, sis?"

I stiffen. "Do you think you guys are the only ones good at math? I'm in this family too."

"That's not what he meant—" Zeph says.

I lift my chin. "Don't worry. I won't embarrass you." My brothers share a look in the awkward silence.

Flustered, I snatch a shop rag from their truck and hand it to Ty. "Not that it'll do much good," I say, but he nods his thanks. "I'm River, by the way."

"Ty is my roommate." Fletch pulls on his boots.

"Tyson James." Ty wipes his face and spits again. "And thanks. That creek tastes like crap." My brothers snicker.

"Yeah? Well." My gaze sweeps over his drenched clothes. "I hope that's an old t-shirt. You'll need a lot of them if you're going to work around here."

He looks down, pinching the sopping shirt away from his body. "I grab a Buc-ee's tee every time I pass through Texas. I think I'm good." He half-smiles. "You must be the one with the sweet pitching area in the barn. Had a lot of offers from schools?"

Zeph steps protectively to my side, as if still harboring guilt for enjoying his college days while I floundered—and sent masses of emails and bounced between exposure tournaments—for nothing.

"Two. The junior college and Northbridge," I say.

"Which one do you want?" Fletch asks.

"They're both good." Zeph turns to me. "The question is, do you want to change schools in two years or stay in one place?"

"Choose the junior college," Kody says from my other side. My head swivels between them, the angel and the devil at my shoulders. "Everyone says you have more fun if you play for a junior college first."

"But," Zeph argues over the top of my head. "It's Northbridge. It'd be worth four years there."

Ty clears his throat, and my brothers turn in surprise. His dark eyes focus on me. "They're both good, right? And you like both coaches?"

"Ty." Fletch shakes his head. "Northbridge is a big deal."

"But." Kody rounds on Fletch. "If she stayed here, we could go to her games. She'd have that hometown feeling."

Ty raises an eyebrow, holding my gaze.

"I like them both," I admit, and feel my brothers' wariness.

"Then—this is just a suggestion—instead of fighting the decision." Ty shrugs. "Flip a coin." Ignoring the hoots and laughter, he raises his voice. "But if you decide on Northbridge and need help with math, let me know. I'm a tutor. I'd be glad to help."

I brace myself and glance at my brothers. But Zeph slings an arm around my shoulders and digs a quarter from his pocket.

"Not a bad idea." He lays it on my palm, then releases me. "All right, people. I need dry clothes. This chafing is annoying."

An hour later, I'm clean and alone in my dark room as doubts circle in an endless replay of the day. We win and what do I do? Break plans with my two best friends. I should be with them, driving into the night, laughing, and talking, and singing.

Why are my choices always either/or? Never just... here, help yourself to both?

But Coach O'Daniel wants... me. He's the one coach in the world I'd die to play for.

So, is tomorrow a try out? Or maybe it's a formality, and he's already sure I'm the right pitcher. That sends a zinger through my stomach. Does Coach O'Daniel really think I can do it? With a groan, I flip over, pounding my pillow.

In a matter of hours, I'll know if my dream is coming true.

On the other hand, he'd said it's a *recruited camp*. Are we all competing for the same spot?

I shove my pillow aside and sprawl on my back. If I sign with him, I might not even play for a year or two. Not like the junior college, where I might play right away and live close enough to go home when I wanted. And... then what? Jaiden will be at college.

Everyone knows I'm not good at being left behind.

I fling back the covers and click on the light. Zeph's quarter taunts from my nightstand. Before I can reconsider, I kneel and pick up the quarter, offering a prayer for divine guidance. Heads—Northbridge tomorrow. Tails—Kansas City, as fast as I can go.

I flip it and slam it where it lands. With a deep breath, I lift my palm.

No mistaking George Washington's profile.

I lean my forehead against the table. What if it's a fluke? What if I did it wrong? Two out of three would be better, wouldn't it?

I straighten and flip it again.

And again.

Then once more, with my eyes closed, to be sure.

All heads.

I climb back into bed and turn off the light.

I knew it.

Chapter 4

We find Coach O'Daniel standing behind a table at Northbridge's indoor facility, and I know immediately that if Dad were here, he'd be beaming. He'd shake hands and march directly in to find a pitching lane so we could show Coach what I can do.

But without Dad, it's surreal. This is O'Daniel's facility, his team, his tribe, and there's no reason for him to notice one more nobody. Parents and athletes pour past me in a noisy stream. My friends are on an adventure that I helped plan, and here I am, invisible and alone. My face heats. I tug down my right sleeve self-consciously because pitching makes that bicep bigger than my left. Another oddity, in case being too tall wasn't enough.

Coach glances up. Then his smile crinkles his blue eyes. "Hello, River."

I smile back. I can't help it.

He's done this before, back at that summer camp. Calmed my fears with a look. Not something most head coaches are known for. I'd been young and devastated after Dad's disappearance, and he'd been patient. No wonder I idolized him.

Two softball players turn with matching clipboards and ponytails. Their stance reminds me of gatekeepers—the kind that guard pearly gates and keep outsiders from entering their sacred college locker room. If O'Daniel wasn't here, would I even be allowed across the threshold?

"I'm glad you made it," he says. "Mia will check you in, and Sarah will show you inside."

The shorter girl hands me registration forms, and my smile slips. I adjust my backpack with its bat rising like a flagpole from the side... and drop the pen. When I pick it up, the registration paper falls.

High school seems so... juvenile right now. These girls are college students. They're elite athletes who've proven themselves and been accepted.

While I struggle, the three of them resume their conversation. When they laugh, I glance up. On the high school team, I'd been the one sharing a laugh with the coach, not gawking like a kindergartner.

"That's okay," the tall one says. "We still love ya', Coach." My gaze swings from the girl to O'Daniel and yearning scratches my throat. I don't know if it's because I miss Dad, but I need to believe that I'll earn a look of respect similar to that someday, doled out by such a genuinely nice guy.

He chuckles and catches my eye. "This is our first baseman, Sarah." He beams at the tall girl. "Our team captain." Then he gestures to the short one. "And Mia is our center fielder. She holds the team record for on-base percentage."

"Hey." I nod, because what else do I have to share? That I'm really hoping to pass high school Algebra II? I wonder what they'd say if they knew about my indecision-busting quarter?

When the paperwork is done, Mom follows me inside, where the sheer size of the practice facility halts us in our tracks. It smells like rubber and paint, the lighted building as tall as it is wide.

"Everyone's warming up. Better get going." Mom gestures to the pitching stations on the indoor turf. Her gaze shifts to the far side, to the brick facade of the stadium visible through an open door. "This is what you've worked for, Riv." She pins me with her gaze. "You're ready. Don't overthink it for once."

But as I change shoes, I wonder what my chances are of standing out in a place this size?

A young girl, nearly the same size as the catcher's bag rolling behind her, settles with a thump next to me. She plants one dainty foot, half the size of mine, on each side and stretches to unzip it.

"Hi." Her dark eyes are bright. "I'm Stephanie."

I finish tying my cleat. "I'm River."

"What grade are you?" She pulls out a shin guard.

"Senior. You?"

"I'm a sophomore." She fastens the hooks and starts on the other leg. "Wanna be partners?"

The odds of me acing this tryout take a nosedive. She's so small. And young. Maybe this would be a good time to flip that quarter.

I scan the athletes for another option, although I can't blame her. She'll get a lot of attention by partnering with an older pitcher. Stephanie doesn't wait for rejection, though. She pulls on her glove, grabs her helmet, and glances back to make sure I follow.

"Be ready," I whisper to the quarter.

Coach O'Daniel introduces the pitching coach, and I'm weirdly intimidated by her perfection. Coach Bosswood smiles politely, every hair in place, and not a wrinkle on her crisp athletic wear.

"Take River to the end lane, Stephanie," Bosswood says, and Stephanie does. *Stephanie?*

She grins as I frown at her. "I've verbally committed already."

I stop in my tracks. Who commits so young? Are those cobwebs stiffening my joints? Should I worry about falling and not being able to get up? Geez. The little weird-o prodigy laughs at me until I catch up with her. The coaches move behind with their clipboards and speed gun, talking quietly.

Of course, Stephanie is a good catcher, and after I've warmed up without actually embarrassing myself, I relax. She frames my pitches and has an arm when she throws it back. Occasionally, she nods at someone beyond my shoulder, and I wonder what the coaches are thinking. Sweat drips down my temples and my legs burn by the time we're done. When she takes off her helmet, I follow obediently plopping down next to her on our bench.

"Coach CJ is the batting coach," she says, startling me from my replay of the tryout. She unsnaps her gear and gestures to the outdoor facility where the telltale ping of bats rings. "And Bosswood is new. She pitched for Northbridge back in the day, in case you hadn't heard."

How would I have heard when I didn't know I was coming here until twenty-four hours ago?

"She jumped on this coaching job last year." Stephanie leans close. "Pretty intense about it. Her sister is the head softball coach at Wichita State, and her dad helped with the Olympic team. Talk about a competitive family." She rolls her eyes and stands. "You don't talk much, do you? Come on, let's ask her what's next."

I hesitate and imagine answering to Bosswood's rigid perfection day after day. A coach who doesn't understand where her pitcher's mind is or how her pitches are working on any day can make her look ridiculous. When I'd been actively trying to get recruited, I'd focused on coaches I thought I could work with. Will Bosswood and I have a productive chemistry, even though I'm only here because of O'Daniel?

Coach O'Daniel leads Mom and me on our tour of the school. The whole time, I second guess whether I belong.

Our last stop is the state-of-the-art dorm for freshmen. O'Daniel holds the outer door of a glassed foyer for two basketball players who make me feel short. But Mom and I share a look of concern as Sarah swipes a card to open the inner door.

"Why the security?" Mom asks.

Coach O'Daniel follows her in. "Even though fifty-one percent of the dorm's residents are not athletes, there are some, especially the football players, who benefit from added security. This discourages the media, for one, from trying to access the players in their off time and, honestly, enthusiastic fans can be as troublesome as disgruntled ones when they forget the athletes are here to get an education."

Mom's eyes narrow, as if she suspects there's more to it than that. She's raised two boys, after all.

That's the last I hear, though, once I step onto the stone floors of the lobby and peer up at the high ceilings. Groups of leather sofas sit at each end, perfumed with brewed coffee. This is *nothing* like the dorms my brothers shared. I run my fingers over the cherry wood bookcases and decide it's calling to me. I must live here next year.

"The dining room is down the hall. They have the healthiest menus institutional kitchens offer," Coach tells Mom.

"I'm glad. This is very impressive." Mom turns to me. "But as beautiful as it is, you'll be committing to an education and a team, River. Not a building."

I think I could commit to a building.

"Don't forget our secret sauce... team dinners at the field house," Mia adds.

"Yup. Coach's wife can cook." Sarah pats her stomach. "It's the highlight of every month."

Mom smiles, but there's hesitation in her eyes. I don't know why she's downplaying this dorm. It's all I want now, to move in here and belong behind these secured doors with all the other important athletes. But what if O'Daniel doesn't ask me to stay?

The quarter is still in my pocket on the walk back to the office. I should've flipped it earlier, just to see if it's on the same page. If it didn't choose that dorm, though, I'd have to chuck it. Is that how Ty meant it to work?

I sneak a glance at Coach. He seems very proud of his athletes. I wonder what I could accomplish in four years under approval like that. I hope I get the chance to find out.

As if he feels my attention, he turns. "What's your favorite sports movie?"

"I love *Miracle*." He blinks at my quick answer, and I ask quickly, "What about you?"

"*Miracle*?" Creases form between his eyes. "Do you play hockey?"

I shake my head. "Not me. But my dad and uncle played when they were growing up. It was our favorite movie to watch together."

"So..." He nods thoughtfully. "Let me think... 'Pass, shoot, score!'? Is that right?"

I nod, uncertain if I've failed a test, but he grins and tucks his hands in his windbreaker.

At the field house, Coach waves to a man and two students on the sidewalk. "Coach Walker. Come meet River." He turns to me. "Walker is the baseball coach. You'll see a lot of him around here. Our offices are next to each other."

The two students trail the coach, one immediately looking bored, but the other draws closer, his backpack slung over a shoulder. He smiles in a way that makes heat rise to my face. I'm tempted to look over my shoulder for a girl who merits a look that appreciative.

"Where are you from?" From under the bill of his hat, hazel eyes framed with long lashes study me. He's close enough I can smell his soap. It's nice.

"Oklahoma."

"Good to meet an Okie. I'm Jace." Suddenly, he flinches as his hat flips off his head. He rescues it before it hits the ground and turns an annoyed frown on his friend.

The guy doesn't spare me a glance. "Let's go, Jace. She's not even a freshman. You've got next year to talk to her."

Coach Walker's lips tighten. "Were you two planning on gracing us for practice?"

"We're going, Coach." Jace repositions his hat and leans closer for my ears only. "And I'll definitely see you next year."

An uncomfortable heat climbs my neck, clinging to my cheeks, and leaving me confused at the unexpected attention. Maybe being too tall won't be a problem at college. I can only hope.

As the two disappear inside the facility, I turn, bemused, to find Mom's gaze narrowed on me. "River, I don't think--"

But a golf cart, heavy with wrestlers, rounds the corner on the side-walk. Coach Walker lowers his chin and points to the street. The cart makes a lumbering U-turn and stalls. I'm afraid to blink in case I miss something as the driver visibly struggles, despite all those muscles, to shift into reverse. Big mistake, I think, watching Coach Walker's bulky mass build up steam and barrel toward them. He's barking orders in a tone that any boot camp survivor would recognize. The guys on the back seem torn between panic and amusement. One of them catches me laughing and grins. Then the transmission grinds into gear and the cart lurches drunkenly, the wrestlers hanging on for dear life.

My fingers itch to text Jaiden about Division I boys.

Inside the office, Coach Bosswood pulls up a chair. "Can you see yourself in this program, River?"

Coach O'Daniel hands me a blue softball t-shirt that smells of screen printing before taking a seat. He's still talking, but I smooth the wrinkles and trace the letters with shaking fingers. My heart thumps wildly. This is what it feels like to be recruited. To know the decision I'm about to make will determine the next four years. A wrong decision to the wrong program could wreck those years. But a delayed decision might waste a golden opportunity and ruin my whole future.

Gradually, I notice the weighted silence and glance from one coach to the other. Everyone is watching me, even the girls on the team's poster. They expect decisiveness and confidence. If they only knew how paralyzed I really feel.

Finally, I ask the most serious question I can think of. "Does anyone already wear the number seven jersey?"

I don't recall that quarter in my pocket until much, much later.

Chapter 5

"Jaiden. You should've seen that baseball player, Jace. He was hot." I turn to lie on the floor and prop my newly painted toes on the side of my mattress.

She closes the pink nail polish, scoots down beside me, and swings her feet up. "Just a guess." She gives me a wry look. "He was big and athletic, right? Maybe Ty's twin? Which should tell you something, Harte. You're borrrrring. What's wrong with flowing hair and poetry?"

I snicker. "Scotty Bacon, the school's free spirit? What do you two even talk about?"

"Who needs to talk when someone's writing poems about your eyes?" She bats those cloudless blues and I fling a pillow at her. She catches it and hugs it to her chest with a laugh.

"Wait until next year." I shake my head. "You won't have time for a boy back home."

"Scotty's not just some boy," she objects, then rolls up on one elbow. "He'll wait. He knows that playing college softball is my life's goal. I told him how I'm going to walk through airports in my team's travel gear, and belong in the field house, and..." She shifts back and clasps the pillow close, her voice soft. "I won't be an anonymous student—I'll be an athlete. A softball player."

Before I can react, she's up on her elbow again. "When are you signing with Northbridge? You know you want to." She suddenly gives a very un-Jaiden-like squeal and pounds the floor, making me laugh. She pauses with a grin. "Maybe our schools will play each other."

"Maybe. But I'm going to miss playing with you, Jaiden."

"I know. Me, too." She leans her head on her palm. "What do your brothers think?"

"You know how they are. They argue, but they're happy for me."

"And Fletcher?"

I roll my eyes. "He's so excited that I'll be on campus."

Jaiden's eyes crinkle. "If I didn't love softball and Scotty, I'd crush on Fletcher."

"No... ahhhh." I gag. "He's like my brother. How can you say that?"

She laughs, then softens wistfully. "What would your dad say?"

I can't answer. It's not as if I haven't imagined what he'd say a hundred times. I shrug, and Jaiden squeezes my hand.

She scoots close to snuggle at my side. "He'd be proud," she whispers, and I nod.

Scotty's ringtone interrupts us. I leave them to their whispers and brush my teeth, but when I come back, Jaiden's changed clothes.

"Where're you going?" I ask.

"Scotty wants to show me his new car. I'll be back." She looks up from putting on lip gloss. "Is that okay?"

I shrug. "Can't you see it tomorrow?"

"He's really excited." She pulls on a jacket. "He's meeting me at the end of your drive."

"Okay," I say uneasily. But we're young. We should sneak out at least once, right? "Leave the back door unlocked so you can get back in."

I climb into bed to wait, but my mind paces like a panther in a zoo. Still, I must drift off between one thought and the next because I startle awake later, wondering why the light is on. When I remember Jaiden, I squint at the clock, then shoot a text with my heart in my throat. Her *back soon* is unconcerned.

With a huff, I toss my phone and curl on my side, hands under my cheek. I wish we were still ten, when my best friend talked and giggled and ate junk food with me all night instead of disappearing with her boyfriend. When our biggest worry had been fitting in at junior high, and college was a vague dream of the future. We were going to do every-thing together.

I guess if I'd ever had a boyfriend, I'd understand. But the fast peck at Jeremy's seventh-grade birthday party didn't count as a kiss because we'd been playing truth or dare, and he had to kiss every girl. And what-ever that was last year with Maddie's brother didn't count. Just the right place at the right time, I guess. I'd tagged along to move him to college and, plainly, his nerves had gotten the best of him.

I turn on my back to stare at the ceiling, my fingers tapping in time to my thoughts. Scotty's kisses may be special, but doesn't he care Jaiden could get in trouble for this? I frown, imagining how her parents would flip out. Would his? She'd be grounded for weeks, even from me. What would his do? I guess nothing if they don't get caught.

I sit up straight. What if she isn't with him? My insides freeze at the thought. I know, with a constantly aching wound, that horrible things happen to good people. She could be stolen away, disappear, like my dad. Just poof and gone. Happy Jaiden tortured and hopeless and...

The sheets catch my ankles in my mad scramble out of bed, and I fall face first. It knocks the breath out of me... and some of the hysteria. I close my eyes, forehead on the carpet, and will the spasm to pass. No one knows that it's been this way since Dad left—worry and fear overtaking me every time someone I love leaves. Two tears drop with hollow pops. Jaiden has to be all right. She has to come back.

I won't sleep until she does.

Dawn coats the treetops, thick as milk over cereal, when headlights flash at the end of the driveway. I nearly melt at the sight. The relief is short-lived, though, as the muffled sound of Mom's alarm breaks the silence behind me.

There's a flash of Jaiden's hair bobbing under the trees as Mom's door opens, and blood drains from my face. Any second Jaiden could be caught.

Mom's soft footsteps cross the hall as Jaiden bounds up the sidewalk to the porch. The bathroom door clicks shut as the downstairs storm door squeaks open.

I tiptoe across the room, peeking down the hall before hurtling for the stairs. The old water pipes knock in the wall, but at the scrape of the backdoor, they stop. Our dog, Charlie, bounds down after me.

The bathroom door opens. "River? Is that you?"

Jaiden freezes in the doorway when I wave my arms.

The floor creaks above my head. "River?"

Jaiden's face pales. I double over to catch my breath, then lift my head. "We're letting Charlie out, Mom." I sound strange to my own ears.

After a long pause, Mom says, "Why are you two up so early?"

Because Jaiden didn't come back until morning. I narrow my eyes at her and hiss, "Ask me to go for a run."

Jaiden is bewildered, but asks.

I raise my voice. "Jaiden asked if we could go for a sunrise run." It's not technically a lie, but I resent the necessity. When the bathroom door closes again, I avoid Jaiden's gaze and trudge upstairs to change without a word.

#

Working Christmas break with Ty and Fletch is noisy between jokes and snow fights. Despite gray skies and wind that punches through our coats to steal our breath, we hunch our shoulders and grin. Mostly.

In February, my Gold fast pitch travel team hits its stride. Jaiden's and Maddie's teams are just as busy. In the lunchroom, we groan about the hours, the coaches, and the girls, but secretly we wouldn't change anything, except maybe to play together again. It's when I'm home that I'm restless. My chores are monotonous and eerily quiet without Ty and Fletch.

In March, my brothers debate their options as they pack for a trip to Costa Rica to search for Dad. Should they go on solo excursions this time, following rumors of hostage sightings, or join a group of grim families on similar missions? Their goals energize and focus them. I slip from the house, knowing they don't consider the other option—to wait and do nothing. Which, for three and half years, has been my only option.

But as they exclude me from their plans, they reveal one detail. Ty and Fletch are returning for the week. *Isn't that great?* And, like checking a box, they're relieved of any troublesome twinges of guilt about abandoning me.

The first morning after they leave, I unlock our small war room in the barn. A map dominates the wall, gouged by pins across Central America. The biggest pin marks the helicopter crash where a roving militia kidnapped Dad before he could be rescued. Relative to the pins, the scale of the map is unnerving. I always remind myself it's a good thing, that there's a lot of room to stay alive. But the uncertainty makes every year drag on forever.

I step closer and trace Costa Rica, the knobby, rutted wood beneath like tiny mountains and valleys. My family treats me as if I'm too young to face harsh realities. It's why they can leave me behind so easily. My fingers curl into a fist. But I'm almost an adult. Not a baby. My brothers had years to do their best. It's my turn. I feel Dad waiting for *me* to bring him home.

I lean my forehead against the wall and imagine his expression when he realizes that I never gave up. But my smile fades. How will he look? Thin? Maybe injured? Maybe blind or unable to walk? And what does he feel every morning as he wakes alone to a full-color nightmare? Is he being tortured? My chest tightens, tears sting. How long does one hour feel to him, let alone a year?

Does he know I miss him?

"Please bring him back, God," I whisper, and feel the weight of how helpless I am.

I grit my teeth and step back before tears can mark the map. There's got to be something I can do to help. But everywhere I look, evidence that he's beyond my reach stabs deeper. I try to breathe around the ache in my heart, but can't even do that. There's not enough air. I'm so freaking useless. With a sob, I turn and wrench the door open...

And crash into a person, like a puck caught by a goalie.

Ty grunts, his jacket rough under my cheek. "Someone's around early," he huffs and sets me on my feet, juggling the fishing pole in his other hand.

"Sorry," I mumble.

His gaze sharpens on my face, then shifts to the map room. I twist free.

He leans the pole against the wall and jogs to catch up. "What's the hurry? You look like you've seen a ghost."

I shake my head.

His voice softens. "River. Are you...?"

"Ty." I stop without warning. His eyes widen as he narrowly avoids my gloves pointed at his face. But... no words come. I swallow and waggle the gloves again. "I'll be gone tomorrow, just so you know."

His gaze moves from the gloves to my face and lingers. "You're taking a day off?" He smirks, and it's almost normal. "You slacker. What is it, a spa day?"

"Dork." I roll my eyes and move to the door. "Jaiden's going to get a prom dress."

His brows rise. "Why do you have to go? Are you getting one, too?"

As we step out of the barn, I tilt my face toward the sun. "I'm not going to the prom." I swear I feel his reaction.

"Why not?"

"It's lame."

"Are you talking about the prom or your excuse?"

"Very funny." I glance at him as we round the corner. He grins and unwraps the water hose, aiming it in the cow tank as I turn on the hydrant. "Just because you loved your prom, Ty, doesn't mean we all do."

"I didn't go to the prom."

I look up, surprised. "Why not?"

"Just didn't." He shrugs, then pins me with his gaze. "But are you sure you don't want to go, even a little bit? Since you're putting all of this energy into shopping for someone else's dress?"

Through the fence, a calf tentatively stretches his moist nose toward my knuckles. "All my friends are taking dates."

"There are other reasons to go..." His eyes widen. "Did you just snort? How rude."

I smother a grin. "Reasons? You mean awkward dancing? Terrible music? Cheesy decorations?"

He mimics my tone. "The end-party of all high school parties? One last teenage dress up before becoming an adult?" But humor dances behind his gaze.

"Is that why you didn't go?" I bat my eyes sweetly. "Because, afterward, you'd have to be an adult instead of a child."

"Look who's talking." He eyes me from ponytail to boots. "You'd have to wear a dress. Ooooh, scary for you."

I laugh, but stiffen. "I like dresses."

The water gurgles as it nears the top of the tank. When I look up, he's watching me thoughtfully. "You don't have a tournament on the day of the prom?"

"Not even a practice," I admit ruefully.

The water overflows, taking strands of backwashed hay. I turn it off as he rolls the hose.

He wipes wet palms on his jeans and shrugs. "I'll go to your prom with you."

It takes a second before I can draw a breath. "I wasn't fishing for a date."

"I know." He smiles.

I'm already shaking my head. "Um, no. I appreciate it and all, but no. Thank you."

"Suit yourself." He shrugs one shoulder and turns casually to the barn, as if he hadn't a care in the world. As if he hadn't just hijacked my head.

Prom? With Ty? Without the awkward conversations or uncomfortable silences? I think, a little dizzily, that maybe I was too hasty to refuse. But, still, how strange. I fiddle with my gloves for a long moment before jogging after him.

"You'd suffer through a high school prom just because we're friends?" I ask doubtfully.

He pauses and squints into the distance. "When you put it that way, no." He looks down at me. "Let's talk cash."

I shove his shoulder and laugh. But the idea has grown on me. I wouldn't be a third wheel. It might actually be fun.

"Too late," I say. "I accept your original offer, if we clear it with the school. And no matter how bad it is, don't forget, you volunteered."

"Not *volunteered*." He raises a pointy finger. "First Responded."

And there's that unbearably cocky humor I've come to know. I narrow my eyes. "Are you implying I'm a disaster?"

The corners of his mouth twitch. "Just pointing out that I'm always prepared."

I smile just to annoy him. "Luckily for you, one benefit of *volunteering* is the chance to improve your social skills."

He laughs. And, during our ongoing jokes about the semantics of volunteering, the strangest thing happens. I forget my brothers keep leaving me behind.

#

The next afternoon, I hurry to start the car before Jaiden can think of something else to shop for.

"That was fun." She buckles her seatbelt.

I try hard not to roll my eyes. "Your dress is amazing. Scotty will love it."

She grins. "And Ty is going to die when he sees yours."

"He won't care," I scoff. But while I'd twirled in front of the mirror, I'd wondered what it'd be like if he did.

I maneuver through Tulsa's busy streets as Jaiden continues to plan my non-existent love life, *ahem,* with Ty. Because, evidently, *eye roll,* the best loves start as friendships. Even at the gas station, she jumps out to help, which means she talks.

"Your eyes will stick that way if you keep rolling them about everything I say," she warns. "And then try to find a date, will ya?"

I laugh. "Then stop acting as if we all have to be like you and Scotty." Scotty. Softball. College. Her entire plan.

"No one can be like Scotty and... Oh. There's one, River." She turns toward me, crossing her arms.

I glance up. "What?" But the gas pump clicks off, and I pulse it toward zeros.

She slants another look over her shoulder. "The guy with the black pickup."

A guy with sunglasses and a hat lifts his chin in greeting. I peer behind us. No one. "Who is he?" I say without moving my lips.

"How am I supposed to know? Nice truck, though." She snickers and grabs my arm. "Maybe he's the one. You can tell your kids he picked you up at a gas station."

I frown, alarmed at the precedence that would set for my kids. "Me? Jaiden, he thinks you're hot for him because you keep making eye contact. Don't make eye contact with strange men or wild bears." I put the pump handle away.

Jaiden giggles, then stiffens. "He's driving over."

"What?" I duck behind her, but she's only 5' 7". A good half-foot of me sticks out above. He stops beside us, wearing a Northbridge University baseball hat, and I straighten.

"I'm not trying to be weird," he says hesitantly to me. "But you look familiar. Do I know you?"

"Worst pickup line ever," Jaiden says, as I say, "Yes." She whips around to stare at me.

"This is Jace." I give her a significant look. "The Jace who plays baseball at Northbridge."

His smile seems pleased. "I do. Have you been to a game?"

While I give the cliff notes of my recruitment visit, Jaiden's slack mouth is replaced with a dawning recognition. It's terrifying.

Jace nods. "But what is your name again?"

Jaiden answers, and although I poke her back repeatedly, she tells him way too much. I'm sure he didn't want my phone number as he was driving away.

"This is your destiny." She sighs once we're back in the car. "He's the first guy you met at Northbridge. And he remembers you." She leans her head back, closing her eyes as if overcome. "Holy cow. I've been waiting for this day."

And... false alarm. She finds a second wind and uses the two-hour drive to explore in detail how much I have to look forward to with Jace at the same school.

At least she forgets about Ty.

Chapter 6

On a brisk day in April, Ty and I stack winter hay in the upper loft of the feed barn. Sprigs of Bermuda crunch under our boots and dusty confetti swirls in the air. I hook a bale and pull as Ty sneezes.

"Gesundheit." I grunt.

He sniffs and wipes his nose on his sleeve. "Thanks. This stuff gets to me."

"I know. Me, too." At a sound below, I stack the bale and step to the edge, raining bits of hay down. "Zeph, are you catching for me tonight?"

He looks up, apologetic. "Aw, River. I'm teaching a Jiu-Jitsu class. Ask Kody."

My shoulders sag. We don't have normal, rearrangeable social lives here. Nope. We have Jiu-Jitsu and marksmanship. And softball. "He's busy. I've got a tournament this week, Zeph."

Ty drops his gloves and picks up a water bottle.

Zeph tips his head to Ty. "Maybe he could catch? You don't want Fletch. He'll kill himself."

I look at Ty's hands as he drinks. They're big and strong. The shin guards would fit around his calves, his chest, though—it'd be a tight fit to get our chest protector on him. I'd never noticed how much more muscular he is than my brothers. His shoulders are huge. I watch him wipe a line of sweat from his jaw. My gaze shifts to his. The hint of wry humor there breaks me out of my stupor. I duck my head.

He shrugs and sets the water down. "Sorry. I won't be much help either."

"I wasn't going to ask," I snap, tugging my glove. "Have you ever caught a ball? You'd get killed. You're a math tutor." His eyes narrow and I turn away to stab my hook in another bale. Ugh. That was a low blow. I actually like that he's a tutor. He fits in with my smart brothers.

"I'll use the screens," I mutter loud enough for Zeph to hear.

"Sorry," he calls and a minute later his pickup roars to life outside.

After an uncomfortable silence, Ty asks, "Do you need help to set up the screens?"

"No." My voice is gruff as I stack the bale, half frustrated and half ashamed. "Thanks anyway." Then I sigh, fiddling with my hay hook. I turn. "About what I said, I'm sorry, I didn't mean…"

He picks up the last bale. "No problem."

"It's just that this is an important weekend. We're trying to qualify for Nationals, and our other pitcher hurt her knee last week."

"So… what? You're going to pitch the whole tournament?" he quips. When I don't answer, he sobers. "You're kidding." He stops stacking hay. "You're going to ruin your arm. You can't pitch a whole tournament. Don't they keep a pitch count?"

"This is softball, not baseball." I glare. "We've got a third baseman and an outfielder who used to pitch, so there will be back up. They just haven't pitched in a few years. No one wants to have only one pitcher.

We don't have a choice."

I grab a wooden post for leverage and shove a bale into line with my boot. A stinging burn rips along my finger. I pull my left glove to find blood welling.

Ty leans in. "That's not your pitching hand, is it?"

I shake my head, but he tugs me to the ladder. "There are bandages in the kit downstairs."

Climbing down the ladder isn't nearly as hard as standing still so Ty can apply antiseptic. I take the bandage from him, out of self-preservation, then struggle to hold one end and take the paper off the other. The clean smell of sweat and hay swirls between us, and I shift uncomfortably.

Ty breaks the silence. "Jiu-Jitsu? Zeph?"

I smile, relieved. "Both of them, actually. Dad took them to a local MMA fight when they were younger and from then on, they were always jumping each other. But Zeph's the reigning champ."

Ty's finger twitches, as if he wants to help with the bandage. "So, Kody moved on to marksmanship instead?"

I nod. "He decided to be a sniper on Dad's Coast Guard boat when Dad was active duty."

I bite my lip and pull, but the bandage slips again. I hiss under my breath. Ty takes my hand, and I frown. "I can do it."

"Mmhmm." He bends over my finger.

"Ty, I can do it myself." But for some reason, I don't.

He smooths down the adhesive, then runs his finger gently over the bandage. "Would I ever say you couldn't?" There's a smile in his eyes when he looks up. He's so close I see streaks of gold in his eyes. "You're tough, Riv," he says. "*But if you spend word for word with me, I shall make your wit bankrupt.*"

"What?" The softness of his voice gives me goosebumps. I take a step back, tucking a strand of hair behind my ear. "Is that supposed to be a geek insult? I said I was sorry."

"Me? Insult River Harte?" He grins. "You've never read Shakespeare?"

"In school." I narrow my eyes. "You quote Shakespeare?"

He raises an eyebrow.

"What play is it from?" I ask, tilting my chin up.

"Two Gentlemen of Verona. Want me to tell you what it means?"

I huff and turn away. "I'm not stupid." I replace the medical kit and close the cabinet. "I get that you're insulting me."

He lays a hand over his heart. "I'm hurt. If I was trying to insult you, I'd say something else, something I can't repeat because you're so competitive."

"Me?" I raise my eyebrows. "Have you met yourself?"

Kody and Mom come into the barn. "Now, kids," she says. "Are we arguing?"

"Mrs. Harte." Ty crosses his arms. "Remind her she's competitive. She doesn't believe me."

Mom laughs and gives me a loving look before sending the guys to fix a windmill that I know will take all afternoon. He glances back as he leaves the barn and smiles when he finds me watching. The barn is unnaturally quiet after they're gone.

Chapter 7

No one should practice pitching in the dark. But it's not until I stop to take a drink that I realize I've nearly done that. While the barn lights hum and pop, getting brighter as they warm, I grab an empty bucket to gather the scattered softballs and sing along to my playlist.

A dark shape detaches from the shadows, and I scream. The bucket lands, spewing balls at Ty's feet as his surprise turns to laughter. He collapses against the wall, a fishing pole in one hand, and I snatch the bucket and marshal the balls back inside with more force than necessary. It wasn't that funny.

"What're you doing here?" I glare.

"Can you do that again?" He tries to breathe between laughs. "It's the best thing I've seen all week."

"Shut up," I snap as he wipes tears from his eyes, which irritates me more. "Don't you have to go home?"

He's still sighing chuckles as he leans his pole against the wall, puts his hands in his pockets, and strolls through my space. He takes an exaggerated interest in my posters. "If you're staying late, I will."

I gather the balls from the screen's pockets and glance over my shoulder. He's moved to one of my favorite photos of Dad and me practicing outside. "It's not a competition," I say.

He raises an eyebrow, still touchy about competitions.

"Won't Fletch and his grandpa be expecting you?" I ask.

"I have the feeling you're trying to get rid of me, Riv," he says mildly, moving to the next photo as if they're the most interesting things he's seen. "And here I was, being nice and coming to get your truck keys so I can do your chores tomorrow."

"Oh." I set down my bucket before he can change his mind and dig out my keys. "Thanks. So, you're going to be here all weekend? Don't you ever go back to Missouri?"

"And give up the chance at extra hours?" he scoffs, pocketing my keys. His gaze flickers across the Olympic softball team posters, then returns to the candid shot of Dad and me practicing behind the barn with native grass in the background. Dad had come home from work to practice that day, then gone back out. He was always doing things like that for me.

"What happens if your team wins this weekend?" Ty asks.

I tear my gaze from the photo and take my bucket back to the pitching mound. I grab a ball and rub it against my shirt as my foot swipes the pitching rubber. "We won't have to play another qualifier, and we'll go to Nationals in July."

"Would it bother you if I stay a while?" He motions to the ball in my hand.

I search his face. His eyes are soft and sincere, if still lit with humor. But the familiar awareness of him slithers under my skin. I shrug and step onto the mound, trying to ignore that it would please me if he stayed.

He exhales hard after my first fastball smacks the screen pocket. He raises his eyebrows when I glance over, but after that, he's quiet as a golf patron. I almost forget he's there as I work through the bucket. Sweat slicks my arms and plasters the shirt to my back. When I finish, Ty pushes away from the wall to pick up balls, his large hands handling two at a time. When he drops them in the bucket, his eyes meet mine, then bounce away. The silence is unnerving.

As we shut off the lights and step out into the night, I stretch my shoulders and gesture to the pole in his hand. "No luck fishing tonight?"

"I caught a good-sized catfish, actually."

I raise an eyebrow.

"Catch and release, Harte," he says.

I hum doubtfully. "If you want, I could show you some good spots next time."

He rolls his eyes.

"Well, I'm starved," I say. "I think I'll run into town and get a burger. See you Monday?"

"Sure." He stuffs one hand in his pocket, tilting his head back to see the stars. Then his stomach growls.

I laugh at his sheepish look. "You want to come? You can, but I'm driving."

He tugs out my keys and holds them up with a grin. We argue all the way to the truck about who's driving. I win.

If only I'd known that everything would change on Monday.

Chapter 8

On Monday, Zeph and I walk to the barn, the sun already bright. Dew clings to Zeph's feet, leaving dark footprints for me to follow. Except Zeph stomps, and his incensed huffs nip any comments in the bud.

Because of a three-day weekend, Fletch and Ty wait on the tailgate of a truck just inside the door, tall coffees cradled in their hands. As my eyes adjust to the darkness, I see Ty stiffen with concern.

"Are you hurt?" He scans my arm, then face. "What happened?"

I adjust the ice bag on my shoulder, shivering against the trickles down my back. "I'm fine. Mom makes me ice."

"She pitched five games." Zeph sounds as frustrated as he looks.

"Three games and parts of two more," I correct.

Ty shakes his head disgustedly, but Fletch jumps down from the tailgate. "You've done that before, haven't you?"

"Not for years," Zeph snaps. "And not at this level. But she's River Harte, so…"

"Why do you use my last name? That's just weird." I unravel the ice bag and drop it in the trash barrel.

"Did you win?" Fletch asks.

"Yup." I grin. "Going to nationals."

"Hey, that's great." But he smirks knowingly when I take his high-five with my left hand.

Ty scowls and pushes off the tailgate to toss his cup into the trash. "What's up today, boss?" He adjusts his baseball hat with a jerk.

Zeph gestures to Ty and me. "You two pick up the feed at the co-op. Fletch, stop dancing around. You're with me."

I climb behind the wheel and start the truck. Ty stalks to the passenger's side, slams the door, and rolls down the window—all without looking at me. I'm fairly certain he can't keep this silence up all day. But the sight of his fist white-knuckled against his thigh prevents me from prodding him right away.

As usual at the co-op, Dennis and I swap gossip while he pulls our order, and it's so normal I forget about my shoulder until I reach to sign the ticket. At that slight hesitation, Ty swears and grabs the clipboard himself.

He pointedly ignores me as he opens the tailgate. But, when I reach for a bag, he cracks. "Don't you even touch it." He pins me with his gaze.

"You can't tell me what to do," I say automatically.

"Watch me." Ty swings a bag up, drops it in the pickup bed, and stares into my soul.

How can a guy make it just as uncomfortable whether he looks at you or avoids you? Annoyed at the heat in my face, I pull a bag toward me, and Ty freezes.

"I swear if you touch that, I'm going to leave and you can do it all."

His voice is low, but Dennis hears and shakes his head before disappearing into the warehouse.

I withdraw my hand. "What good will that do?"

"I won't have to watch you ruin your arm. It even hurts to drive, doesn't it? Stubborn little..." He mumbles under his breath as his next fifty-pound sack shakes the truck.

"You don't stop working when you're sore." I squint against the sunshine, fighting a ridiculous need to laugh and cry at the same time. "So why the fuss? Because I'm a girl?"

"Give me a break." He jerks the next bag over, fitting his hands around it. "I'm not a big-shot softball star using my arm to nail a college scholarship."

Sweat beads on his forehead and, for a second, I wonder if he'd actually walk away. But this isn't about stubbornness, it's principle. Mostly. I yank the last bag, riled enough that I barely feel the twinge in my shoulder. "I'm not arguing with—"

Suddenly, I'm face-to-face with a dark frustration in Ty's eyes that mirrors my own. Well, good. We're even. He opens his mouth to say something, and I will him to do it. I step close enough to touch and gaze up into his face and *dare* him to pick this fight.

But as we glare at each other, his long lashes distract me, framed the way they are around the rich deep brown of his eyes. Heat ripples off him... and my temper shifts into a sizzling awareness. He lets out a breath. His gaze drops to my lips. I forget where we are.

"Please don't hurt your arm," he whispers, soft as his touch on my shoulder.

I sway, undone by the plea in his voice. "Ty," I breathe.

He slowly bends. But stops, his breath torture on my skin. With a small sound, I stretch up and press my lips to his.

The kiss is short. And... the longest, most perfect moment of my life.

When he pulls back, I stare at him. He looks a little surprised himself.

He gently scoots me back a step and picks up the last bag. It lands in the truck, and he wordlessly slams the tailgate before climbing in the passenger side. I stand there, a stupid smile on my face.

I don't have the nerve to look at him until we're out of town. His face is expressionless under his baseball hat, but his ears are red, which sends a jolt through my stomach.

I bite my lip and stare at the road. It's all I can do not to embarrass myself by fanning my face. But after a few miles with only the rattles of the truck, the loaded silence swells uncomfortably.

"It's really okay to pitch that much," I say.

He makes an irritating, non-committal sound which, perversely, makes me feel better.

"Fine." I raise my chin. "Be a grump if you want to. Just don't take it out on me."

His jaw drops, and he turns to stare. "You have no idea, do you?" He closes his mouth and breathes through his nose. When he speaks again, his voice is even. "Coaches don't always look out for you, Riv. My brother broke his back in high school doing squats. You have to watch out for yourself."

Broke his back? "Wow. I'm sorry."

"But this is different, right?" His lips twist.

"That's not fair." I scowl at the road. "I wanted to pitch this weekend because my team needed me. No one made me."

He adjusts his hat and turns away.

"Come on, Ty, softball is what I do."

He holds my gaze until I shift uncomfortably. Geez. I need to learn how to do that.

"Since you don't play sports..." I clear my throat. "It might be hard to understand, but part of what I love the most is that pitching makes me dig deep, mentally and physically. It's taken a lot of work to get where I'm at. I've learned how to take care of my arm. Pitching that much over two days sucks, but it doesn't happen often. When it does, I can handle it."

A strange expression crosses his face but, once again, the ditch seems more interesting than me.

Suddenly, I'm tired of this whole passive-aggressive I'm-not-looking-at-you thing. Maybe we should just sock each other in the arm and get it over with. Except my shoulder really is sore. If it was one of my brothers, I'd...

"Um," I clear my throat. "You have a brother?"

The muscle in his jaw jumps.

"Is he older or younger than you?"

Ty gives me a sidelong glance.

"Hey, you know everything about me." I grin. "Your brother can't be worse than both of mine, can he? Or wait, worse than Fletch?"

He rolls his eyes. "He's okay, I guess. Typical firstborn."

At once, my perception shifts from the stoic Ty I know to annoying-little-brother Ty tripping through adventures behind an older version of himself. And he becomes even more irresistible.

"I have an older sister, too," he says into the quiet. "She'd like you."

I rear back. A sister. Not once in the months I've known him has he brought up a sister. Although, that explains his unflappable ease around me... but there's real pain in his voice.

My earliest memories of my brothers are of two identical faces smiling at me, gently leading me by the hand, or kneeling to share treasures cradled in grubby palms. When I stood between them, holding each of their hands, they looked huge and capable. When they took a step, I did too, thinking that I was as good as they were. They've always watched out for me.

Why does Ty never talk about his own family?

When we get back, Fletcher is sweeping the feed room. He sets the broom against the wall and gestures toward Ty. "We'll unload this, Riv."

I narrow my eyes. Is every male crazy today? But when I lower the tailgate, Fletch elbows me aside.

"There's some hang up with payroll. Your mom probably needs help to figure it out."

I study him suspiciously, but the two of them are already unloading the feed with a rhythmic efficiency.

When I go in the house, their checks are in the kitchen, and Mom is nowhere to be found. Grabbing a water bottle and the checks, I stomp back out, slamming the door. Charlie bumps my leg, and I bend down to ruffle his fur. At least the dog's still normal. Then I overhear the guys in the barn.

"How'd it happen?" Fletch asks.

"None of your business," Ty snaps.

My heart sinks as I turn from Charlie's brown face to the barn door. There's a grunt and the sounds of boots scuffing the dirt.

"What were you thinking, man?" Fletch says, slightly out of breath. "Watching out for her means keeping your hands off. It's the co-op— her brothers are going to hear about this. Dennis called me because he knew people would talk."

I close my eyes, but Ty makes a disgusted sound, followed by more scuffing. "Get off, dude." His voice is strained. "You don't know what you're talking about."

"She's the baby of the family. How do you think this'll end?"

"There's nothing to end," Ty grunts. "Let go."

I straighten at the sound of something big hitting the truck. This is all my fault. Their tailgate slams, and I look around wildly. They can't find me like this.

When they appear out of the depths of the barn, I'm watering our potted plants, my pulse jumping ninety miles an hour. They're both sweating and avoiding each other. If they were horses, their ears would be laid back against their heads. Ty straightens his wadded t-shirt, and I can't bring myself to meet his gaze after he endured that embarrassment.

They pluck their checks from my hand, but we're saved from small talk when Kody rounds the barn with shovels. As soon as they're gone, I slowly turn off the water and press my palms to my temples. When will everyone stop treating me like a baby?

If only growing up was just about how many birthdays you've had. Instead, I'm locked in a bubble cage by the people who love me most. When will I be an adult? After I break out? When I poke the eye of everyone who refuses to see who I've become—who I'm meant to be? Does someone have to cry?

<h1 style="text-align:center">Chapter 9</h1>

The next Saturday, Mom raises her camera, eyes bright. "Hold still."

I freeze, hand extended, my gaze locked on the corsage box in Ty's hand. I haven't been able to look directly at him without losing my breath since he walked in. One glimpse of Ty in a white dress shirt and black jacket, and my stunned heart jammed in my chest. That box is my lifeline.

Then Ty shifts it out of reach, and I glance up in surprise... and see his lips.

My body flushes with memory. Will he kiss me tonight? While we're dancing? Or when he walks me to the door? Would it mean that he *really* liked me, not just *kind-of* liked me?

My gaze rises to his, and... it's all I can do not to laugh at his exaggerated expression.

"Do not move," he whispers.

"Okay," Mom says, enjoying her photo shoot. "Open it."

Ty lays the box on my palm. "Open it," he overstresses under his breath.

"Shut up," I whisper back, and he snorts.

I lift the lid on the mauve and purple orchid wristlet that perfectly matches my dress, and something melts in my chest. Ty's fingers tap the side of his leg and he leans forward slightly, as if checking that the flowers are still all right. I smile up at him. "It's beautiful."

His eyes soften.

"Hold it so I can see." Mom points her camera.

Ty grins and we both turn toward her. Me, covering my mouth in rapturous surprise, and Ty pointing at the corsage with a cheesy smile while she shoots away.

"Put it on her wrist," Mom says, still looking at her screen.

But when Ty reaches out to steady my wrist, I jolt at the contact. He slides the wristlet on and I keep smiling and Mom keeps shooting and no one knows how the touch of his skin on mine overwhelms my every sense.

No one except Ty. Because I had felt his hand tighten for an instant at my jerk, as if he meant to calm me.

"Prom pictures. Check," he says from the corner of his mouth, as if my reaction never happened.

On the way to town, Ty's truck rumbles over the dirt road as his fingers tap in time with the radio. When we pass an oncoming truck, I lift my index finger in a wave. He chuckles.

"They can't see you." His eyes glint in the dashboard lights.

"It's called southern hospitality."

"How'd you do it?" He slouches, wrist on the steering wheel, and makes a peace sign.

"Not like that. Say hello. Okay, tilt your chin down, you're not dragging Main Street. Yeah, that's better." I fake smile and say under my breath, "City boys are hopeless."

He laughs. "What? There's a wrong way?" He practices again. "So, what's the deal? They teach this in Driver's Ed around here?"

"Don't be a jerk," I say primly. "My dad taught me when I was ten and driving in pastures." There's a pang at the memory. Ty straightens and an old rock and roll ballad curls from the radio.

"How old were you when he went missing?" he asks quietly. And I really like the way he always sees what's important.

"Not quite fourteen."

He presses my wrist above the corsage. "I'm sorry. I hope he's found."

Not trusting my voice, I nod and look out the window. You and me both.

He shifts, moving his arm back to his side. "I don't think I've ever seen your hair down before." His smile flashes. "And you're usually wearing a ribbon at work."

"I like ribbons." Dad had liked them too. Well, Dad had liked whatever I liked. Jeans and boots, uniforms and cleats, dresses and sandals. "Dad always told me to be myself. So, I tried."

If only he knew his words had helped through my teenage years. The time I tried to offset embarrassing pimples with a ribbon and fake diamond earrings had been especially awful. A girl I'd thought was my friend sent a laughing note about it to the boy she knew I had a crush on. And later that day, an upper classman on the softball team trashed those same earrings as too soft for the field. Knowing that Dad would've been proud that I was true to myself kept me from being crushed. That, and realizing girls will always know how to hurt you.

Ty clears his throat. "*Time is wasted that's spent trying to see yourself in someone else's eyes.*"

I blink. "Shakespeare again?"

He shakes his head. "No. That's all Henry." He parks in the school parking lot and turns. "A friend."

And that's typical of a friend; whether good or bad, their words tumble into your life like Velcro balls, bouncing around until a few stick.

He opens his door and music spills in from the gym. "Wait there."

He rounds the hood and opens my door, holding out a hand to help me down so I don't trip on my hem. The satin material cascades to the ground as I straighten, shimmering between French mauve and purple as the light hits it. He tightens his grip when I try to let go, and I glance up.

"You look beautiful," he says, and I resist the urge to tug up the deep v-neck of the form-fitted bodice. It's funny that flashing too much skin on the front is more uncomfortable than the softball uniform tan lines spoiling the view on my back.

I smile, ducking my head. "You too." Light reflects on his neatly combed hair and smooth jaw as he shuts the door. It's all I can do not to reach up to see if his cheek is as soft as it looks. Then I remember that we're just trying to get through this rite-of-passage. It's not an actual date. I release him and take a breath. "Prom compliments. Check."

He catches my hand and tucks it at his elbow. "Take me to the punch, princess."

The gym looks exactly like a bunch of kids on a budget decorated. My heels click hollowly on the wooden floor. Light spills from the lobby and glistens on the confetti covered lunch tables with their fold out chairs. Fairy lights twinkle through glittery sheer curtains hung on rods.

There are no secrets in a small town. Everyone knows Ty, knows he works for us, so he returns the head nods from the other farm boys and the appreciative smiles from the girls. That's probably not all they know, if the guys from the co-op have been talking.

Across the room, Maddie pats the space next to her. I slide in gratefully.

Ty leans down to ask over the music, "Do you want something to drink?"

"Sure." I turn to Maddie. "Do you want anything?"

Her boyfriend jumps up before she can answer. "I'll get it." He claps Ty on the shoulder, and they weave their way to the refreshment table, tall and handsome.

"Where's Jaiden?" I ask.

"I haven't seen her." Maddie frowns, then moves to tip the last two chairs against the table for Jaiden and Scotty. She sits again and cranes her neck toward the door. "They must be running late."

When the guys return, Ty hands me a cup and watches over the rim of his own. "Are you ready for some dance lessons?" He tilts his head toward the dance floor.

"Sure." I stand, eye the crowd, and turn to Ty. "What've you got?"

"No." He leans closer to set his drink beside mine on the table, and my breath catches at his nearness. "I mean, are you ready to give me some pointers?"

I grin. "Another thing I have to teach you?" I count on my fingers. "How to feed the animals, how to hook up a trailer, how to—" He rolls his eyes and pulls me to the dance floor.

I don't know what people are thinking when they dance by themselves. The ones who twirl gently on a sandy beach with a flowing dress and a salty breeze. That's not what we're doing. Half the fun of a school dance is being in the middle of the crush of all of your friends, the girls, the guys, the music, the heat. That no matter where you look, there's someone. Music pounds through the floor. Hairspray, and sweat, and bridal shop fabric scents the air. A corner of the decorations peels off the wall and hangs limply. It's the best night ever.

By the time the music slows, I'm out of breath. Assuming that we'll sit the next one out, slow dances being what they are, I turn toward the table, glancing back to be sure Ty is behind me. At some point, he'd taken off his jacket, and his sleeves are rolled up. But instead of leaving the dance floor, he holds out a hand.

The whole gym stands still as I look from his palm to his eyes. My smile falters. I lift my hand to place my fingers on his. In slow motion, he draws me to him, looming larger and larger until we're face to face. Up close, he's definitely bigger than he's seemed from a safe distance—from all the way out in the friend zone. This might make me lose my mind.

As Aerosmith croons, Ty's hand rests on my back and mine molds to the rounded muscles of his shoulder. I'm really fond of his shoulders. He must be the strongest math tutor ever. Then his grip tightens on my hand and I'm distracted by the callouses on his palms, so similar to my own.

My eyes are level with his nose, but I don't have the nerve to look higher. I duck my head and discover that's an even bigger mistake. The area between his ear and his jaw draws me closer, making me want to press in to that vulnerable spot. I never knew that small space could be so tempting. It's all I can do not to set my lips there. He smells like woods and meadows, and I close my eyes.

This is Ty. My friend. My coworker. I squeeze my eyes tighter. We're just having fun. Don't think about the kiss. Don't think about the kiss. Don't...

He pulls away, his brown eyes almost black in the light. "You okay?" His fingers tighten around my hand.

I try to smile, to act normal, when there's nothing normal about being this close. "Yes." It comes out a whispered croak and I clear my throat. "Yes. I'm..."

Beyond his shoulder, Jaiden walks into the gym, and I forget what I was going to say.

She searches the crowd, dismissing each face faster and faster until she lands on me and stays. My heart skips a beat. I come to a stop. Her face, her every mood, is so familiar to me, but I've never seen that look before.

"Um, excuse me," I say and let Ty slide through my fingers. Without a backward glance, I cross to my best friend and, as I get closer, it's not the pallor of her skin that scares me. It's the buckshot tinge of shock.

Chapter 10

"What's wrong?"

She grabs my hand and pulls me to the bathroom. I watch with growing concern as she checks every stall.

"River. I..." She leans against a sink and puts a hand over her mouth. "I'm..." Her eyes are huge and dazed. My heart thumps painfully.

"What, Jaiden? You're scaring me. Are you okay?"

The door bursts open. Maddie slows at the sight of the two of us.

"What's going on?" she says. "River took off from the dance floor like... Dang, Jaiden. You look like you're going to puke. What are you? Pregnant?"

"Shut up, Maddie," I say, but Jaiden turns green and runs for a stall.

Maddie inhales. "I was kidding." I don't look at her.

Hesitantly, she moves closer to lean her cheek on my shoulder and squeeze my arm. "You don't think she's really pregnant, do you?" she whispers, and it isn't funny this time either.

"There's no way." But is there?

When Jaiden comes out, mascara smeared under her eyes, I hand her paper towels after she rinses her mouth.

"You're pregnant?" I ask hesitantly.

She nods, not looking at me.

"Maybe the test was wrong. Do it again." Maddie runs a hand over Jaiden's hair.

Jaiden dabs under her eyes once more, then lets her hands drop. "I took three, just now." She nods at the trash and we stare at it as if it'll cast the tests back onto the floor.

Her lips are bloodless, and her hands shake. I can't stand to see her this way and wrap my arms around her. "Does Scotty know?"

Her eyes fill with tears as she shakes her head. "I couldn't... before I knew for sure."

"What're you going to do?" Maddie looks stricken as she rubs circles on Jaiden's back.

Jaiden takes a shuddering breath and straightens, lifting her chin. "Talk to him."

"Can I help?" I ask, even as she pulls away.

The door opens to a group of giggling girls, and Jaiden stiffens.

"No," she says, then shoulders past the girls and out into the hall, propelled by the same stubborn strength that never let a ball pass behind the plate.

I don't know why I wash my hands—I can't even feel them. Maddie waits for me to meet her gaze, but when I don't, she gives up and slides silently out the door. The new girls flutter between stalls and primping in the mirrors, casting curious looks at me. But I close my eyes, unable to meet even my own soul in the mirror. Tonight is truly the goodbye of our youth. How could our dreams have died so soon?

I shouldn't have come. I hate that I have. Prom isn't a rite-of-passage. It's a stupid dance, a faint shadow of the important things in life. Things that slip away when you aren't watching. I toss the paper towel and open the door.

I don't have to go far to find Ty. He's alone at our table, one arm over the empty chair at his side. His smile dims as I sit stiffly.

"Is everything ok?" He rests his hand on my back, his gaze warm and concerned.

I lean out of his reach. "I'm ready to go, if you are."

He studies me. Then something in his eyes shutters, and he shrugs. "It's your dance."

We gather our things and make our way to his truck. It's a silent ride home, although I barely notice. All I see is Jaiden's face. When he parks and tells me to wait a second, it startles me into looking at him, but he's already closing his door. He opens my door, and I take his hand to get out. This time, he lets go as soon as my feet touch the ground.

"I'm sorry about the dance," he says.

"Why? Prom? Check." Bitterness tinges my words. Was tonight ever carefree? I can't remember.

Ty steps back and tilts his head toward the front door. He follows me to the porch and reaches around to open the unlocked door. His face is so close that the gold flecks in his eyes surprise me. If I leaned in, we would touch. The heat of his body lingers as he pulls back.

"See you at work tomorrow," he says.

Suddenly, I want to tell him to wait, to give us a minute alone here under the moon.

But he's already out of reach and, without looking back, he drives away. I close my eyes as the moment evaporates for my first real, end-of-the-night, I-see-you kiss. The possibility of it aches inside me, though. What would it've been like? What would've happened between us tomorrow? And the day after that?

And what am I supposed to do with these feelings when he doesn't feel them back?

I can't even ask Jaiden. Instead, I have to figure out how to help my best friend while dealing with my own drama alone.

I rub my forehead. How about that? More questions about growing up now than there were before the stupid prom.

Chapter 11

Jaiden gets her phone back on a hot Saturday in June. I think her parents finally realized it was too late to lock her in and gave up.

All the way to the pond at the back of our farm early that morning, I remember Jaiden as she'd been at her fifth birthday party, wearing a princess dress and playing softball. Even then, we'd been best friends. We've spent years doing everything together. The past several weeks since graduation have been the longest of my life without her.

I back the pickup next to Jaiden's car, crushing ankle-high grass, and turn it off. My door slams loudly in the sudden silence. Jaiden looks tired and thin as she gets out, but she smiles, and I'm reassured—she's going to be fine. Then I hug her and feel her ribs.

"How are you?" I ask.

She had said little on the phone except to ask me to meet her, in a voice so quiet and unlike herself that I didn't question it.

She turns away, heaves herself onto my tailgate, and swings her feet. I join her and sit shoulder to shoulder. Blackbirds and swallows swoop across the pond in front of us.

"I'm still pregnant, if that's what you're asking." Even in the rising heat, she wraps her arms around her middle.

"But you're so skinny." I frown.

She laughs without humor. "That's because I'm sick every day."

I cringe. "Really? That's the worst." It takes a second before I remember who else might be sick. "How is Scotty?"

"You knew he asked me to marry him," she says flatly. "Well, he keeps asking."

How can she be so calm? Then I realize Scotty is a natural romantic, so a pragmatic proposal from him isn't what she would've expected. Where's the big production and the photos? Where's the burning desire to say yes because it's the right time? Her hands tremble, and I'm struck by the enormity of how her life has changed. Marriage and a baby for college and softball.

"What'd you say?"

She takes a big breath. "I said no." She turns to look at me. "I don't want him to feel he has to marry me. I mean, both of our parents were sitting right there. It was a group decision; not him asking because he can't live without me for the rest of his life."

"But you love each other, don't you?" Her expression is full of such pure pain that I touch her arm. "That was a dumb question."

Creases form between her eyes. "He's mad that I said no, swears that he's not going anywhere. But our parents want us to get an education first, so I think they're on my side."

After a long pause, I ask, "Are you keeping the baby?"

Her face softens as her hand glides gently over her stomach. "Yes."

She shouldn't be old enough to be a mom. Aren't we both still just kids trying to figure life out? Then I think about my plans to look for

Dad. This is about as grown up as you get.

"What about softball?" I ask quietly.

To my surprise, her face crumples, and she starts to cry. I want to kick myself as my own eyes fill. I scoot closer and pull her into my arms.

"All I ever wanted was to play softball, you know?" She sniffs.

I do know. I can't talk past the lump in my own throat. She's worked so hard, for years, to get recruited to play in college. Every sacrifice and injury were worth it for the privilege to play at the next level.

She leans her head against my shoulder. "My parents made me call the coach and resign from the team."

My heart breaks again. She won't be a college athlete walking onto campus. We're never going to play against each other. We're never going to meet halfway between our schools and act as if we've never been apart.

"I'm so sorry," I whisper against her hair and hug her tight.

She reaches up to grip my arm with whitened knuckles. Locusts rattle in the bushes by the pond, and there's not a puff of wind. Everything is supernaturally still except Jaiden. Despite the shaking, she swallows hard and sits up, pulling away.

"Maybe you could try to play again later?" I swipe my nose with the back of my hand.

"Of course not," she huffs a laugh, wiping her eyes. "I'll be a mom. All of that's over. I just wanted you to know what I've decided."

It sounds final. Too final. As if she's telling *me* goodbye, too, casting me off with the rest of her youth. I pull at a loose string on my shorts' hem and blink away new tears. "If you don't already have someone else," I say, "I'll be a godmother or something, if you want, like in the princess movies." I sigh morosely. "Minus the magic."

She actually laughs.

\#

Before I know it, it's August.

On my last night at home, I cross the empty barn to my practice corner to pack a few things. Summer radiates through the wood walls. Crickets chirp. I flip through the stand of bats and pull out my favorite Mizuno.

The 2004 Olympic softball team poster has a thin film of dust. I brush it off with my forearm and study the athletes. Cat Osterman, Jessica Mendoza, Crystl Bustos, Lisa Fernandez, Jenny Finch, Natasha Watley, and the others. They have always inspired me to practice harder, to push beyond fatigue, and to blast my music until it vibrated through my chest.

Beside the poster is the picture of Dad suited up to catch and smiling at a younger me. I tap the corner to straighten it. It'd made sense to my teenage brain that if his picture witnessed how hard I'd worked while he was gone, he'd know it somehow. As if he'd been here.

I lay the bat and my backpack to the side and sit on the lip of the five-gallon bucket to search for the best balls to take. Most are streaked or nicked. I run my finger over the red stitches of one, trying to imagine what's ahead. All I can think about is what I'm leaving behind.

The calves grunt and jostle one another on the other side of the wall. I suppose one of my brothers will haul them to a new pasture after I leave tomorrow. Life will go on without me.

"Kody wants to know if you're taking his lucky baseball hat to school?" Ty asks out of the dark. Startled, I turn to see him stride across the barn.

"Tell him no, but thanks."

A smile tugs at the corners of his mouth. "You don't want a little extra luck? What kind of ball player are you?"

"Have you seen it?" I say wryly, pulling my backpack to me. "There's an expiration date on luck, and his hat passed it a long time ago." The hat hadn't worked out so well the last time he'd left it with me, anyway. It hadn't kept me from breaking my collar bone trying to ride my bike fast enough to keep sight of the twins leaving for college.

Ty pulls a bucket over and sits with his elbows on his knees. My shoulders tense. It'd taken a while after the prom for us to find safe footing again. But the long hours over the summer and the hard physical work lent itself to joking and comradery, and we'd made it. I glance at his boots, scuffed from slogging through miles of pastures with me. And it still makes me laugh to remember his expression when he'd torn those holes in his jeans building a barbed wire fence. Even his ratty beaver t-shirts have grown on me, or desensitized me anyway, after seeing one every day. I swallow around the knot in my throat. It takes a lot of effort not to ruin it all by showing how much I'm going to miss him.

"Do you know how to find your dorm tomorrow?" he asks. "I could draw you a map."

I huff a laugh. "With crayons? Oh, please. And color code it?"

"Whatever will help," he says solemnly. "Your mom said—"

I hold up a finger. "Careful. Don't lie. My mom would never say a bad word about her only daughter."

He grins. "She mentioned you might be directionally challenged, that's all."

I level my gaze. "North is up, Ty. What's the big deal?" Over his laughter, I say, "Besides, you and Fletch volunteered to show me around, remember?" I narrow my eyes. "And I don't want the plain ol' school-brochure tour either, so up your game."

Behind the teasing glint, there's a wariness. As if he feels the same tension I do. But that doesn't make sense. He's the one who made it clear we're just friends.

A car door slams, and florist shop owner, Bella, marches into the barn with a large bouquet. "River? Got something for ya."

"Back here."

Ty trails me to the door where Bella hands me white daisies tied with a blue ribbon. Dad had been the last person to give me daisies. He said he'd always think of me when he saw them.

"Daisies are my favorite." I smile, lift the card and read out loud, "*Congratulations. Northbridge is lucky to have you.*" I turn the card over. "Who's it from?"

She peers over my arm. "Is there not a name?" She shakes her head in disgust. "Doug took that order. Said some kid ordered them. I'll find out and let you know. Sorry, dear."

A kid? Who could possibly want to welcome me to college? My mind races through possibilities, then stumbles over Jace. He'd repeatedly said he'd look for me on campus.

"How weird," I mumble.

"You have an admirer and you're not even at school yet." Bella winks and leaves Ty and me in an awkward silence.

Flushed, I fumble the daisies into the crook of my arm and retrieve my backpack. Ty slips the strap out of my hand and over his own shoulder, but I can't meet his gaze. He follows as I turn off the lights for the last time and walk to my car. He settles my backpack inside, then retreats so I can close the door.

"I'll see ya at school." His voice trails off.

"Okay." I twist the flowers' ribbon around my finger. Why is this so hard?

He tucks his hands in his pockets and studies my car. I squeeze the ever-livin' life out of the flowers, painfully aware of his every move. But he finally nods and leaves without a backward glance.

#

The next morning, I shove my suitcase in the car and slam the hatch. I check each tire, pointedly ignoring our farmhouse and the familiar acres of native grasses that are the background of my childhood. The country air is filled with trills and tweets, songs that I would recognize anywhere.

The four guys come out of the barn, batting dirt from their hands onto their jeans and laughing. Kody reaches me first. I duck, but he pulls me in for a hug.

"We're going to miss you, Li'l River," he says in a baby voice.

I pat his shoulder. "Want me to stay, Kod? Are you scared?"

"You're so sweet." Then he tickles me until I gasp and squirm.

Zeph rescues me, sending Kody back a step, and I lean into his hug.

"I really will miss you. You'd better call," he says quietly.

"I will. Maybe you could visit. I'll introduce you to all the cute girls." I tilt my head toward Kody. "He can meet your rejects."

Zeph laughs. "Like they'll be able to tell us apart."

Kody smirks. Ty watches, arms crossed, the ghost of a smile on his face.

Fletch hugs me loosely. "See you at school in a couple of days."

"I'll be waiting." I smile back.

Mom comes out of the house with a bottle of water and a bag of snacks for the drive. "Are you sure about this, River?" She assesses me. "The boys can handle the farm. I can jump in the suburban and follow you to school, help set up your room."

"It's okay, Mom. There's not that much to do before my team meeting this afternoon." I focus on the bag of fruit and crackers she hands me, feeling the noose close around my neck. I'm almost gone—tied to a school far from here. Kody grabs the bag and opens my car door.

"It's Mom's special snack, the kind we had on the bus ride to camp, remember?" He ducks in, then pauses. "Where are you going to freakin' put it, River?"

I rescue it from his big paws and push him out. "Don't mess up my packing."

He smirks, letting me drive him back several steps. "Easy there, you brute."

"Kodiak, stop teasing," Mom commands. For a minute, her using his whole name eclipses the sadness of leaving.

"Me? I'm not doing anything." He nips the bag from my hand and tosses it to Fletch. I sigh and roll my shoulder. I can't win playing this game—at least not playing fairly. I stalk toward Fletch, noticing how he stays away from my stronger right arm. He can't use his wrestler's moves on me in front of my brothers, so he'd have to just stand and take it if I catch him.

He laughs and tosses it back to Kody. Zeph snags it and I turn doe-eyes on him.

"Zephyr," Mom says. "Put it back and leave her alone."

"The story of my life," he groans. "I'm the one who's trying to help."

Mom hugs me instead of fussing, and that's when I realize that they're all trying to make the leaving easier. Chaos and teasing—hidden tears. I avoid Mom's eyes, trying to keep my expression cheerful, but Ty's sympathetic face over her shoulder is almost worse. He smiles with his arms crossed but lifts a finger in a wave, just the way I taught him. Mom grips my shoulders and waits for me to meet her gaze.

"You're going to do great," she says. "I can't wait to watch you and your new team. Call and tell me about your roommate, okay?"

"I will." I avoid the tender brightness in her eyes and try to remember to breathe. As if I have this all under control. As if I'm ready for this.

And then it seems like just a heartbeat later, when I'm looking at them in my rearview mirror from the end of the driveway, that I'm sure I'm not ready for this at all.

Chapter 12

My new catcher is a freshman. Lily lifts her helmet from her thick red braid and stops beside me. Coach Bosswood yanks up the adjustable netting separating the three pitching lanes and approaches sophomore pitcher Zoe. As I open my water bottle, I catch the glance Zoe flicks at me before she turns back to the coach.

"What's going on?" Lily asks quietly.

I shrug. "She hates me."

Lily nods. "Which she? Zoe or Bossbaby."

Good question. Coach Bosswood demonstrates a spin for Zoe and varsity catcher Abbey. On our other side, Liz picks up balls with her catcher, Kim.

"Bosswood. It's like she already knows I'll fail, so I might as well go ahead and live out of my car and beg food on a median," I say darkly.

"I hate to say it, but that may not be your only problem. I don't know Zoe well, but I'd recognize jealousy anywhere."

I groan. "I know. She watches me all the time. She even made me change lockers because she needed more room. What did I do to her?"

"You're the shiny new object, and she's not."

I huff and wipe my jaw against my sleeve.

Lily faces me. "Just pitch, Harte. That's it. The more Bossbaby gets on to you, the better you do. Take it as a gift."

"Am I supposed to ignore that?" I gesture as, of course, Coach beams at Zoe.

Lily studies them. "'There's no crying in baseball,' right? But maybe Zoe would, if Bosswood was tough on her." She leans closer. "Bossbaby's dad and sister coach, too. She probably knows what she's doing."

"I can't believe you call her Bossbaby."

It pisses me off, though, that Bosswood makes me doubt myself. Does she think I'm good enough to be here or not? It'd all be so much easier if she'd recruited me herself.

"You've got two choices," Lily says. "Stick it out and eventually get game time, or crumble." She looks pointedly from my feet to my head. "And that would be some fall."

At the end of practice, Bosswood sets up two pitching mounds and assigns a catcher for each. Rotating the pitchers into the spots, she calls out game situations. Every time she yells "next" after one of my missed pitches, I feel as though I've failed a midterm.

Bosswood lays out the scenario for Zoe and me. "It's a 3-0 count. What pitch would you throw?"

"I'd throw a fastball on the inside corner," Zoe says.

"Screwball on the inside corner," I say and hate that it sounds like a question.

"Go." Coach points to Zoe, but even with Abby framing the pitch, it's a little off. "That was high. Go again."

When my screwball is a little outside, she calls, "Ball. Next."

Bewildered, I trade places with Liz, who shares a sympathetic look. It's hard not to slump.

After practice, Lily drags me to lunch and sits across from Fletch. I sit numbly beside him and go through the motions of unfolding a napkin across my lap. Inside, I replay every second of Coach's disapproval of my pitches. I'll show her. I'll fix my spins. And hit my spots. And once I'm good enough, I hope I get the chance to prove I know what I'm doing. *It'll just take more practice.* More than I'm getting daily with the team. Even more than the four extra nights a week I've added. So... every night then.

Fletch's stare bores into my ear. I look up and he raises his eyebrows.

"One guess why you're so quiet," he says.

I shrug a shoulder. "You already know."

He nods and studies me. Then he turns back to his overflowing tray framed by his forearms, as if to ward off theft. Stir-fried chicken, vegetables, three rolls, and a slice of chocolate cake. He digs in his pocket.

"What're you doing?" I ask.

He leans back, holds his phone over his plate and snaps a picture. Taps his phone. My phone chimes as he scoots forward again to pick up his fork.

I roll my eyes and turn the screen to Lilly. "Do you take pictures of food?"

She gives Fletch a diplomatic grimace. "I'm sorry. I haven't thought about it."

"That's a no. Don't apologize." I turn to look at his pleased face. "Does anyone else you know send food pics? Or is this because you were a wrestler?"

"You can't tell me this doesn't look perfect." He circles his fork over his plate. "And it's not just me. Ty took a picture of his steak on Saturday."

My heart twists. I haven't seen or heard from Ty since the day I left for school. At least now I know he made it safely to campus.

"You were a wrestler?" Lily asks him.

I pick up my spoon. "Yes. Fletch was fast as lightning. But one wrestling season, I flipped through his phone—twenty-seven pictures of food. They weren't all his. Some were from the internet. Just food."

Lily giggles, and Fletch smiles as he chews. "When you can't eat as much as you want, it's all you think about," he says.

"Yup." I shake my head sorrowfully. "Not cars. Not girls. Only food."

"I had a picture of you, remember?" He points his roll at me before taking a bite.

I narrow my eyes. "I was eating ice cream."

Fletch nods as he chews. "Good times." Then, while I'm still smiling, he leans close. "Made you forget." He winks and returns his attention to his food.

I bump his shoulder as I steal one of his rolls and take a bite. *This* is why I love him.

#

Coach O'Daniel adjusts his windbreaker during the last thirty minutes of pitching practice. He paces thoughtfully, pausing behind each pitcher while we run drills.

"Rapid fire!" Coach Bosswood calls and sets the timer. "One minute. Three times."

Lily and I work back and forth, concentrating on every pitch.

"Good one," she says, and rises to one knee to throw the ball back. I barely hear her over the staccato of pops echoing between the lanes.

I can't tell if my pitches are faster as they skid across my callused fingers, but my legs burn as if they are. If I could just find one more burst of strength to overcome this fatigue.

Then Bosswood yells from behind me, "Explode off the mound, River! Use those legs."

I grit my teeth. Sweat trickles down my temple. Trying to ignore my quivering muscles, I bear down, drive off the mound, land, snap, follow-through. There's no time to enjoy the gratifying pop in Lily's glove.

Finally, the timer sounds, and my damp glove slides to the ground with a thump. Coach Bosswood ducks into Liz's cage. Zoe tracks her while she picks up her water bottle. Then she turns and frowns when O'Daniel enters my lane. Lily and I share a look.

"River." O'Daniel tilts his head as Lily and I pick up loose balls. "I saw you in here late last night. What's up?"

"Just working on some things, Coach." I wipe my cheek on my shoulder. Haven't other pitchers needed as much practice as I do? Maybe it's just that all the work hasn't improved my pitching yet.

"Who told you to come in every night?" he asks.

I blink in surprise that he'd noticed. "No one." I dump the balls in my arms.

He waits until I look up. "I've been doing this a long time, you know. Obsessive practice isn't what makes the difference. Purposeful practice does. You need to focus on your snaps and relax after releasing the ball. Follow through." He narrows his eyes. "I recognize that you're a hard-working athlete, but don't forget that progress is made during rest periods. You're too tense. It's defeating the purpose."

I shift my weight uncertainly.

"Go do something fun," he clarifies. "Give your mind a break. I don't want you in here after hours the rest of the week."

Well. Shoot.

Chapter 13

Relaxing is for the birds. As I avoid puddles on my way to the student union the next day, I decide that telling someone to relax is like telling them not to think about the color blue. My feet may be dry for the first time since our early morning practice, and I may have spare time on my hands, but all I think is Blue. By the time I enter the student union, mist clings to my lashes and frizzes my hair. Blue. Blue. Blue.

Flipping back my hood, I leave wet footprints across the bookstore, snagging a pack of notecards on the way to the lanyards. Mumbling darkly about "fun" and "resting," I squeeze between racks of sweatshirts and turn the lanyard display to snatch one color, then another.

I'm almost done when a hand snakes over my shoulder. I squeal and flinch into the sweatshirts, sending hangars clattering to the floor. The clerk cranes his neck to eye me suspiciously.

Ty is bent over laughing. "What's wrong with you?" he gasps.

"Are you kidding?" I huff and don't know if my heart is jumping from the scare or the shock of seeing him in person. I pick up the sweatshirts and rehang them. "You're what's wrong with me. You always do that on purpose."

"I'm sorry," he says, unapologetically. Drops of water glisten in his hair and dot his sweatshirt. He grins at my expression. "I was going to say you should get the blue one."

I roll my eyes and replace everything except the red one and hear his soft huff of a laugh. "Where have you been?" I ask, but what I want to know is why he hasn't called. "I thought you were going to show me around? I've been here for weeks."

He smirks knowingly. "There's this thing called school…"

"Forget it." I wave him away and veer toward the front.

He follows. The clerk glances between us as he scans my purchases.

"Let's go now," Ty says. The clerk narrows his eyes at how Ty has crowded my space. Not that Ty notices. He looks up from a basket of lipstick-sized LED flashlights and meets my gaze.

"Fan-freaking-tastic. Let's go."

His brown eyes light with laughter as he studies my face. "Have you been to the tower?"

"At the library? Not yet." I pay, then stuff the bag into my backpack.

"Have you heard its story?" He swipes his card for a package of gum and a pink flashlight.

Pink? I hide a smile as we walk out. "What's the big deal? Did someone jump?"

He shrugs and glances down at me. "Well, not just one." He stops when I do and lifts my hood against the mist. "It was a lover's pact, you know."

"Are you joking?" My voice rises as he turns to the door.

He reaches back and tugs me forward. "Serious as a renegade."

Despite the weather, the tower's square copper roof is visible above the library. I eye it with fascinated horror. "How long ago did they die?"

"Back in the 1940s, I think. The campus would've been different then, but the tower has always been the tallest building."

The library is photogenic, even in the rain. And the landscaping at the base of the building begs to be used as a digital background.

"Were they students?" I ask as we climb the concrete steps.

"He was a German on a student visa." He opens the door. "And she was a Polish Jew."

"In the 40s?"

He nods. "You'd think if there was one corner in the world where they'd be safe, it would've been here. But it was during that part of the war where the government set up encampments like Crystal City and filled them with Japanese, Germans, and Italians."

Crystal City? I don't remember hearing that name before. We weave through the library and up a rich wooden staircase. Mute amber light streaks from a stained-glass window, bleaching spots on the wood. At the landing, an older hall dotted with doors sprawls to the right. We turn left and continue to climb.

"So," I huff as we pass cherubim hovering in the red-gold design of the window. "Why did they jump?"

"Kind of a Romeo and Juliet story." He's not even breathing hard.

"I knew you'd bring up Shakespeare as soon as you could."

He raises his eyebrows. "If you don't want to know what happened…"

I chuckle breathlessly. "Sorry. Carry on. It's your story."

He gives me a look. I press my lips together, point at them, and am rewarded by a faint twitch of a smile.

But Ty climbs a couple of steps in silence, as if contemplating how to continue. "They revoked his visa," he says softly. "He didn't want to leave—not with the Nazi party-thing waiting at home. As for her, where could she go in Europe with a German boyfriend and be safe?"

We round the corner at the top. Benches are bolted to the floor facing walls of full-length windows. The view steals the rest of my breath. Mist covers the tops of trees and buildings. Had it looked this haunting back then?

"It's beautiful," I murmur. But the unhindered panorama also feels isolated. Like we're alone in this world caged by glass. I lay a hand on the window frame, fighting vertigo to peer down to the ground. My feet tingle and my palms sweat. "I couldn't do it. I couldn't jump."

Ty leans to study the drop, too. "I wonder which of them decided. Or maybe, by the time they climbed all the way up here, they thought they didn't have another choice."

"I don't know," I say thoughtfully. "Maybe jumping together wasn't just an option, but their goal."

"I don't know," he counters. "What kind of guy lets the girl he loves die?"

"So, maybe it was an accident?" I try to work it out in my head. "Lots of things happen you don't mean to."

His lips pull to the side. "It would've had to be an epic accident. No. The story is they committed suicide together and, if they had changed their mind, we'll never know because the consequences were permanent."

"Maybe they didn't have hope." I raise my gaze, looking out across the multicolored trees. "They thought they'd reached a dead end, but if they'd had any reason to hope, they'd have run with that." I can't help thinking that hope is the one thing I can't live without. Otherwise, Dad might disappear for good.

Ty frowns as he studies me. "Maybe they didn't know how to find hope."

I get the feeling he's not talking about his story.

The low wispy clouds stretching to the horizon remind me how small I am in the universe. And maybe that's why I've been able to keep hoping—I've lived where the sky was endless. It takes a lot of faith to survive where everything is bigger than you.

Voices echo up the stairs. I back out of the window and smile softly. "Thanks for showing me, Ty."

We go down single file, the voices getting louder. Rachel, a sophomore left fielder on our team, and two of her friends appear around a curve. She acknowledges me, then her gaze slips past my shoulder. I can imagine the impression Ty makes. He feels like a solid mountain at my back, and she raises an eyebrow as she passes.

"How's softball going?" he asks once we're outside.

"It's okay. Our first scrimmage is next week." I push my hands into the kangaroo pocket of my sweatshirt.

He leans a hip against the back of a bench and studies me. "What's wrong? And don't say nothing, because you rarely say softball is 'okay.'"

I'd forgotten how perceptive he is.

"It's an adjustment." I avoid his gaze. "I'm learning a lot about pitching…" I straighten. "Oh. Guess what?" He brightens, a mirror of my excitement before he even knows what I'm going to say. "We're going to San Diego for spring break."

"Who's we?"

"The team." I poke his shoulder. "Don't you wish you were as cool as us?"

"All the time." His skin holds the same sun-browned hue from this summer, but it's his eyes that hold me in place. The longer I look at him, the less I notice the cold, and the more I recall how strong he'd felt the day we'd kissed.

"Ahem."

I jump and find Fletch, a book under his arm, glancing warily between Ty and me.

"Did you remember index cards for the research paper, River?" he says.

I pat my backpack and gesture to his book. "Is that all you brought? And you're late."

He ignores that. "I thought you had to take an ice bath."

"Done."

"Okay, then." Fletch tips his head to the doors. "Our papers are due the day after tomorrow."

Ty smirks. "How did you two end up in the same class?"

"Just lucky for Fletch." I adjust my backpack. "I'm sure he hasn't started on his American history of social class and politics paper, have you?"

Fletch leans toward Ty. "She's writing about how there used to be fewer chances for girls to play sports."

A gust of wind sends droplets of water drumming from the branches overhead. I pull my hood higher, and Ty's shoulders hunch.

"You're such a tattletale. I'm not going that far back in history," I say. "I'm writing about Dr. Dot Richardson, the Olympic softball player."

"Which Olympics?" Ty asks.

"1996 in Atlanta and 2000 in Sydney. She was on the 2000 poster by my practice mound."

"Why her?" Ty asks.

Fletch narrows his eyes. "Sucker. You had to ask when you know the only thing she loves is softball. I'm going to get a table." He climbs the steps, but winks at me before disappearing inside.

Ty nods for me to continue. Where to begin? "She's done it all...

played on boys' teams." I press a hand to my chest. "I only played on a machine pitch boys' team. She was picked for a women's team when she was ten. *Ten.* Her book describes attending college, then med school while trying out for the American team, practicing, and competing." I shake my head. "Nothing stopped her. No matter how hard it was. And training for the Olympics was no picnic. There wasn't Title IX when she started. We've got more support now because she and all the other women paved the way for us."

The campus clock chimes. The tip of Ty's nose is pink with cold. Then, to my shock, he steps closer and kisses my forehead under my hood. Heat floods me again.

He holds my gaze as he slowly backs away. "I want to read it when you're done." At my dazed look, he smiles and turns to go.

When I reach for the handle on the glass library door, my goofy, flushed face reflects back at me—evidence of Ty's effect. But my smile fades. This exhilaration could easily become addicting. But Ty is just a friend—one who distracts me completely while not seeming bothered himself.

I pull the door open, displacing the image. I don't have time for that kind of complication.

Chapter 14

"Twelve triangles?" Kim asks at the end of practice later in the week.

Coach O'Daniel nods and taps the ground with the Fungo bat that he's used for infield practice, a sheen of sweat on his forehead.

"And check your email today, ladies. The list of hotels we'll be staying at this fall is there, along with game times. Your parents shouldn't call me to ask for information. You're responsible."

Lily glances over, her face flushed under her damp red hair. I give her a thumbs up. We'll be printing those schedules in my room as soon as we get back.

"Also, not that anyone cares, the Friday before our first scrimmage will be the team dinner." He stifles a smile at the whoops and cheers and glances at Coach Bosswood. "Top ten coaching tip: learn what excites your team."

She grins. "And your coaching staff."

He checks his watch. "Okay. Respond to the email. Got it?"

"Are we having jambalaya, Coach?" someone asks.

"Of course." He gestures to Coach CJ with a straight face. "And Coach has volunteered to keep me from overeating, so we won't have a repeat from last year." His mustache spreads with his smile at the laughs.

Then he straightens and tucks his clipboard under his arm. "Good job today." His gaze passes over us, catching each eye as we quiet. "All the talent we need is here, believe me. But remember, everyone gets knocked off their talent at some point. The exceptional pull themselves back up with their heart. That reserve of strength comes from your work ethic and your will, your teammates... and the hope of what you believe." He nods. "I see a lot of heart out here."

He glances up at the sun. "It's hot and you're tired, but you're not finished. So, it's going to take courage to attack these last little things with enthusiasm, even running triangles." He lowers his chin, his voice quieting so that I lean in to not miss a single word. "Outsiders will see your success, but the knowledge of the work you invested to get there is all yours. Your reputation is what others think about you." He pats his heart. "But you have to live with who you are. That's why I leave this part to the honor system." He nods at Sarah and turns away.

The coaches leave the field, picking up water bottles and clipboards. For a moment we don't move, just stand in a sweaty huddle under the humid afternoon sun.

"Let's go." Sarah threads through us, taking the lead. "You heard them. Start at home plate. It only counts if you touch both the out-of-bound poles before heading back to home. No shortcuts or we have to start over."

I toss my glove, the soft leather falling open under the weight of the ball. Twenty-three pairs of cleats make tearing sounds on the grass as we run.

By the tenth triangle, blood pounds in my face. Lily is alarmingly red except for a white outline of her mouth. We make the turn at the pole and see Chelsey, a sophomore who didn't play much last year, make a U-turn half-way and go back. I grimace at Lily. She shakes her head. The other freshmen, Andy, Katie, and Emma, are faster and run in a pack ahead of us. I wonder what the upper classmen will say about Chelsey.

Before we make the twelfth pole turn, Sarah and Abbey are already coming back. With a whoop, Sarah high five's everyone she passes. Everyone except Chelsey, who is already at the dugout. When we straggle in, Sarah, Abbey, and Mia gesture all of us closer.

"Huddle up," Sarah says over the sound of heavy breathing and the huge metal fan at the other end. The other seniors besides Sarah—Kim and Liz—don't make eye contact. "So, Chelsey didn't finish the run."

Next to me, Mia drinks from her water bottle. She and the other juniors, Abbey, Callie, and Bree, look grim. No one responds, and the silence grows.

I clear my throat. "We noticed."

"If we tell the coaches, will we have to run that again?" Lily gestures to the poles.

"That's the rule." Mia wipes her chin. There are mumbled curses and groans. "But no one asked what happens to Chelsey if we rat her out."

"Because we don't care," someone says behind me.

"The coaches take care of their own business." Sarah shares a glance with Mia, and a chill runs down my spine. "Let's just say that they enforce their rules."

"But it's not fair to us," Dawz says, leaning forward with one knee on the bench to see around Katie. Dawz (I don't remember her first name,

Juliet or something weirdly girly), Rachel, and Zoe are sophomores, like Chelsey.

"The alternative is to keep it to ourselves." Sarah's hands are on her hips, a challenge on her face. "Do we let this slide? Coach always says to take care of the little things, so is that the best we can be?"

"What do you think?" Abbey asks, looking from girl to girl. "We have to decide as a team. We're all going to live with the consequences."

"Tell her to freakin' finish." Bree wipes her face on the neck of her shirt.

"She's already in the locker room," Sarah says. "If she cared what we thought, she wouldn't have cheated."

"I don't want to run again." Katie sighs, looking beat.

In the silence, metal cleats scrape the concrete. Someone drinks from a squeeze bottle with a gurgle. Our groundskeeper, Old Whit, whistles a mindless tune from across the field as he pulls water hoses and rakes from the shed to work the dirt infield.

"I think we're going to have to tell the coaches," I say reluctantly. Behind me someone whispers, "Suck-up."

Zoe turns speculatively from Sarah to me. Lily wipes sweaty hair stuck to her forehead and nods. "I agree. If we let things slide now, where will we be in the spring?"

I meet Sarah's gaze over the others' heads. Then she scans the group. "What do the rest of you think? It's our team, our season. What's it worth?"

"If someone cheats and we let them," Andy says. "We won't be able to trust each other."

Dawz curses. "The coaches won't trust us either."

"I didn't come here to lose," Callie says. "I came here because it's a great program. We can't settle."

"So, let's vote," Abbey says.

"We don't have to vote," Zoe interrupts. "Our honor is on the line. Let's just do it. If you don't want to tell the coaches, say so now. Otherwise, team unity comes first."

Sarah shakes her head. "We vote. We're in this together. We listen to each other."

"Hands up if we should vote?" Rachel asks. It's unanimous. "Should we tell the coaches and run the triangles again as a team? Raise a hand."

It's unanimous, again, of course, but deep sighs fill the air, along with a few more curses.

No one moves. Finally, Sarah clears her throat. "I just want to say…" She throws an arm around the girl at her side. "That I'm so proud to be on this team with you all. There's no one better. Love you guys."

I put an arm around Lily's shoulders and the other around Katie's. Our circle tightens despite the heat, and I feel the dread of running again lifted, less heavy somehow because it's shared. Goosebumps rise on my skin.

Abbey asks softly, "Who are we?"

We start to sway side-to-side. "The Fighting Fishers."

"Who?"

"Fighting Fishers!" And I clench my fists in their shirts as we sway hard and fast.

"Who?!"

"Fighting Fishers!"

We break a part with whoops and fist pumps. Then, we run again.

Chapter 15

"River." Coach O'Daniel appears outside the athletic office at the football stadium. I turn toward him. Then startle. He smiles at my delayed reaction.

An hour in the Athletic Academic Center has left me in a lingering, foggy stupor. Any place that can lay your life out so bleakly should come with a warning.

"I was just thinking about you." He joins me on the sidewalk. "How're your classes?"

Good? Bad? Revolting? One problem class sinking my boat. And I can't tell anyone, especially my family. I glance at Coach and manage a noncommittal sound. He probably already knows about algebra. A squirrel pauses on the sidewalk, giving me the brown eye.

"Last time we spoke, you said your weakest subject was math. Are you having problems?"

That startles a laugh from me. This brain fog finds saying *math* and *problem* together hilarious. But a glance at Coach reminds me he's serious and the misery returns. "I bombed the test last week."

"I saw that on my weekly report," he says calmly. "And I heard you've found a tutor."

My eyebrows rise. "Really? The AAC just worked that out. We start tonight after batting practice."

And thank the almighty goodness the AAC scheduled the tutor themself. Saves me from admitting to the one math tutor I know how badly I'm failing. If Ty doesn't know, maybe my brothers won't either.

"What about the rest? Your room? The other players?"

"Everything's great." I avoid his gaze.

After a pause, he says, "I've coached a long time." There's humor behind his familiar words, the ones he says before imparting wisdom. "I know it's difficult to adjust, that's why I check on my players. But you're going to be fine, kid, trust me. I've seen it all. You're going to sail right through the next four years with me."

I honestly don't think he means sail. It's four years of this, and I've barely started. He means I'll back country hike the John Muir Trail—barefoot—with him. But I'll enjoy it.

"Good," I mutter as we join students waiting at the crosswalk. "Mom won't want me home early." Especially if it's because I flunked out.

He startles me with *his* laugh this time, then leans close. "If she says that I've talked to her, don't believe it."

My lips pull to the side at the twinkle in his eyes. "Oh, so it's a conspiracy?"

He shrugs one shoulder. "I make the same deal with all the parents. We agree to save my job."

Now I smile. "I should've known."

He nods as if pleased, his mustache twitching. After we cross, he turns serious. "River, have you heard Wayne Gretzky say, '*The highest compliment that you can pay me is to say that I work hard every day.*'?"

I almost choke. He's quoting a hockey icon?

"You're already ahead," he says. "Your heart has been in this for a long time. College may not be easy, but remember that I'm here to help in any way I can. We all are."

He may be, but Bosswood is different. "I would like to know if there's anything I should work on? For pitching, I mean."

"The staff has talked about this." He smooths his mustache and assumes a head coach's tone. "Coach Bosswood notes your hard work. I'm sure you're doing a good job."

I frown. "So, there's nothing?"

"Coach Bosswood will tell you if there is. She's not shy. If you have questions, just ask her." He winks. "In its own way, this time of year is grueling as we practice day after day without live games. It'll get better." He watches my unconvincing nod. "Coach Bosswood knows pitchers, Riv. Take my word for it, she's smart, insightful, and understands more than you think. In fact, we were just discussing you, our farm girl, putting your mark on everything you do. We refer to you as our own branding iron."

Wow. He's *really* good at this… at making you feel confident. I'd recognized that the first time I'd met him as a thirteen-year-old at camp. But as much as I need to know if he remembers, I don't have the nerve to bring it up.

Lily and Emma appear ahead, dressed for after-hours batting practice. Coach waves, then winks at me. "It's been a good talk, River."

He leaves. As I approach the girls, the smell of fried food saturates the air.

"We've ordered onion rings." Lily gestures to Doc's Dogs and Burgers.

"I thought we were going to practice." I frown and calculate how much time I have.

"Get with the program." Emma snaps her fingers. "We're sharing onion rings first."

I surrender, hands up, and join them at a round table inside. A chalkboard lists all the athletic events for the next week, including our scrimmage.

"So, do families usually come to scrimmages?" I ask, taking a seat.

"My parents are," Lily says.

"Mine aren't." Emma sits across from us.

"My mom and grandma will come," I muse. "But probably not my brothers." Our number is called, and I jump to retrieve our food.

"You have brothers?" Emma calls after me.

I turn to Lily with a questioning look. "The twins. We've talked about this."

When I return, they descend on the basket before I can sit down.

"Brothers?" Emma prompts, already reaching for her second ring.

"They're twins." Lily says, mouth full. "Mega-millionaires jetting around the world."

"No one told me." Emma pauses, looking hurt.

"Because Lily is a liar." I laugh. "They're poor college-graduate farmers."

"River doesn't talk about anything. Ever," Lily says from the side of her mouth.

I lick my finger. "Nothing to tell." I eye the last two onion rings.

"Why's she so secretive?" Emma whispers loudly. My jaw drops, and she swoops in, taking the last rings and handing one to Lily. I roll my eyes.

"No guts," Lily says.

I smirk and snatch the onion ring from her fingers. "Bite me..."

Then the door opens and my mind goes blank. Lily steals her onion ring from my limp fingers, but Ty pulls off his sunglasses. His dark green t-shirt fits snugly across his shoulders and biceps as he tucks the glasses into the neck of his shirt. Mud speckles his boots and jeans.

"Nice," Emma says, following my gaze.

He doesn't see me at first, until Lily's backhand against my arm catches his eye. He pauses, then threads between tables. Lily and Emma gawk as I lean back and grin at his small, crooked smile and crinkling eyes.

"Working hard?" he asks, and I beam as if he's quoted Shakespeare.

"Carb-loading for practice." I gesture to the others. "Do you know Lily and Emma?"

He's got very good manners, I notice, as I introduce him. Then we watch him make his way to the counter.

Emma leans in. "Who is he, and how do you know him?"

Lily pulls her gaze back to me and glares. "The long answer, Harte."

"He worked with us this summer." At their stares, my cheeks warm. "On our farm."

"Uh-huh." Emma studies my blush. She turns and raises her hand to get his attention. "Ty, I have a question."

His head swivels from Emma to me, and he smirks. But he comes over.

"I told them you worked on the farm this summer," I say helpfully.

He sits next to me, crossing his arms on the table. "Yeah. Me and Fletcher."

"Oh." Lily nods and leans past him to glare. "Fletcher, too?"

"So, you've known River for a while." Emma settles in to chat.

"Mmm, almost a year, I guess," he says, looking thoughtful.

"He's a math tutor." I mimic his crossed arms with a strange anxiety about this interrogation. "The best."

Ty picks up a straw wrapper and wads it into a ball.

"Do you play a sport, Ty?" Emma asks as he flicks the paper at my face and I bat it away. He smiles at her.

"No." He turns to me, eyes twinkling. "And how do you know if I'm a good math tutor?"

I take a drink. Why did I bring this up? "You said you were good." I tip the cup at him. "Are you saying I shouldn't believe you?"

"When have you ever?" he asks. "And I thought you were going to call about algebra."

I shake my head. "I never said—"

Lily leans forward. "River sucks at math."

"I do not."

She drums her fingers on the table. "What did you get on the last test?"

"I've got it covered, okay?" Out of the corner of my eye, I see Ty studying me.

"It's just as well." He slouches back in his chair. "My last tutoring spot has filled."

I frown. It hadn't occurred to me he'd run out of time slots. Him, surrounded by his happy students, all basking in his undivided attention.

A number is called. "That's mine. Nice meeting y'all." He scoots his chair back, hands braced on his legs to stand, but he meets my gaze. "You're still scrimmaging on Saturday?"

I nod. "Are you coming?"

He squeezes my elbow as he stands to leave. "I'll be there."

The pressure of his fingers lingers as Lily and Emma trade looks across the table, as if I won't notice. But what does that matter when he's coming to my scrimmage? Leaning back, I stretch for one last glimpse through the window.

And I get one, just not what I expected.

Zoe, the softball princess, has pulled out her phone in the middle of the sidewalk, right in his path.

Chapter 16

Zoe is oblivious to the world for the time it takes Ty to reach her. Then, with impeccable timing, she comes to life and turns into his path. He dodges the collision, reaching out to steady her with the hand that'd touched me seconds before. He releases her, but they linger, two beautiful people laughing and talking in the sunshine. But I tense as her attention sharpens on him—a focus as intent as a great white coming out of the deep.

Zoe's flush rides high on her cheeks when she walks in. "Guess who's coming to my scrimmage?" She drops into a chair. "Just the hottest guy I've ever seen."

"Our scrimmage," Lily says. "And, yeah, that's Ty. He's a friend of—"

"Speaking of softball," I interrupt. "We better get going."

Zoe frowns. She glances out the window, but Ty is gone—I feel it.

"What are you doing, Zoe?" Emma asks.

"The Athletic Director is a friend of my dad's," Zoe says slowly. "I'm babysitting their two-year-old tonight."

"Perfect," I blurt. Emma nudges my foot under the table. "I mean, have fun."

Zoe's eyes narrow. She's smart; she'll figure it out. Maybe she already has because she studies me from ponytail to fingertips, as if measuring me for a casket.

Lily rises. "Ready? Time's wasting."

I give a half-hearted flap of a goodbye as we leave Zoe alone in the restaurant. Outside, it's hot, the sun burning my eyes, searing the image of Zoe and Ty. We're halfway to the batting cages before Lily breaks the silence.

"He won't ask her out."

He might. He could. How will I survive if he does? I clench my teeth. "Not my business."

Emma launches into a story from class but, for a second, Lily leans her head on my shoulder as we walk. I love her for that.

#

At practice, Emma cracks balls off of tees with the easy rhythm of a metronome. Across the building, baseball players blast their music. Their voices are a low throb around the tings of their bats as Lily perches on the lip of a bucket and soft-tosses to me. I'm winding up for the next swing when a movement in Coach's office catches my eye.

"Lily," I hiss. "Look. Hurry!"

She jumps up. Coach O'Daniel crouches over his desk. He seems absorbed in his work—then the chorus starts. And to our glee, his head bobs, and his left hand rises to the beat.

"Those are the moves from the music video." Lily giggles at my side.

The chorus ends and Coach flips a page.

"What're you doing?" Emma asks as we wait expectantly.

I point, and she backs up until she can see over our shoulders. At the next chorus, up goes his hand, and Emma squeals. He turns, suddenly, and Emma squeals again, collapsing into giggles.

Coach gestures for us to get back to the tees, but I swear his mustache twitches. I pick up the bat and dance the rest of the song with Lily before she plops onto the bucket with a laugh.

So, when she fumbles the first toss, I chortle, ready to give her a hard time, but she's staring at the tee.

"What was that?" I ask.

"Don't look, but Jace just came in," she says.

I glance over my shoulder. "Do you have a crush on him?" I tease.

Her pale skin flushes. "Shut up. Everyone has a crush on him."

That's probably true. He's drawn our attention, and all he's done is drop his baseball bag and talk with his teammates.

"Too bad he's here to see me," I joke and tap my temple. "We've got a connection."

Lily rolls her eyes, and I grin. Truthfully, he's forgotten I exist. The few times I've seen him from a distance, there was no hint of recognition.

"You wish." Lily picks up a ball. "He can't stay away from me. I see him twice a week."

"Because you have the same Spanish class." I laugh, setting up and swinging at the toss. "He sent me flowers once." I wiggle my hips. But, really, why had he done that?

"Liar. Liar. Pants on fire." She smirks, tossing another, and I swing.

I nonchalantly glance at him. His confidence is sexy. His laugh. The way he shakes wavy brown hair out of his eyes, then slowly scans the room. His gaze passes over me—then returns. My heart skips a beat.

He tilts his head, and his smile changes into something dangerous. Lily gasps as he crosses the room and ducks into our lane.

"Hi, Lily," he says as she leans around me to wave. Then he blasts me with a megawatt smile. "It's River, isn't it?"

Lily chokes.

"You're a hard person to find." He steps closer. His voice, slow and sweet, sweeps over my body. "When you're done here, you wanna hang out?"

The bat that I'm tapping nervously against my shoe slips and smacks my shin, though I hardly notice. "Thanks." I step back. "But it'll be a while. You don't have to wait—"

"Fifteen minutes," Lily's disembodied voice pipes up helpfully, and I swat at her behind my back.

Jace runs a hand over his t-shirt and down his abs, drawing my gaze. He tilts his head toward the guys. "No problem. A bunch of us are hitting the food trucks behind the field, if you're interested."

Lily shoves me forward. "Okay," I stutter.

"Great." He gives me a heated gaze. "I'll meet you outside." He wraps an arm around my shoulder and squeezes, then leans past me to Lily and Emma. "You all come too."

When he lets go, I tuck a strand of hair behind my ear and squeak a goodbye.

As Jace leaves, Lily ambushes my arm, leaning against me to watch him go. "You... I thought you were lying."

"Ha." But it lacks volume. I clear my throat. "I forgive you for your lack of—"

She shoves me unexpectedly, and I nearly fall as we break into giggles.

#

The crowds around the food trucks remind me of the State Fair. Lily, Emma, and I order grilled cheese. Jace appears with a carton of pizza.

He picks up a slice and leans to see my sandwich just as someone bumps him, jostling both of our dinners. He must have a lot of friends, because it seems people are always messing with him. Sarah and Mia arrive with their own meals.

"Hey, Sarah," Jace says. "I heard O'Daniel is sixty wins from breaking a school record for career wins."

She frowns. "How do you always know so much about the softball team?"

"The guy has eleven hundred and forty wins at one school in one sport. Everyone is talking about it. He'll take the record at twelve hundred."

"Wow," Lily says. "I didn't know that."

Mia shakes her head. "We don't talk about it." She glares at Jace. "It's bad luck."

Sarah rounds on Lily and me. "It's not our job to aim for a record. Our job is to play the game the way Coach tells us to, that's all." She gives Jace a disgusted look. "Are you trying to jinx us?" They bump Jace's shoulder as they leave, but he just grins.

"Jace," I ask. "What do you get for breaking the record?"

"A plaque. In the University's Hall of Fame. And maybe an invite to the State's Hall of Fame if you're lucky. His record wouldn't be broken soon, either."

"How do you know?"

"Because those are major numbers. My dad's college football team only held their record for five years." He shrugs. "It takes something special to last."

"Where's the Hall of Fame?" I ask.

"What are you ranked this year?" Jace asks instead and stuffs the last of the pizza in his mouth.

"We're twelfth," Lily says helpfully. "But it's early."

Early? Oh, no. I glance at the time and wince. "I have to go... math tutor."

"Yeah?" Jace rolls his pizza container like a towel. "I'll walk you."

"No," I blurt, then flush. "I mean, thanks, but no."

"I don't mind. I'm not doing anything else." He takes my trash and drops it with his into a bin, then gestures for me to lead. I look to Lily for help, but she grins and mimics for me to call her.

At first, all I think about is suffering through this faceless tutor's pity. But as we walk, Jace fills the silence with random stories, until we're in the library and winding past small glass room after glass room, scanning the cubicle numbers.

"Here you are." Jace points, not noticing that I've already stopped in shock.

All the dread of meeting my tutor morphs to horror as, from the table inside, Ty gives me a familiar two-finger wave.

He's wearing a clean t-shirt and a small smile. My mouth goes dry. Oblivious, Jace nudges my reluctant body to the doorway, then leans past.

"Sup, man. You're still tutoring?" His hand slides lower on my back as he smirks. "I've gotta go clean up after practice. Take care of my girl here, okay?"

Ty's smile disappears as he lifts his chin in greeting. His dark gaze swings from Jace to me, as if we're strangers and didn't laugh over onion rings just hours earlier.

Then Jace presses his lips to my temple, and I start violently. He whistles as I watch him disappear around the corner.

"Did you bring your book?" Ty asks, drawing my stupefied attention back. Are these freaking guys trying to drive me crazy?

I sink onto the chair, hugging my textbook like a shield. "How...why are you here?"

He frowns. "What do you mean?"

"I'm supposed to meet my tutor. Are you filling in?"

His eyebrows rise. "I am your tutor." His mouth twists as he studies my face. "You didn't know that this afternoon? I thought you were just being secretive in front of your friends."

His words slosh through my thick brain. I think he said he tried to protect my pride? I close my eyes. Can this get any worse? "There must be a mistake," I murmur.

His face goes carefully blank. "We can have the AAC reschedule you with someone else." He straightens and gathers his papers, tapping them together. Collects his pencils... as if he can't wait to leave.

I wish I had Coach O'Daniel's windbreaker right now, so I'd know what to do with my hands. Instead, I fidget as Ty's face flushes and my heart sinks as if I've slapped the niceness right out of the best guy I know.

"No." I squeak, my head nodding in a confused circle. "This is great."

He winces, then leans his arms on the table. "You look like you're going to puke. It's messing with my head, Riv. What's going on?"

Pockets. I need pockets. "Nothing." At his impatient huff, I sit back, choking the life from the book. Maybe I could slide under the table. If I can't see him, he can't see me, right?

"This is going to be fun," he mutters. Then, as he studies me, his eyes soften. "You know I don't discuss my students and what we work on." He scratches his chin. There's a hint of humor now. "But no one else is quite as competitive as you, are they? How bad is it?"

"I'm not competitive," I say automatically.

He pins me in his gaze, deliberately reaching for an eraser and dropping it in his backpack. My eyes widen.

"Okay," I choke, and he stills. "It's just…" Inhale. Hold. Glance at the corner of the room. Wish I could die. "My brothers are geniuses at math," I say in a rush.

He squints. Shakes his head. "Everyone's different."

"Yeah." I frown. "But I'm as smart as they are. We've got the same parents."

He snorts. "Boring." And… zips one side of the backpack closed.

I groan, toss the textbook on the table, and cover my face with my hands.

"How bad, River?"

I mumble into my hands, "I'll lose eligibility if I don't get this grade up."

After a beat, he says, "No problem."

I look up. "You say that, but you haven't worked with me yet."

He gives me a withering look. "I worked with you all summer."

"I hate this." I cross my arms again. "I really hate that you're going to see how much I suck at math."

"Noted." He nods solemnly.

But I narrow my eyes at the suspicious way he rubs his lip. Then he moves his hand.

I've touched those lips. Felt them move against mine. Tasted their shape. His lips part on an exhale, and I glance up as his eyes darken. I take a quiet breath. He'd felt so strong when I'd pressed myself against him. What would a real kiss be like if he had all the time he wanted? I shift on the chair.

Ty tears his gaze away and swallows. "It's none of my business, but I hope you know what you're doing."

"What?" I say faintly.

He nods at the door. "With Jace."

I glance at it, confused. "We're not—we're just friends."

He shrugs, avoiding my gaze, and pulls my book over. "What Chapter are you in?"

I blink. He flips pages, and I lean in, but instead of the book, I see that soft space under his ear. That warm skin that had tempted me before, the scent of woods and meadows.

He shifts back, taking the book with him, and clears his throat. His ears are pink, but he picks a page, then settles the book like a hedge between us, and asks if I brought scratch paper.

I'm not sure how I survive. Not with the way those hands hold a pencil, the way they move over a page, the way his brows crease as he gauges my understanding. How can I want to lean closer and run away at the same time?

But an hour later, Jace returns. Ty closes my book and stands. "See you Thursday."

And, with a dry mouth, I watch him stride toward the vending machine down the hall.

Chapter 17

I roll out of bed with a twinge of shame at the sleep wrinkles in my practice t-shirt and shorts. Dad always said I was perfect the way I woke up, so if I primped, it wasn't because I lacked something. As I squint against the light to pull my hair into a bun, I'm sure he hadn't intended it the way I'd taken it and run. But fifteen extra minutes of shut-eye before six a.m. weight lifting is still fifteen minutes. So, thanks, Dad.

The empty weight room echoes our invasion before being drowned by Abbey's music. Nickie, our much-too-cheerful trainer, swaggers between our smith machines, barking and coaxing. Lily and I rig for bench presses as conversations rise above the thumping music and clank of metal.

"Riv, who would *you* bring if we had a party?" Rachel asks from the next machine.

"No one." I slide under the bar, lift it off the hooks, and lower it to my chest.

Lily peers over the bar. "What about Ty?"

"Who?" Rachel tilts her head, her eagle-eye not leaving Dawz's presses.

"Nothing." I shoot Lily a warning as I finish, and we change places.

"Wait," Dawz frowns as she stands. "Does River have a boyfriend already?"

"Boyfriend?" Zoe's saccharine-sweet laugh drifts across the aisle. "Is there really anyone tall enough?"

Rachel chuckles. "He'd have to pass the stilettos test." Catcalls and laughs ring out.

"Sorry," Lily giggles. "But you with heels? A deer on stilts, Riv."

"She'd make a deer look graceful," Zoe crows.

I nod good-naturedly, like it's funny, like I haven't heard all the jokes.

Zoe's changed since she met Ty. Not that she was friendly before, but everything she says now leaves paper cuts. Competition for starting positions is one thing—and maybe getting the guy is a competition to her, I don't know. But what if she needs me to feel bad so she can feel good?

"Stilettos, platform boots." I shrug and gesture to my full height. "I stand out in a crowd. Just saying." New laughter and whoops.

Lily is suspiciously red when I glance down. "You, too?" She shakes her head, and I sigh. "That's eleven, Lily. C'mon, one more."

Her expression falls. "I'm sorry," she mouths.

"Who's Ty?" Rachel asks from her bench. "The guy from the tower?"

I rack Lily's bar. Is Rachel trying to stir up trouble?

"Ty who?" Dawz raises her voice, then her arms. "No one tells me anything."

Sliding back onto the bench, I can only imagine the fallout from Zoe if this continues.

"Wait. Ty James?" Zoe's spotter, Sarah, calls, and I close my eyes. "He's nice. I had a government class with him."

"I thought River was into Jace," Emma says.

"You're a bunch of gossips," Lily calls as I finish, and she guides my bar back. But it's too late. Zoe's face is stormy when I stand.

"Ty James?" She crosses the aisle. "You mean the guy I told you about the other day? You knew I liked him." Silence ripples down the room.

Lily shoves forward. "River knew him first. They're friends."

Zoe leans past her. "You went after him behind my back, didn't you? Because he said he'd come to my game. Sisters are supposed to come first."

"Hey." Nikkie plants herself between us. "What's going on here?"

The others are suddenly busy, and Zoe slowly retreats with a wounded pout. But girls track her, then glance at me and murmur quietly.

#

The strain lingers at pitching. Bosswood clicks her stopwatch. "Go!"

With his arms crossed, her dad, the Olympic coach, silently dissects every pitch. It's hard to ignore the weight of his stare.

Lily feeds me ball after ball. Pitches thread past the obstacle tee but bounce off the screen instead of into the pocket. *Smack. Smack.*

"Harte," Bosswood barks from behind. "Your elbow is out. Visualize where you want that ball to go."

I miss again. Tied in knots and losing the spin on the ball, I slow enough to place the ball, knowing it's the most ineffective thing I can do, but desperate to try anything to break this cycle. Bosswood's disappointment sends tears prickling to my eyes.

She moves to Zoe's lane. "Thatta way, Gibson. Don't fall off at the end."

When practice is finally over, I jerk the ball cart behind me and scoop up the evidences of my failure. To top it off, Bosswood and Zoe talk as Abbey cleans the lane alone. I huff softly.

"Not your problem," Lily says.

"I know," I snap. "I'm trying."

"Bring it in." Bosswood raises her arm. When we're gathered, she says, "We're coming off a great season last year. Sometimes when that happens, we have a hard time starting the next year."

She purses her lips and looks at everyone but me. "I'm seeing inconsistency in our pitching. You're each going to have to get hungrier, want it more, bring the next level of skill to your game. That's what I'm looking for, what I'm hoping you can find in yourselves if you want to take this team into its first Women's College World Series. Dig deeper and come ready to practice tomorrow."

Dig deeper? That's what I've been trying to do.

Lily hustles to class while I rehash my curveball for so long that I'm the last to leave the locker room and only Coach Bosswood and her dad are left by the pitching cages. She's probably picking apart our incompetence, and I duck my head to hurry past, then frown. At second glance, he's the one gesturing from lane to lane—as if critiquing the practice. She's straight-backed and nodding stiffly. She... she almost looks my age.

"Are you coming?" Coach O'Daniel asks from the lobby.

I hitch my backpack higher and turn. "Sorry, I was thinking."

"It's a splendid exercise," he says with a twinkle as I pass. "I do a lot of it myself. Anything you want to share?"

We fall into step outside, and I'm tempted to admit my frustrations.

But is that something a college athlete does?

"I remember the first time I saw you," I say instead, shocking myself.

Surprise lights his face. "I think I saw you first, since I was in the stands."

"Actually." I swallow and look down, careful to avoid the cracks in the concrete. "I came to Northbridge's softball camp the summer before eighth grade. The first time I saw you, we were sitting on the grass, and you were telling us how glad you were that we'd come."

"Is that right?" Sunbeams streak through his white hair as his mustache twitches at the corners. "Well, it's a small world. When was this?"

"Four years ago."

"Ah." He studies the horizon, then glances at me. "Yes, that was a rebuilding year for us. I was looking for corners. We had a senior at third and were moving the first-baseman to second. I wish we'd met, River."

"We did." I can't quite form a smile. "You sat with me on a bench."

Coach stops walking. He tilts his head and holds me in that blue gaze for a long moment. "That was you?" he says softly. "The one whose dad was missing?"

I nod and look away. He dips his head and walks again. "Well, well. I've found my brave little pitcher." A wry smile crosses his face. "Not so little anymore."

Nope. I've gained six inches and thirty pounds over the years. He tucks his hands in his pockets in that familiar way.

"I don't think I would've stayed at camp if you hadn't talked to me," I say.

"Is that so?" He glances up. "I rarely sit when I'm running one of those camps—as you'll discover. But you were on that bench all alone and unsupervised." He shrugs, as if he still can't believe it. "And I had a surprisingly serious talk with an admirable young lady." He jingles the keys in his pocket once, then asks in a conversational tone, "Any news about your dad?"

I hesitate, but this is Coach O'Daniel. "Last year, officials wanted to declare him deceased for the death benefits. Mom said absolutely not. We believe he's alive somewhere."

"Good for you," Coach says firmly. "Hold the hope. If he can come back to you, he will, I promise. Just keep living and doing your best. You'll have something to show when he returns."

I laugh, but tears sting my eyes. "That's what you said last time."

"Trust me, River." He pats my shoulder. "There's not a dad alive who wouldn't fight heaven and hell to get back to you. And your curling up in a ball won't make a bit of difference if he can't."

He glances away, and I hurriedly wipe my eyes. "River," he says with a thoughtful frown. "Did you send me recruitment information back then?"

"Um, no." I take a deep breath. "I got behind. I broke my collarbone before my sophomore year and missed travel ball. Then I rehabbed and didn't play for the high school varsity until I was a junior. So, I only wrote to smaller schools close to home."

"How did you break it? Were you in an accident?" He shifts so I don't have to duck under a branch.

I roll my eyes. "I was a klutz—flipped over the handlebars of my mountain bike." My smile fades. "I was racing to the top of a hill to watch my brothers leave for college."

Coach drops his chin and nods. Then he clears his throat, and the only sound is the whisper of his track pants with each step, and I have no idea what he's thinking.

Chapter 18

Every step on the field for our first double-header scrimmage is surreal, intense. The sun is too bright for October. Fall season is always short, a sprint rather than the marathon of the spring. For some parents and fans, it's a reunion, but for new fans? I try not to glance at Mom, Grandma, my brothers… Ty.

Happy tears well at the first ball I catch. I blink furiously and listen to my teammates laugh while they work. It hits me hard that I almost didn't make it to this moment. Without one amazing coincidence, I wouldn't have. Everyone had said no to me, except O'Daniel. I'm so glad I didn't quit.

And I realize the tears are for that little girl whose dream came true.

The game starts, and those of us not playing parade back to the dugout to cheer our team on. But, despite the crowd and the announcers, Zoe's voice stabs low and viciously at the beauty of the day.

"I should get to pitch these games," she says from behind me. "They don't count toward our record, and I need the mound time."

My smile fades. Then I can't help it. I stomp my cleats down the concrete to put acreage between us. Does Zoe expect to monopolize the fall mound time? Is this how the next years will be as her teammate?

"These games matter to all of us, Zoe, and you know it." Emma crosses the dugout and drops softballs into a bucket. "We all need playing time."

Some girls lean to see my reaction, but I won't give them the satisfaction of even a raised eyebrow. Zoe can be a spectacle by herself. I glance at Coach, though, and wonder if he changes lineups when players think they deserve more time. I guess we'll find out.

"I'm just saying that our infield needs to get used to each other," Zoe says. "That's why I should pitch."

What the heck? I turn, and she pauses, water bottle lifted. Her expression changes. "Gotta get our big-deal freshman on the field, though." She gives me a such a sickly sweet smile that I probably catch diabetes. "You've got this, Seven."

I turn back to stare blindly at the field, arms clenched over the top rail of the dugout's five-and-a-half-foot safety fence. There was always a fifty-fifty chance I wouldn't play as a freshman. I could as easily warm the bench as take the mound because I'm the new girl paying her dues. Yet now, I can't help thinking about playing time.

The infield throws the ball around the horn, ending with Liz. She's the varsity pitcher; Zoe's number two. That makes me number three. Last. Youngest. The baby. What else is new? Wearing the uniform on the sideline has to be enough for now.

Slowly, I notice Andy's weird stillness at my elbow, with her forehead pressed against the fence in a way that's got to block her view. Studying her only confuses me more. "What're you doing?"

"I'm deciding," she says.

"Deciding what?" I frown. "Can you even see?" But I brace myself. It's Andy.

When she turns, her rueful expression is comical. "No. So, I'm deciding exactly how jealous I am of your height."

I huff a laugh. "Or you could just get something to stand on." I drag a bucket up for her. "You drama queen." She grins as the game starts.

In the fifth inning, Coach Bosswood says, "Harte, warm up."

I glance at the scoreboard, then at her retreating back. We're tied 2-2. But Coach O'Daniel gestures for me to hurry. "Pass, shoot, score, Riv."

That makes me so happy.

Zoe and I avoid eye contact as I stride for my glove and shift foot-to-foot as Lily gears up. Even though I've warmed up hundreds of times, jitters run under my skin as we wind through the dugout and out to the bull pen.

Lily tosses her helmet aside and starts talking the way she's throwing—enthusiastic and fast. I try to swallow, but can't get past the sand dune in my throat. We're sweating by the time my pitches are warm, and Emma calls through the fence.

"Ready, Harte?"

Lily meets me at the gate. "Oh-my-gosh-this-is-real," she whispers, and I don't think she's talking to me.

I feel taller than usual when I run onto the field, bigger than I did in high school. Although, it's understandable since everything is bigger in college. The stadium. The stakes. My nerves.

The stands are a blur as I focus on Lily's glove for my first batter. Number Four grounds her cleats confidently in the batter's box and looks at me. And, somehow, I throw a strike, then bite my cheek to keep from grinning. Lily glows as she throws it back, and Coach O'Daniel nods, as if that's exactly what he expected. Three batters and three outs later, Lily high-fives me in front of the dugout.

But it's when I'm back on the mound for the seventh inning and lean down to swipe the dirt that I see my own cleat mark and pause. I'd been wrong, I realize as I stand and look around. A Northbridge uniform alone wouldn't have been enough no matter how grateful I was—not now that I've sweated it out with a batter bent on hitting my pitches, or received a pat on the back from O'Daniel. Nothing compares to being on the field with my team.

We win that game.

Zoe starts the second game and plays until Coach Bosswood sends me in for the sixth inning again. Bosswood's inspirational coaching follows me out, "Get it done, Harte."

And despite the warm endorsement, we win that game, too. But when we swarm the field in celebration, I'm so caught up that I glance over my teammates' heads, scanning for Dad's grin, the way he towers over the other parents... before I catch myself.

I know better. I hate the weakness that made me look and the wave of grief that followed.

All my life, he kept track of my stats and we'd talk about them on the ride home, whether I wanted to or not. No one else has ever been invested as deeply, interested enough to watch that close. But I tuck those feelings away and manage to smile, anyway. A skill I've had to learn.

When the athletic trainer finishes wrapping ice on Zoe's shoulder, Zoe picks up her backpack with a toss of her ponytail, and the trainer turns to me. Beyond the dugout, Mom visits with other parents, and Zeph and Kody dwarf the exit wearing baseball hats and shorts instead of blue jeans and boots. They scan my teammates with open curiosity. Despite the swing of my emotions, I shake my head, a real smile forming at the way their presence makes itself felt in my world.

Then Zoe saunters out of the dugout, and the sadness turns as cold as the trainer's ice. I lean forward, narrowing my eyes as she nears my brothers. The trainer pulls me back, but not before I see Kody's slow smile of appreciation. And Zeph? His surprised look is somehow worse.

If she knows what's good for her, she will not flirt with them.

Of course, when I'm released, she's still talking to them, and my jaw tightens. Are my brothers so shallow that all they see is a pretty girl? Can't they tell what she's really like?

Kody notices me and lifts his chin in greeting. Zeph turns and wraps an arm around my shoulders. I'm instantly enveloped in the feeling of home I've been missing. It's such a luxury for someone as big as me to feel small and protected, even for a second.

"Are these your brothers, River?" Zoe asks coyly.

Aaaand that's all I can take. I turn and slide a protective arm around each of my brothers to steer them away. "Who? These two? Gross." The twins laugh, but I bear down. "Gotta go, Zeph. Mom's waiting."

"Wow." Zoe's voice is breathy. "You don't meet many people whose name starts with Z." My brothers turn back, drawn by the husky tone. She smiles. "I'm Zoe."

Wait... is she batting her eyes?

Zeph looks a little dazzled. "Zoe with a Z, you've—"

"Hi." Kody steps forward, offering his hand. "I'm Kody, with a K."

Zoe laughs delightedly, and they both puff out their chests. Gag.

"Mom?" I say pointedly. "Have you seen her?"

Zoe flips her ponytail as if to go and gives them a look under her lashes. "You guys are funny. Will you be at the next game?"

"Definitely." Zeph grins.

She glances back as she leaves, and he doesn't budge until she disappears around the fence. Ty, the warthog, laughs at my expression.

But when I finally have all of them to myself, Zoe doesn't matter. Having them here in person reminds me it's been a long time since I've been this content. I don't have to keep my guard up. I can let down and lean on them.

Then I spot another achingly familiar person through the crowd of families and stop mid step.

Jaiden wears a maternity shirt and capris instead of softball pants. As I hurry to her, she examines the dirt on my uniform and the number on my backpack before meeting my gaze, and my breath catches at her wariness. She's never had that expression before. Surely, she doesn't think anything has changed just because she has a bump under her shirt?

I wrap her in a hug. "I didn't know you were here."

She pulls away, tucking hair behind her ear. "I was late."

"Perfect," I say. "Because I only played the late parts."

She smiles. "You did a great job. I like your drop curve. It's different. Whatever you've changed, it really works."

I pause, uncertain how much to share, unwilling to hurt her. Then I see the hunger in her face for the details, the descriptions that would let her live my experiences in place of her own. So, I start with Coach Bosswood and how much she hates me. I don't even embellish much, and Jaiden laughs, chasing the shadows from her face.

We pull her along with us to the pizzeria, where, not for the first time, my family is the loudest one there. When the pizza arrives, and it's quieter, I notice Ty's frown.

"Something wrong with the pizza?" I ask.

He looks up. "What? No. But what's it called when you run in the batter's box?"

"Slapping?" I give Jaiden a knowing look.

"Yes!" He lowers his voice. "Why isn't that illegal? There's no slapping in baseball."

Kody leans on a forearm to see around me. "And runners aren't allowed to steal in softball, either, like baseball. They can't take off until the ball leaves the pitcher's hand."

Jaiden counters, "That's why our games are faster. We don't play around off base, wasting time. When we steal, we mean it." The boys groan.

"The cheers are better in softball, too." Mom says with a smile, cutting her pizza with a fork. Kody makes a gagging sound.

"River, do you remember the one, when you were little?" Zeph squints. "Something about a cow?"

Jaiden and I lock gazes. "Holy cow! It's a foul. Mooooove it over!" Our voices gain volume as we go, then we dissolve in giggles at the tortured looks on the guys. We bump fists across the table.

My smile fades as I look down at my plate. "The only person missing is Dad. If he could've seen us today, I'd have told him how much I love playing for Coach O'Daniel."

Ty nudges my foot. Leaning over, he says softly, "You'll get to tell him."

Chapter 19

The stadium bleachers seem extra short on Friday evening as I slowly lower myself to sitting. Lily grimaces as she settles next to me, then flips her hair behind her with a sigh.

"Did you see the visiting recruits at lunch?" she asks.

Hundreds of students crowd into the football stadium for the pep rally. I glance down our row to the softball recruits, herded there by teammates I hardly recognize in real clothes.

"I had algebra for lunch." I arrange my short skirt, but am already wishing for my sweatpants.

She winces. "I know a good math tutor."

"Ha, ha. He's trying, but look what he has to work with." I raise my arms and groan at the sore muscles as I lower them.

Lily's giggle turns into a whimper. "I hate weight training."

Cheerleaders tumble onto the field and everyone gets to their feet around us. I debate remaining seated for my quads' and glutes' sakes, but the others push upright, so I rise, reaching back to help Lily. When I'm sure she's stable, I hold out a hand.

"You're such a pain, Riv," Lily grumbles.

"Not me. That's the sore muscles talking."

She opens her bag of sunflower seeds in the kangaroo pocket of her sweater and casually slips me a handful. I sneak all of them into my mouth with a fake yawn. Seeds are hot commodities in our way of life.

The bear of a man on my other side suddenly punches the air with a bloodcurdling yell. I nearly swallow the seeds and collapse, half-laughing, half-choking, on Lily, who groans at the movement. The bear's eyebrows rise as we untangle, still giggling.

But as I straighten, I glimpse Ty's familiar head three rows below. I smile, the bear forgotten. Maybe Ty's with Fletch. If only I were down there with them, it'd be like this summer. I crane my neck, my smile stretching into a grin. But it's... it's not Fletch. I blink as a dark-haired girl turns to look up into Ty's face.

He says something and she laughs, shoving his arm. I know that teasing look of his, how it lights his eyes and makes me want to lean closer. Humor softens his face as he tilts his head to focus on her. But it's the affection in his gaze that slices my heart. I jerk upright. With a pang, I realize Ty hadn't been flirting with me this summer. Not like that.

Lily jars me from my thoughts. It takes a minute to realize she's pointing to Jace threading his way down our row. When he's close, I scoot back to my tiptoes to give him room to pass. Instead, he stops, and I wobble. His hands settle helpfully on my waist.

"Hey, girl." His attention travels down my body. "Got plans tonight?"

I try not to swallow my seeds as Lily snorts. "We've got a team dinner," I manage.

He considers the bulge in my cheek. "Are those sunflower seeds?"

He shifts closer. "Got any more?"

Lily, suddenly generous, shares her seeds without a grumble. The bear shifts impatiently at the intrusion. His glare passes between the three of us, and I smile apologetically. Jace doesn't notice.

"A dinner, huh? Do you want to skip out early for me?" He leans into my personal space. "I mean, a party with athletes sounds like more fun, right?"

I stiffen and avert my face. "Yes. It does. Big of you to admit that."

He blinks, surprised, then smiles. "Good one." Suddenly boyish, he says, "I mean, cut me to the quick, but no worries." His eyes linger on my lips. "Next time." And he winks.

As he leaves, I tug at my skirt and watch Zoe, farther down, say something that makes Jace laugh.

"Two hits on you in one week?" Lily asks. "He's moving fast."

His smile is visible, even from this angle "He probably says the same thing to all the girls."

"He didn't say it to me."

I bump her arm. "Not helping, Lily."

Zoe glances at me, then pulls Jace into the space beside her.

It's all... confusing. I fight the urge to stare down at Ty and his date, too. Will he take her to a party tonight? There's no shortage of Friday night options. In fact, some of my teammates will no doubt end up at Jace's party later. I curl my hands into fists. Next time, maybe I'll say yes.

After the rally, the sunset glows pink above the stadium despite the bright field lights. The air is autumn cool, a warm and cold tug-of-war that makes you wish for a sweater.

Our team gathers outside the stadium, where Coach acknowledges each new arrival. Streetlights blink to life between trees as students pass in groups of twos and threes. Music blares from cars.

Sarah says something in Mandarin Chinese, and we all laugh at Coach's expression. "I said I'm hungry," she explains.

"Sure, you did." He nods sagely. "And you should be. My wife's been cooking all afternoon. Wouldn't want to disappoint her. Ah, here he is." He glances past us.

The athletic director shoulders into the group, reaching to shake Coach's hand. His square jaw and strong shoulders give the impression that he's a former athlete himself.

"I can't wait to meet these talented girls you've been telling me about," he says, then turns to us. "You'd think, to hear him talk, that you're the best team he's ever coached."

Coach Bosswood flips her folder closed and announces that we're all accounted for as the crossing light changes.

"Dinner time." O'Daniel catches my eye, and the happiness in his expression lifts my heart. He steps into the crosswalk, and we're all pulled into his wake.

Lily, Sarah, and I are to his right, far enough from the intersection that I skirt a parked car to step off the curb. The walking-man light burns bright on Coach's white hair as he looks both ways and starts across the street. He sends an approving glance back at our group's forward movement.

At first, in all the chaos, I don't hear the rev of engines echoing down the road.

Coach lifts his head and squints. A distant squeal, shrill as stallions neighing at rivals, pricks my country-honed senses before I know why I've turned that direction. Then the growl of engines reverberates across my skin. Headlights flash over Coach.

Someone screams.

A car honks. My shirt is jerked. I stumble backward, trip violently, and throw out my arms to keep from tumbling to the ground. My elbows scrape on something sharp.

With a wide sweep of his arms, Coach shoves everyone near him back from harm's way. Mia staggers, windmills into Liz, who loses her balance, and they both land in a heap. A Mustang and a Charger appear, tires locked in a banshee shriek, the roiling smoke of burnt rubber wafting behind. They skid through the red light, neck and neck. In a flash of light, Coach's head jerks. There's a dull thud, and he disappears.

I struggle to my feet. Across the intersection, a heavy crunch is followed by a hot tick, tick, tick. When I glance over the top of the crowd, the front wheel of the Charger is bent unnaturally on the sidewalk.

Sarah squeezes my arm and pushes, but I realize she's just using that energy to start moving when I see her stumble through the crowd. She drops to her knees beside Coach, who's sprawled on the road. I stagger into the street in front of them and fling my bleeding arms wide.

I'm big, generally, but I don't know if it's my six-foot wingspan or the look on my face that stops traffic. Over my shoulder, I glimpse Coach's leg bent at an odd angle and turn back, heart galloping with a fierceness that dares anyone to come closer.

Car doors shut. People silhouette against blinding headlights and take slow steps forward, uncertain of where to stand, but unable to look away. I start praying, begging even. Coach has to be all right. Nothing can happen to him, not now that I've found him again. No one is performing CPR, which is good, but he's not moving. I stay there until the intersection is lit with blue and red, and I'm pushed to the side.

Then I don't know what to do.

Chapter 20

No one tells our team anything once the emergency crews arrive. They leave those of us uninjured huddled and miserable as they rush around dealing with those of us that need help.

The back of the ambulance opens. I watch them scoot Coach inside. The EMT pulls a sheet over his twisted leg and settles it at his chest. I stand on tiptoes and almost wilt with relief that he doesn't pull it over Coach's face. That must mean he's okay. He looks like he's sleeping on that board, the neck brace a duller white than his hair. I try to read the EMT, but I don't know his normal work expression. This one is tense and focused. He reaches for something just as the doors close. The siren winds up and the ambulance speeds away, dragging our hearts behind like cans on strings.

Liz leaves in an ambulance, too, and in the sudden quiet, my mind is numb, but my body is restless. I don't know what to do with my hands, what expression my face wears, where to look. I can't close my eyes without seeing the cars roar down the road again. I wish I could've grabbed Coach, pulled him to safety. It's a knot in my chest, suffocating and hard.

Then Lily slams into me, and I lose my breath. I think she's fallen and reach down to steady her, but her arms wrap around my waist, and I realize she's hugging me.

"It's going to be okay," she says into my shirt and lifts red-rimmed eyes. "But shouldn't we go to the hospital? They're both alone. And what if Coach wakes up and no one's with him?"

I re-hear the horrible thud again and imagine the hit he took on the concrete. The awkward angle of Liz's ankle is no less devastating.

Lily is warm under my arm as we stagger back to our cars. Her rib cage seems fragile as it expands against my side with her breath. I straighten, taking more of her weight, letting it give me a purpose, some way to make a difference. Because the horror is real. And I'm pissed.

#

"The surgery on Coach's leg went well," the athletic director says hours later. "But..." And everyone freezes, happy murmurs dying on our lips. The A.D. rubs the back of his neck, his face pale. "He's in a coma."

#

The A.D. comes back to our locker room on Monday.

"We've moved this week's double-header scrimmage to next week," he says, dark circles under his eyes. He pauses and his Adam's apple bobs as he stares at the paper tortured in his hands. He clears his throat and straightens to face the room, but his gaze lands on Liz and the cast on her right ankle.

"Coach O'Daniel would want you to continue your season..." He looks away from Liz. "So, Coach Bosswood is now your interim head coach. Questions?"

At our silence, he tucks the paper in his pocket. "There is one more bit of business." He sounds brisk now, as if on familiar ground. "Even though the students involved in the accident have been charged, the media is watching you as a team. This will cool off but, as usual, what you say on social media and what you do in public will be of particular interest. You are role models to many young people who hope to be in your shoes someday. Keep that in mind. And I don't need to remind you we have a zero-alcohol tolerance on campus. Because of the suspected role that alcohol played in this accident, new discussions about what goes on around campuses, and ours specifically, are being held. You will be the ones who'll make a difference in the aftermath of this tragedy— you will be the ones who live it."

Coach Bosswood stands. "I know there are a lot of parties next weekend for the home football game, but for the good of the team, you have a curfew. Do not take part in any questionable activity. We must have a united front. Understood?"

She says something about armbands on our uniforms, but I'm distracted by an uneasy feeling at the look Katie and Kim share.

#

A tree-shaped air refresher hangs from Jace's rearview mirror. It rocks back and forth with each stop and turn. The radio is on, but it's nothing more than white noise because all I think about is how empty Coach O'Daniel's office is. When the pickup stops, I look around at the houses and yards, surprised. I thought we were going to eat. Although I haven't had much of an appetite, the idea of getting off campus had been appealing when he'd asked.

"Why are we here?" I ask.

"I need to pick up something." He takes the keys from the ignition. "Want to come in?"

Coach O'Daniel's wife tried to be optimistic this morning when we went by to check on him in the ICU. I wonder how long someone can stay in a coma?

"River?" Jace frowns, one hand on his door.

"I'm coming." I open my door.

Jace flips a light in the house's entry. Shoes and a game controller spill out of an open coat closet.

"My roommate's." He nudges a pair of cowboy boots out of the way. "The door jambs. He's supposed to fix it since he broke it." He glances into the living room and back at me. "Wanna sit down?"

I study the furniture doubtfully. I don't know. It's just... too hard to decide.

"Aw. Come here." He wraps his arms around me. "What a crappy week."

I sigh against his shirt. "It doesn't feel real."

"I wish I could make it better." His voice lightens. "Did you see the flowers the team sent?"

All the teams from Northbridge had sent flowers. It's a regular garden of Eden in the hospital.

"They were great." I rouse enough to pull back, smiling politely. "And I never thanked you for the flowers you sent this summer, either. I love daisies."

"What?" He smiles quizzically.

I look at his clear hazel eyes, my brain slow to comprehend. "I thought you... um, never mind. It must have been someone else."

"You thought I sent flowers?" He runs his hand down my back. "I wish I'd thought of it. I couldn't get you out of my head all summer."

I duck my head in embarrassment and try to step back, but he pulls me tighter. I look up, confused, as his kiss on my cheek becomes a trail to my lips. My body stiffens. For the first time all day, I am truly awake. I push against his chest, but it's the doorbell that causes Jace to let go to peer through the peephole. He jerks back. After a quick scan of the room, he pulls me toward the broken coat closet.

"Do me a favor?" he whispers.

"What...?"

"Shh," he says. "I'll explain later, but could you just stay here for a minute? I promise I'll explain." He pushes me into the closet like an unneeded snow shovel. The doorbell rings again. "Be quiet," he says and shoves the door closed with a heave of his shoulder.

Stunned, I move a hanger that's poking my neck and listen to the creak of the front door. A girl's voice, "Hi, babe."

Jace's chuckle is strained. "This is a surprise. When did you get back?"

And I don't need any other explanation. He has a girlfriend.

My breath whooshes out. How could he do this? Bring me here. Try to kiss me. Push me out of sight into a closet? I turn my head to follow their voices as they fade into the house.

I'm River Harte. I have friends, and family, and a team to belong to, and... and it'd serve him right to get caught cheating red-handed. I don't have to put up with this.

The doorknob is cold to the touch, but a thought makes me pause and close my eyes. She won't see what he's done. All she'll see is me slinking out of hiding.

How had I utterly misread him? I wipe my mouth and all the parts he'd touched. My only explanation is his attention had flattered me. Flattered. I lift my head. What about this summer? I stare into the dark and recall the flowers. So, he didn't send them, couldn't have because his brain isn't that big. But who would send them and not sign their name?

I'm so focused, I almost don't hear their voices approaching again. He chuckles, and I imagine he's thinking of me when he does it. I nearly wrench the door open and rip into him, but humiliation keeps me still. The hateful heat of shame sears my courage, although none of this is my fault... except being too proud to jump out of the closet.

Then it occurs to me that if I wait, Jace will open the door after she leaves. He'll be letting me out at his own convenience.

They're right outside the closet. It has to be now. I take a fortifying breath and twist the knob, but the door doesn't budge. I shove it with my shoulder. Nothing. He'd said something about a broken door, and with horror, I realize he meant seriously broke.

Jace's voice rises, as if to cover the sound of my struggle while he escorts her out of the house. When the door finally gives way under the assault of my kicks and shoves, I stagger out. I narrow my eyes at the empty room, then yank open the front door.

On the sidewalk, Jace looks resigned above the small blonde, who turns with a curious glance.

I glare at him. "You freaking player."

"What?" the girls says.

I march up to him and shove his chest, cutting off the girl's faint question. "You small, insignificant excuse for a—"

"Hey." The girl knocks my hand away and steps between us. "What's wrong with you?"

"Guess," I scowl, and her frown slips. I round on Jace. "Don't you freakin' talk to me. Ever. Again." I punctuate each word with a jab at his chest, because it feels good, then I stomp across the lawn.

It takes two blocks before I realize I need a ride. And another before I have the nerve to call Fletch.

His voice sounds muffled, as if the phone is against his shoulder. "Come get you? Sure. Where are you?"

I read the street signs, but he sounds distracted. "Where?" he asks. "What's it close to?"

"I'm in a neighborhood, Fletch," I say bleakly and glance up and down the road. "I think it's the road by the bike store."

He pauses, and I imagine his head coming up. "A neighborhood? Why?"

"Fletch." My shoulders hunch.

"I'm leaving. But talk, Riv. What's going on?"

I lower myself to the curb, head in my palm. It's got to be easier if I can't see his face. So, I tell him. He arrives grim and deceptively calm.

"Which house is it?" he asks as I climb in.

"It doesn't matter." I bend to the seatbelt, suddenly weary. "Just take me home."

"Huh uh." He chuckles darkly. "Not happening."

I sigh at the wrestler in him who has never met a fight he didn't like. "Fletcher. I will walk home if you go back to his house."

He studies me with a steely gaze, then shakes his head and pulls away from the curb with a squeal. "I'll come back later."

"Yeah. That will make my life less embarrassing. You have to let it go."

Fletch's white-knuckled grip on the steering wheel doesn't relax, even when we park at the dorm. I close my eyes and brace for the storm, waiting for him to pick up where he left off. Instead, Fletch's shoulders slump and he rubs his face.

"I should've warned you about him." He sighs.

I frown. "How could you have known?"

His gaze slides away, then back. "I've heard him bragging. Ask Ty."

"Absolutely not." But Ty had been very tense around Jace.

"They went to high school together, Riv." I'm still dealing with the shock of that when the slow, almost gleeful, smile that appears on his face fills me with dread. "I just realized you might think I'm bad." He huffs a laugh. "But wait until your brothers hear."

With a groan, I get out and slam the door

Chapter 21

Late Friday night, sitting with my head in my hands at my desk, I realize I'd forgotten about the aftermath of tragedy. The landscape it creates of emotional landmines. It explains why I've been a little unnerved when people with sad, compassionate eyes radiate trauma when they realize I play for O'Daniel. And why others avoid my gaze altogether, afraid to get too close, as if misfortune is contagious.

But solitude is no better. Studying is fruitless. Paragraphs blend together. Minutes evaporate. Sleep evades. Deadlines stack and grow. Softball practice that was once a haven, turns brittle and grim. It's exhausting. All starting and stopping, never escaping. I'm a wreck.

I'm so gutted that the smell of popcorn in the dorm makes me nauseous. Echoing laughter gives me a headache...

Or maybe the problem is Andy and Dawz aren't answering my calls.

I'd caught them whispering about going out and told them all the ways it was stupid. Now I hope against hope they aren't tagging along with whatever Kim and Katie had planned, despite Bosswood's orders.

A car honks outside and I jolt. A round of midnight serenades starts below, tipsy songs all the more cheerful under a full moon. I reach over and slam the window.

My cell phone rings. Finally.

"River?" Andy says. "Is that you?"

I close my eyes and lean my forehead on my palm. "Why haven't you answered my calls?"

"My phone was off."

Her words are slurred enough that I frown. "Are you okay?"

She doesn't answer, and I'm about to check the connection, when I hear her small voice. "Can you come get me?"

Her vulnerability is a stab to my gut. They told us not to go out. Not to give the media fuel against us. But I'd known by the way the girls had avoided my eyes that they were going anyway.

"Where's Kim?" I demand.

"Gone. Can you come? I don't have anyone else to call. I love you."

I sag against my chair and scrub the creases between my brows. Why do people say they love you when they want you to do something? When I try that, my brothers laugh. And yet, a part of me is stupidly relieved she's okay.

"Are you alone?" I ask.

"Katie and Dawz are here somewhere."

I knew it. Well, if they're so smart, they can just call their own ride service.

Except, seared in my mind is the image of Coach's awkwardly bent leg. I sigh. "Where are you?"

"Matt's house. Next door to Jace's. You remember Jace? Oh, yeah, you like him, don't you?"

I grit my teeth. Sure. I'd *like* Jace to wash my car with his tongue.

"Andy, I'm leaving. Watch for me out front. Do you hear?" She's still thanking me when I hang up.

I pick up my keys and hesitate. The thought of seeing Jace... of him smirking... I chew my fingernail. This night is bad enough without that. But I can't leave the girls. I heave a breath. Screw it.

On Jace's street, I weave between cars parked like large blocks tossed in a toddler's fit. Somehow, I find a parking spot without seeing his pickup and slump in the dark to text Andy. Music from the party echoes between the cars. After minutes pass without a response, I curse and get out. Slam the door.

Dry grass crunches under my feet as I stalk past a group of three who follow me with their eyes. Overflowing trash cans line the gate. People crowd the back yard, milling in groups or lounging on cheap plastic chairs under an enormous oak tree.

I start down one side of the fence and work my way to the back gate with no sign of Andy's light brown hair. When I finally find her, she's curled small with her head on her arms.

"Andy." I kneel in front of her. "I told you to stay out front."

She looks up, and the dim light reveals all the grief and shock of the past weeks under her smeared mascara.

"Never mind." I pull her up and, gripping her securely, turn toward the front.

Dawz appears, eyes wide. "We have to go." She takes Andy's other arm and twists toward the back gate.

"What're you doing?" I tug, as though Andy is my doll instead of one of the best hitters on the team.

"Someone reported the party," Dawz hisses. "Let's go!"

Beside us, a boy stands and overturns his chair. Panic spreads through the yard.

"Dawz, I'm parked out front."

She gives me a frustrated look, then spots Katie and disappears after her. The shadows of the back yard roil as people swarm the gates.

"I don't feel good, Riv," Andy says.

Tugging her hand over my shoulder, I heave some of her weight and doggedly push toward the front.

"Remember when you pitched to me at the state tournament?" She looks up, her face inches from mine. "I didn't want you to pitch, did you know that? But I got a hit, didn't I? Yeah, I got a hit. And we almost won. But we lost."

I make an affirmative hum. We near the gate, only to see red and blue lights reflect on the side of the house. I reverse toward the safety of the alley.

"I didn't like you then. I'm sorry, River." Andy's still lost in her own world, oblivious to the chaos. "But don't worry, I love you now."

"If you love me, hurry!" I grunt as someone sideswipes me.

Before we reach the back, loud voices sound in the alley. My chest heaves as I look around. If it was just me, I'd scale the fence into Jace's yard and disappear, but... I adjust my hold on Andy and it's the familiar scent of her sunscreen over the stench of beer and trampled soil that rips my heart. She'll be toast if Bosswood hears of this. I pivot. Fence it is then.

With some effort, I haul her onto a picnic table and lean her against the fence, arms over the top. "Step into my hands." I crouch and look up. "I'll help you over."

She moans and picks up a foot. But nothing about this year has gone as I planned. The next thing I know, we're both on the ground, with someone's abandoned beer soaking my back, Andy's solid weight crushing my chest, and the breath knocked clean out of me. Then a flashlight blinds me, and I squint.

"This isn't what it looks like," I rasp. Andy stops moaning and vomits by my ear.

"It never is," comes a resigned voice behind the flashlight. "You kids need to come with me and we'll check you out."

"Sorry, Riv," Andy whispers.

I don't know who helps who to the car, but Andy and I wait in silence until her phone rings. I smell worse than a barn full of calves.

"They found another ride." She wipes her phone on her shirt. I avert my eyes and try to breathe through my mouth as I start the car.

At the dorm, in this semester chalked full of days that keep getting worse, Andy asks in a small voice, "Can I stay with you?"

She's measurably cleaner than I am, but when I study her, she's just as miserable. My irritable response dies in my throat. I shrug, then wince as the wet hair on my shoulder slides forward.

"Fine," I say. "But I get the shower first."

We keep our heads down and clear the lobby without drawing attention, then the elevator, and down the hall. But as soon as we're inside, I cross my arms, suddenly cold.

"I'll be done in a minute."

Andy glances up from her phone and nods.

Not until the water is hot and my forehead rests on the shower wall can I take a full breath. The truth is, Andy's expression is the honest one. I'd know because the same emotion has haunted my own mirror. We all need help to work through this limbo of suffocating grief.

Yet, when you tell people they're making bad choices, why is it you're the one covered in... I pull off my wet t-shirt, careful not to let it touch my face, and toss it on the floor.

Water runs over my matted hair, and after I wash it twice, it finally smells better. The heat pounds my shoulders. The windows steam over. But I still don't want to face the world. I pick up the shaver and start grimly on my legs.

Andy and the others are immature. Bad things happen in life. They need to get used to it. Toughen up. The blade twitches in my hand. I flinch at the sting and rub the welling blood.

If only it was that easy—just rub the hurt away.

My shoulders slump. She's young. She hasn't lived through the heartache I have. I'm sure I didn't handle it well in the beginning either. Even thinking about the devastating pain of Dad's absence still makes me want to run. Maybe, instead of hoping to grow numb, we can let the wreckage remind us we're alive. With a sigh, I turn off the water.

I dress, then pause, comb in the air. I should brew her some hot chocolate. That always helps me feel better. We've all made mistakes, but at least she's safe. My good intentions last until I open the door and hear voices.

Katie and Dawz are on the sofa in the living room. Andy stares at me wide-eyed. Behind her are two guys I've never seen before.

"What's going on?" I ask.

"The party got busted," one guy says, reaching for a bottle from a six-pack on the floor.

Incredulous, I glare at Katie and Dawz. "You brought them here?"

"Do you mean the boys or the beer?" Katie says. "Because we didn't bring the beer."

"What are you doing in my room?" My voice rises. "You can't have this stuff here. You'll get me in trouble."

"Oh, we do this all the time," the other boy says with a confident smile. "Just chill. Have some fun."

"There's nowhere else to go," Dawz says. "Can't we stay for a while?"

"No," I say. "Go. Now. Take them with you." I flip a hand, encompassing everything on their side of the room as I march to the door. Andy hands the six-pack to the boy. Katie and Dawz have the grace to apologize as they put on their shoes.

I fling open the door and jerk to a stop. The dorm director stands in jeans and a rumpled shirt and lowers the hand he'd raised to knock on the door.

Chapter 22

The next morning, I'm summoned, along with the other three, to Bosswood's office. My eyes are gritty and my hair pulled in a rough bun. After Coach learns what happened, I hope she'll back me up with the dorm governance, then I'm going back to bed.

The fluorescent lights aren't kind to the girls. "Sit," Coach barks and their tail bones hit the chairs; though, if they had real tails, they'd be tucked under. I stand against the wall with my arms crossed. Hopefully, I'll be out of here before Coach really starts in on them.

Her large desk is immaculate, like its owner. The bookcase bulges with books, posters, and small trophies. She taps a pencil on the desk and turns furious eyes on me.

"I have been trying to think of what to say to all of you, but there's nothing. We just had this conversation, yet you're caught in an underage drinking situation off campus and on. I could've let this slide, but— don't ask me how—It's. Been. Reported. In. The. Media." Even I squirm as heat climbs my neck.

"All you had to do was fly under the radar for a couple of months. We have alumni and compliance people on our tails about Coach O'Daniel's accident. There is no wiggle room. None. So, believe me, you cannot imagine how disgusted I am with the four of you."

Startled, I drop my arms. "Coach, I wasn't at the party..."

Her gaze burns. "Did I ask what you were doing? No! I don't care."

"But—" I say, and she points a finger. Her voice is menacingly soft, honed to the right inflection to keep twenty-three girls in line at a time.

"Harte, if you say one more word, you can go home. Do you understand?"

The floor disappears under my feet. I reach back with shaking fingers, searching for something solid. My face, flushed with the pressure of unspoken words, pales. It becomes painfully clear we each have done our part to embarrass the program and shame the school. The others by trying to have fun. Me by answering my phone.

"You're suspended until the last scrimmage, and you'll attend another compliance meeting on our drug and alcohol policy," she says. "I don't want to see any of you until then. Now get out."

#

Dawz and Katie whisper on the way back to the dorm. Andy takes one look at my face and hunches her shoulders. There's not much to say, anyway. Kim escaped all consequences by leaving the party early. If only they'd all done that.

There's a soft rustle as Andy shifts closer. When I peek at her, she furtively wipes her cheek. But it's the red and blue flashing lights I can't stop seeing. The smell of beer. The panicked rush of bodies.

"It's my fault you're here," she says hoarsely.

I bite back unhelpful words. If only I could talk to Coach O'Daniel, he'd know how to fix this.

The housing director comes out of the office when we enter the lobby, as if he'd been waiting. "I need a word with all of you." He holds the door as we file past. It closes with a soft click, and I realize this is going to be much worse than I'd thought.

"Considering your recent activities," he begins as he sits behind his desk, "the housing board has no choice but to sever your contract with the dorm effective immediately. According to our rules of conduct, you have twenty-four hours to gather your belongings and move out."

"But—" I stutter. "Isn't there a warning first? You're going to kick us out the first time we mess up?"

He looks away, as if he'd rather be anywhere else. Then he straightens. "I know you regret what's happened, but you've broken dorm rules. This decision has come from beyond the housing department. The school is taking a hard line, and it's legal. The rules are spelled out in the code of conduct you signed with your lease. My hands are tied. I'm sorry."

Dawz leans forward. "This isn't River's fault. You shouldn't—"

"There's nothing I can do," he interrupts firmly. "For any of you." He lays out papers for our signatures.

I fold my hands in my lap and blink at the blurry paper. "Can we return later?"

"This is the freshman dorm. You'll apply for housing next year as usual."

My lips tremble. I've never been homeless before. "Where should we go?"

His eyes soften, and he reaches behind his desk for a list. "You might try one of these places. And..." He looks at each of us. "The school is bound by privacy laws. We can't contact your parents and tell them what's happened. I would highly suggest that you take care of that first thing. Parents have a way of finding out."

He releases us out into the lobby that still smells of coffee and leather. Only it's not my lobby anymore. And, once upstairs, it's no longer my room that I unlock. The living area with its big window will belong to someone new. No more lounging in the sun there, watching traffic below.

In my bedroom, I lay the picture of my brothers face down, so they won't see what I have to do. I straighten a stack of 3x5 cards. Put a pencil back. Sink to the floor and curl over my knees with the list of apartments crumpled in my fist.

A hesitant knock from the other room interrupts the quiet. When I hear footsteps, I realize I didn't lock the door. Andy, Katie, and Dawz file into my room. They don't look surprised to see me on the floor, but drop beside me, their knees nearly touching mine in the small space.

"My grandma lives in town." Katie tucks hair behind her ear. "She said we could live with her."

"You should come," Dawz says solemnly. "She has bunk beds in one room and a queen bed in the other. I'll get an air mattress. You can have the queen room to yourself."

I lean back against the desk, the drawer handle poking my spine, and feel the walls close in. *Suffocating.*

I lift the list. "Actually, I'm going to stay at..." I read the first name. "Greenleaf Apartments. Furnished efficiency rooms, with reasonable rent."

"Won't you be lonely by yourself?" Andy frowns, dark circles under her eyes. "I could room with you."

"Efficiencies only have one bed." I fold the paper. "There's not room for two."

Life's going so fast that I'm dizzy with it, and there're no brakes. The past two days—no, the past few weeks—have been eclipsed by an overwhelming helplessness. Actually, it goes further back, like four years. But I'm done being tossed about. If I live by myself, I'll at least have enough control over my life to shut and lock the door. There's a measure of power in that, right?

"I appreciate the offer," I say. "But you three stay together. It's a great deal."

Dawz sighs. "We're really sorry, River. It was stupid. I don't know why we did it."

Andy sniffs, trying not to cry. Katie's shoulders slump. If only I could relieve this crushing weight on my chest.

"You know why you did it." I lean forward, planting both hands on the carpet. "And so do I. It's been crazy around here."

Andy says dully, "You didn't go. And you've had the crazy, too."

I pause, then squint at her. "*Had* the crazy?"

"No. I didn't mean—"

"What... like, do I need an antibiotic?"

Dawz chokes. "Andy!"

Katie giggles. "The crazy—it's contagious."

Andy's face turns red. "I mean, you weren't immune."

"Oh." I try not to smile. "You think I'm a super spreader?"

"Stop." Andy waves her hand, choking on a laugh. "You're messing me up."

I push her shoulder. She topples into Katie with a giggle.

Just an hour ago, I thought I'd never smile again. Look at us.

#

Twenty-four hours later, Greenleaf Furnished Apartments becomes my new home; though, if they were ever green, it was during one of the world wars. I climb the wooden steps of the two-story old barracks that resemble an outdoor-access hotel. At the second apartment, I juggle a pile of clothes with my pillow to unlock the faded tan door.

The efficiency has a kitchenette, desk, Murphy bed, sofa, and a bathroom, all with a clean but thread-bare carpet in shades of tan and blue, and my heart dies a little at the impersonal space. I dump the clothes on the desk and sink to the sofa, my pillow in a death grip. The meager room blurs. I blink to clear it, but it blurs again. Maybe I'll quit softball. It can't be worth this misery.

Would Grandma understand if I quit? A tear escapes. Would Dad? He'd been my first coach as a four-and-a half-year-old in a princess dress. He'd said I'd be the best softball player someday. He'd said not to let your team down.

What could I have done differently? Meeting Coach O'Daniel had started what I'd thought was an adventure but was really a misadventure. No, that isn't fair. He didn't choose to be hit by a car. He wasn't responsible for the decisions made. With a sob, I toss the pillow aside and head back out to get another load.

When everything is put away—pictures on the desk, softball backpack by the door—I pick up my glove and sit down. In that stillness, the coming night looms over me. The long, dark hours of nothing. I open my phone's alarm clock and think about the morning instead, but that's even worse.

What time should I get up without weight lifting or practice to go to? Should I sleep in? My fingernails dig into my glove as I eye the bed that doesn't feel like mine. The life that doesn't feel like mine.

Hopeless. That's what I am. One of those lovers who'd jumped. No sign of relief.

I hug my glove and decide, from now on, oblivion is preferable—as many hours unconscious and sleeping as possible. Either that or maybe I should start drinking since they've accused me of it. Pass the suspension in a stupor.

Best softball player, Dad had said. *Don't let your team down.* I hadn't known to ask what happens after you've done your best and your team leaves you behind, anyway. I close the alarm without setting it and turn out the lights.

My last thought as I lay in the dark with my glove, on an unfamiliar mattress, listening to the creaks of a building older than my grandma, is that silence is loud.

But at seven-thirty in the morning, I open my door to a cool mist with a banana in one hand and room keys in the other. It turns out my body wants exercise. Now. So, I pull the door shut, then freeze at a movement next door.

Ty's head jerks up from where he unlocks a door and we stare at each other. He slowly straightens, flushed, the neck of his t-shirt wet with sweat.

"What're you doing here?" I breathe.

Chapter 23

He frowns, glances at his door and back at me. "I live here. What're you doing?"

"I thought you lived with Fletcher." It's cruel that Ty, of all people, would witness my failure before I've even come to terms with it.

"Last year. Now he lives downstairs." He narrows his eyes, stepping closer. "What—"

"I just moved in," I say, shrinking back a step.

His eyebrows rise. "Why?"

"I'm going for a run." I turn quickly and lock my door, literally ready to run away. I try to slide past him, keeping as much distance as possible, but his large hand snakes out to block my way.

He studies me. "You want to tell me what's going on?"

I avoid his gaze.

He touches my upper arm, his thumb rubbing circles on my t-shirt. I clench my hands, all the muscles in my body so rigid with emotion that I might shatter. As usual, Ty seems to understand and releases me.

"The bridge is out on the trail to the east." He takes a step back. "Go west and it should be okay."

I nod with relief.

He clears his throat. "Maybe I'll see you later?"

My eyes sting as I pass because he'll see me a lot. I have nothing else to do.

Later, when I get to class, my usual seat is taken. If I hadn't gone the long way to avoid crossing paths with athletes leaving the indoor facility, I wouldn't be late. And I wouldn't be hungry if I'd gotten to eat with the team this morning. By the time I'd showered after my run, there hadn't been time to get food. Another thing to blame on being isolated in every way. The trip from sisterhood to solo-hood overnight is just such a joy.

The first empty chair I find is directly behind a row of football players. Once I sit down, I realize why no one else wanted it. I'll spend the next hour twitching from side to side to see the board. I don't even have my pencil out when the professor announces a pop quiz because too many of the football players will be on the road on Friday when the quiz was originally scheduled. I drop my head into my hands.

"I can't stand athletes," a girl says behind me and, for a second, I agree with her.

"I know," another one says, "they're so privileged. Why doesn't someone just come in and take their tests for them on Friday and not make the rest of us suffer?"

Okay. Wait. I raise my head and narrow my eyes. I completely feel their frustration, but how can she insinuate we don't do our own work? Even if it means that we do it on buses or over lunch or on Friday night when everyone else is out having fun, we get our work done or the AAC has something to say about it.

"Yeah. It's not like anyone even looks at their grades anyway," the first says.

"Right. They have life so good. Everyone caters to them," the second says.

I glance over my shoulder, expecting to see bitterness dripping from their lips, but they don't notice. Do they think that just because we're athletes, life is somehow roses? I could prove that isn't true. It's in the school's best interest that we succeed, so they provide tutors and accountability, but there are a lot of strings. We have extra rules, extra scrutiny, extra work. Our full-time jobs honing our skills, competing in our sport, and representing our school pays for some of our education, but doesn't give us time off in season, and not much in off-season either. And a lot of us have student loans just like everyone else. Worst of all, there's no one to talk to when access to the teammates that we've sweated and bled with is taken away.

"And it costs the school to take care of them. Where's my money?"

The football player in front of me heaves a sigh and slouches in his seat. A strip of kinesiology tape is visible under the neck of his t-shirt. For a second, I feel the weight of the ice bag that's usually wrapped to my shoulder. I'll probably have old-man shoulders by the time I'm thirty.

The football player rubs the back of his head. He's probably been to an early workout while the girls behind me were still sound asleep in their warm beds—beds in buildings that are partially funded by the money football brings to the school.

They don't stop their rants until the quiz starts and, by then, my hands are white-knuckled on my pencil. I'd love to flip this class off, just for once, and walk away from the stress. But, ironically, as an athlete, I'm not allowed to do that. My missed classes are reported to my coaches, then we have a *talk*. At least on any normal day. Today, they'd probably take away my cleats and tell me not to let the door hit me as I leave.

The quiz goes fuzzy in front of me, and I blink quickly. I have no choice but to keep my mouth shut and my grades up. No choice, because I have to play. The game drives me, the skills, the belonging, the challenge, the niggling thought that I can do better next time. Or at least it had.

But by the time class is over, I just want to climb into bed and hide under the sheets. Instead, I find... the bench.

It's not my usual route, so the sight of it jolts me. I make a reckless U-turn into the empty parking lot and stop haphazardly, straddling two spaces, afraid to blink. I get out and cross under the trees slowly. The bench looms larger and larger until it's close enough to touch... and I'm thirteen again.

Reaching for the seat, I lower myself, facing the grassy space in front of the public softball fields with light poles and chain-link fences. With an inhale, I slide back and sense under my fingers every scar and letter etched in the planks. But the bench fits differently. I glance down to see my feet flat on the ground and smile. This would've been impossible back then.

I raise my head. Coach O'Daniel had crossed the field that day, eyeing me with a tilted chin. What had he seen on my face? Something that, instead of him telling me to join a group, had made him ask what was wrong. And, surprisingly, I'd told him about Dad.

I lift my feet to the bench and hug my knees. Coach is still in the hospital. Still in a coma. They say that's not necessarily bad, but they don't always look as if they believe what they're saying. If he were here, he'd understand what I'd done for the girls. If he were here, I wouldn't be in trouble.

But what a pathetic mantra: If he, meaning Dad or Coach, were here, things would be different. How many times have I told myself that, especially when I'm neck deep in self-pity? That's what I'm good at, self-pity.

Dad had known how to deal with my moods. When I was younger, I'd get flustered on the mound, and he'd yell the most annoying thing possible from the dugout, "Just throw strikes." Then he'd grin when I glared at him—his mission accomplished. He knew I played better angry than scared.

And the one time he'd needed me to be there for him, I'd been horrible. I drop my head to my knees and groan with pain. That last horrible practice before he left. Before I lost him. I know he loved me, but I didn't deserve it. I'd been such a brat that day, pitching to the screen in the barn, and mad because he was late.

He'd said we needed to talk, but where was he? Like I didn't already know something was wrong. Heat radiated from the wooden walls and rolled off my face. Pitches smacked into the mesh pockets of the pitching screen as fast as I could throw them.

It's not as if I can't practice by myself. *Thunk.*

I'm almost fourteen. I don't need anyone. *Thunk.*

When I reached again, the bucket was empty, so I kicked it, then swiped a stray ball from the dirt floor and set up again. I wiped my cheek on my sleeve and glared at the lower right pocket. People shouldn't say they're going to be somewhere if they aren't.

The ball ricocheted off the metal frame with a crack.

My glove hit the ground and sent up a shower of dust and then more dust as I kicked the dirt floor.

The sound I'd been waiting for, a diesel pickup, grumbled to a stop outside the barn, then died with a growl. I froze, my breath caught in my throat. With a small sound of distress, I rushed to the old boombox, turned it on, then hurried to gather a few balls and set up on the mound again.

I couldn't have said which pitch it was, but I'd thrown two of them before footsteps sounded close by. I blinked to clear my eyes.

"River," Dad said. He walked to the boombox, turned it down, and grabbed his bucket with the padded cover and pockets stuffed with batting gloves. He didn't meet my gaze as he settled in front of me and motioned for me to sit, too.

There was no point in refusing, as much as I wanted to. I hugged my glove and perched on the rim of my bucket. My heel bounced.

"You know I'm proud of you, right?" he asked, and I wanted to bolt for the door even more because this couldn't be good.

"When do you have to go?" I asked bluntly.

He sighed and rested his elbows on his knees. "The end of the month."

My stomach dropped, and I stared at his lowered head. "You're going to miss—"

"I know." He looked up. "I'm sorry. Text me, okay? Let me know how Nationals go."

Text him instead of catching his gaze from the mound and sharing a smile? Let him know how it went when he usually understood how I felt before I said a word? And who cared about the tournament? What about our long walks after supper? Or our usual summer trip to the lake. Or our family fishing competition? Or reading together? Or...

"You've never missed a tournament before," I said numbly. Softball was our thing. It was supposed to be protected. Somewhere deep, I knew it wasn't his fault, but I couldn't seem to stop.

"I wouldn't now either, but there's a big humanitarian mission, and they need experienced helicopter pilots. You know I gave my oath. I can't say no." His eyebrows rose. "I'm good at my job, Riv. And people need my help in Costa Rica."

"Do the twins know?"

Guilt flashed behind his eyes. "They were with me when I got the call. You were in the middle of the qualifier—"

I jumped up and kicked my bucket out of the way. I was the only one who didn't know.

He rose and slipped on his catcher's glove. The pitching screen was replaced with his bucket, then he sat behind home plate. I threw a hard drop ball that he caught with a flick of his wrist.

"Good one. Don't bend over so far." He tossed the ball back.

"Dad…" I flung my glove aside and stomped to my water bottle. "Don't coach me." My voice hardened. "There won't be anyone to do it. I need to learn to fix things myself." I swished the tiniest bit of water in my mouth, but there was no room to swallow past the lump in my throat.

Dad's big shoulders were there when I turned, but I stiffened. I will not cry. I—Will—Not.

Then his arms were around me, and his shirt was soft under my forehead. His voice rumbled deep in his chest as he squeezed me tight. "River, honey."

My breath hitched. "Don't baby me."

He huffed a laugh. "I'm not. I'm babying me."

The corner of my lip lifted, then flattened. "Then don't go."

"Honey, as much as this stinks for you and me, you know I'm proud to go and do what I'm good at. And while doing the right thing this time is going to cost both of us, we'll be brave together. Okay? Because you and I don't let our teams down, do we?" He leaned to see my face, but I turned away.

"I just want you, Dad. Let someone else be brave."

He sighed. "I'd forgotten... well, that's not true. It's just been so long since I had to deploy. You kids were little last time." He sounded like it hurt him, this leaving. "Hey, I'll be one hour behind you, so we'll talk every evening, okay?"

My eyes filled then, because I knew. Nothing I did would keep him home.

Slowly, my arms rose to wrap around him. I already missed him. "I'll send you pictures when we win." I sniffed.

He rubbed a circle on my back. "Deal." His voice was rough. "You're going to blow them away. I'll wear my number seven jersey under my gear on Saturday for you. You're such a fighter. I'm so proud that you don't quit."

I squeezed his shirt in my fists and nodded. Then I did the hardest thing I'd ever done. I pasted on a watery smile and leaned back. *"What will you bring me?"*

Looking back, what else could I have done? He'd thought I was tough. I couldn't let him—

"I don't mean to bother you," a raspy voice interrupts.

I lift my head and blink. A hunched bag of dirty clothes, the same gray as his long hair and beard, is standing at the end of the bench.

"What?" I wipe my cheek.

"I don't mean to bother you," he repeats. His shoulders stoop like it's too much effort to stand. "It's just... this is where I sit. Are you going to be here long?"

It takes a second for that to register, then I stand. "Sorry." I wave at the bench. "I'll go."

"No. No, I don't mean to run you off." But he looks longingly at the bench.

"Here, sit down," I say, still unsettled, but smart enough to stay more than an arm's length away. Although, after studying him, I'm confident that I could outrun him if needed.

He sits gingerly on the end and leans on the wooden armrest as if pushed beyond his endurance. I look back at the field. It's just an empty softball complex.

"It's a nice view, isn't it?" he asks, and I nod.

There's no one else in the park. It's still early. As the scent of unwashed male wafts toward me, I wonder if I should worry about how isolated we are. He seems harmless.

"Do you come here a lot?" His voice cracks, probably from not being used.

I sink slowly to the bench. "Not since I was thirteen. I played softball here once."

He nods courteously, his grimy fingers clenched against his dirty canvas pants. "Is this a happy place?"

I have to breathe deep to answer that. "It's mostly happy. Good things happened here."

"Good things." He studies my red-rimmed eyes from behind clumps of dirty gray hair.

Is he hungry? I look around, but of course there's no one but me.

"Do you have any..." I start over. "Do you need anything?"

The man smiles, I think—his mustache moves. "That's kind of you." His eyes squint dreamily. "I used to have a nice daughter like you."

"Oh. Well." He needs something, but what? I can't think of what to do. I don't have cash. Then I remember the two unopened Gatorades and the bag of chocolate almonds I'd just bought at the gas station and have an idea. "Hold on."

The drinks are cold when I press them and the almonds into his hands. He thanks me profusely, but I tell him it's no problem. Then I wave awkwardly and get in my car. He stays where I'd left him, shoulders hunched, looking out at the empty softball fields. It's a peaceful place, at least until little kids start showing up later.

But I wonder what it is about that bench that draws all of us sole survivors?

Chapter 24

When I park my car at the apartment later, I stare at the red pickup with mud-splattered in a wing-shape behind each wheel. The 'EIEIO' sticker on the back window had been a joke, and I'd giggled while I'd waited for their reaction. My weird brothers had kept it. I put my car in reverse just as Zeph comes out of Ty's apartment and looks down at me. Fine.

"Is there any way to keep you two from butting into my life?" I ask when he meets me at the top of the stairs.

"Why do we have to come all the way over to find out what's happening?" he asks.

Kody appears at the door and I glare at Ty. "You called them?"

He looks wary but doesn't deny it.

"What've you done now?" Kody follows me to my apartment. Inside, I drop my keys and perch on the edge of a wooden chair. The guys surround me, Kody across the table, Zeph on the sofa, and Ty on the corner of my desk.

I tell them in short, choppy sentences about the party and Coach Bosswood.

"I wouldn't put up with it," Kody says when I'm done. "You should come home and go to that junior college that wanted you. Screw this."

"She won't quit," Zeph says. "Will you?"

"Maybe I should." I tuck my hands under my thighs. "What good is it to sit out two weeks of a three-week fall season, not practice, and then return to a coach who hates me?"

"Exactly." Kody leans back, crossing his arms.

"Man, River. I never thought I'd hear you say that." Zeph rubs the back of his neck. "What about Coach O'Daniel?"

"He's still in a coma."

Kody taps a booted toe. "He'll back the interim coach anyway, when he wakes up."

Ty studies my face. "It's your decision. You're the one who'll be playing, not us. What do you want?"

Over the rumble of my brothers' opinions, a voice inside whispers that leaving the team would be the biggest mistake of my life. Is that stubbornness born of my brothers' interference? Maybe.

I look down at my hands. If the worst happens, and I emerge on the other side of this suspension and never take the field during a game again, who will I be? Will I contribute to the team from the bench or will I lose heart? If I quit now, will softball become a touchstone of bad memories that I'll avoid for the rest of my life?

Then I remember how the mist had covered me as I'd run by myself this morning. Grittiness had gotten me up for that. I haven't lost myself. I am still a softball player. An athlete. Part of a team. They haven't kicked me off completely. Yet.

I raise my head and meet Ty's gaze. "I'm staying."

He smiles slightly. "And you can't keep your spot on the team with-out practice."

I sigh. "I can do a lot by myself, but I will need a catcher."

"I'll work out with you." He sits unnaturally still. "I'll catch for you."

"I don't know," Zeph says, unaware that I'm studying the intensity on Ty's face, the tension in his shoulders. "You haven't caught for her before. It's not easy."

"Can't your regular catcher help?" Kody asks.

I tear my gaze away and shake my head. "It wouldn't be fair to ask her to practice with me in her spare time. We barely had free time before."

Ty clears his throat and braces his hands on his thighs. "I am, was, a baseball catcher in high school. I can do it."

All three of us gawk at him. He shifts uncomfortably. "I'm really good."

My brothers burst out laughing, but I know him. He's serious. I narrow my gaze. "What happened to the 'I can't catch you' from this summer?"

"I didn't say I couldn't catch, I said I wouldn't be much help." He shrugs one shoulder. "Now I will."

"You're not that good," Kody says, chuckling. "Her drop-curve will take out your knee and her rise ball will take off your head."

"Kody's right," I say. "You might get hurt. I'm sure there are batting cages around where I can find someone to catch for me."

Ty pushes off the desk, as if it's suddenly too hard to sit on. "I was the MVP at the Missouri championship where we won state. I broke school records." He huffs an unamused laugh and leans toward me, his voice low and intense, every word torn from some place deep inside him. "I broke state records. Professional teams were trying to draft me right out of high school, for Pete's sake. Believe me, I can *catch* for you."

Stunned, I watch his unblinking eyes and the way his nostrils flare with each breath. Then, as the magnitude of what he's said sinks in, I surge to my feet. Pain curls through me at the realization that he's treated me like a fool. I'd liked him, accepted him just as he was, and he'd cold-heartedly lied in return. Something hot and ugly rises in me. Who does he think he is?

"Believe you?" My voice shakes. "You lied."

"I didn't lie to you." Ty's face is pale and stormy. My brothers straighten, glancing between us.

"You know you did." I squeeze my fists. "Why didn't you tell me?"

I may be blindsided, but he's been getting ready for this fight for the last half-hour. That's why he's standing. That's why he's upset.

He takes a deep breath and pulls back. "I thought," he says in a low voice. "I was done with baseball. It wasn't who I was anymore."

"So? We talked about sports all the time. There were plenty of chances to tell me." I throw my hands up. "I don't even know what to think right now."

I need space, but when I step out of the apartment, I realize I don't have anywhere to go but back into my own room. I whip around in the doorway and point to the parking lot. "Get out. The whole bunch of you. Go."

Ty looks straight into my eyes. For a second, he looks vulnerable. Like he knew I was going to kick him out all along, and that's why he'd been standing. Then he pushes past me.

#

The thing about an efficiency apartment is there's nowhere to go to get away from someone who's talking to you through the door.

"I know you can hear me, River," Ty says from outside. I sling the pillow I've had over my head to the floor and stare at the ceiling.

"I'm getting weird looks." He raps a quick beat on the door.

"Your brothers left," he says after a pause. "They said to tell you they'll call later."

Still crickets from my side. I hear Ty's huff. Then he lowers his voice. "I haven't told anyone about baseball, if that makes you feel better."

I grit my teeth, then stand and walk quietly to lean my forehead against the door.

"You should understand better than anyone why I don't talk about it," he says.

I turn my head to the side. "Why'd you quit?"

He sounds closer, as if he's leaning his head on the door, too. "Can I come in?"

I hesitate, then slide the deadbolt free and swing the door open, keeping my gaze at t-shirt level. He pauses, as if waiting for me to look up, then slips past, crossing to the sofa. The door closes with a soft click.

"Did you get hurt?" I ask, crossing my arms.

He shakes his head. "It was a family problem." His shoulders are stiff, and the effects of strong emotions are clear in the tight lines of his face. "I have something to tell you." He watches as I cross to sit beside him. "I've never told anyone this, either."

"I won't say a word."

He swallows and shifts uncomfortably. His hand clenches. "My dad is Johnny James from the Cardinals. He played—"

"Centerfield?" I jerk upright. "Johnny James, the center fielder? He retired two years ago?"

Surprised, he nods and opens his mouth, but I hold up my hand, shielding myself from whatever shocking thing might come out next.

"Hold on," I say, squeezing my eyes shut and replaying what he said. "Your dad was a pro baseball player?"

Chapter 25

"See?" he says. "Everyone gets stuck right there."

I hold my hand on my forehead. "Ty. You have to admit it's the biggest shock. I've known you for most of this year, worked beside you for eight to ten hours a day all summer, and had no idea."

"I guess it is." He runs his fingers through his hair. "But it's not the important part."

"Oh." I eye him warily, dropping my hands to my lap. "What else is there?" But there's something that floats just out of reach, some event, some incident, that I should remember.

"Johnny is an alcoholic—recovering alcoholic," he corrects himself cynically. "He was drunk my whole high school career and didn't come to my games until I started getting attention from Division I programs and scouts. Then he became this proud father in public, except father-and-son time meant drinking together. Not that he was mean, really. It was more that I was invisible unless I would drink with him or unless people wanted to talk about my future."

"Which makes him a jerk," I say softly.

He shrugs. "I loved baseball. *Never* considered not playing," he says. "But when I realized playing made me like him, it wasn't that hard of a decision. I wanted things to change.

"He called from Los Angeles one night. They were in the middle of a series. Asked which direction I was going to take for baseball." He studies his hands. "Probably because reporters were asking. I told him I was quitting unless he got help with his problem." Ty smiles humorlessly.

"And he jumped right on that chance for rehab?" I say.

He glances at me, acknowledging that as the sarcasm I meant it as. Then his gaze moves restlessly over my room, although I'm sure what he sees has nothing to do with my apartment.

"What I regret the most," he says finally, "Is that my mom was with him that weekend."

I flinch as a memory surfaces. "Wasn't there a wreck?"

He gives me a sidelong look. "Sometimes you are scary, River." Then he sighs. "He walked away. Mom is in a wheelchair."

My breath whooshes out. "I'm so sorry." I lay a hand on his arm.

He presses his hand over mine, and I don't know if he's going to push it off or hold on. "So, I've been at Northbridge ever since."

The weight of what he's not saying would probably sink a boat.

I study his hand, the clean nails, the wide knuckles, a dark freckle above his thumb. "Except when you were on my farm." I look up.

He gives me a lopsided smile and squeezes my hand. "Except then."

"Are you sure you want to help me?" I gently pull free. "Will it bring up bad memories?"

Ty leans his head back on the sofa, gaze rising to the ceiling. "Actually, I've been going to a batting cage." He tilts to look at me from under his lashes. "Since I got back from spending the summer with you."

#

"I don't care how good of a catcher you are, or were, you aren't catching me without equipment," I say, pacing the room in short, quick strides. His cavalier attitude has broken the peace of a few moments ago.

"Okay." He steps in front of me, capturing me by the arms. "We'll get equipment."

"How?" I wrench free and wave at his body as if that explained everything. "Have you seen how big you are?"

A smile spreads across his face. He crosses his arms smugly. "We'll get baseball equipment from Northbridge."

Horrified, I stare at him. "We can't steal catching equipment."

"We won't steal it. We'll borrow it while they aren't using it."

I press my hands to my head. "Stealing equipment will get me expelled for real. You don't think I've been in enough trouble?"

"I think you haven't deserved the trouble you've had," he says grimly. "Might as well earn it if you're going to pay the price."

"That's an asinine thing to say." I round on him. "Who do you think I am? And who said life's fair?"

We measure each other, re-weighing what's been said. Then Ty shakes his head. "We won't steal it. I said we'd borrow it, that's what I meant. We'll ask Jace."

I turn icily on my heel and march to the door.

Ty pulls on my arm to stop me, but I shake free, and he raises both palms. "Okay, you're right." He returns my glare. "I think it'd be more fun to steal it, too."

I moan and collapse onto the sofa, propping my head in my hands. He sits close, facing forward and careful not to touch me.

"You and Jace... what happened?"

I shrug and rub my face.

"Look, I know it's not my business, and some things are hard to talk about. We've both had our issues," he says dryly. I peek at him sideways, mouth quirking up despite myself. His brown eyes are warm. "But at least we're honest with each other, don't you think?"

I snort. "Besides you not telling me you're a freaking talented baseball player?"

I frown then, and straighten, finding a thread on the hem of my shorts suddenly fascinating. His other deception had bothered me all summer. It feels wrong to pretend that my brothers hadn't coerced him into babysitting me, but it's also completely humiliating.

"What's wrong?" he asks.

I roll my eyes and sigh. "It's just... I wish you'd told me that my brothers were making you stick around."

He looks lost.

"Oh, come on," I say, embarrassed. "I don't care, except I wish you'd told me."

He shakes his head. "I don't know what you're talking about. Your brothers never made me do anything with you besides chores. Never. We ate together almost every day, Riv, and I saw you virtually sun up to sun down. What're you talking about?"

I spring from the couch to glare down at him. "Do you remember after my tournament? And the next morning when we... we..." My hand waves helplessly, but I can't say the word, so I point at him. "You wouldn't let me unload the feed? Well, I heard Fletch."

He stands, his ears turning pink, and I know he's thinking about the kiss too. His brows lower. "I remember everything about that morning." He holds my gaze. "And Fletch wasn't there. So, what you are accusing me of?" He squints. "And why aren't you picking this fight with him instead of me?"

Flustered, I wonder if he can see the memory of our kiss in my eyes as well as I see it in his? "Why did Fletch jump you in the barn if there wasn't some rule about River guard duty?"

He pauses, then slowly, his frown disappears, and a hint of amusement crosses his face. "Oh. That's not... that's a guy thing." He looks away. "It didn't come from your brothers. That was all Fletch. I assumed you knew he was over-protective of you."

"A guy thing?"

He rubs the back of his neck with an embarrassed laugh.

"What?" I shrug impatiently.

"What do you think is the best way to ensure that a girl is respected?" He turns, and his gaze softens. "Have the men in her family..." His eyebrows rise and we both know who he's talking about. "Have them look a new guy in the eye and spell out how special she is to them. It's like that country song about the dad telling his daughter's date that he'd be waiting all night, cleaning his gun while they're out. He wouldn't use the gun. He's just making sure the guy has something to think about before he lets himself get too carried away."

"And that works?" I ask, intrigued.

"Like you wouldn't believe."

I smile.

He shakes his head. "Is that it? You're good now?"

"I guess so." I tamp down a grin.

"Great." He clears his throat. "Then what about you?"

I blink, and the humor fades. "I've never lied to you."

"No. I mean, is there anything I need to know?"

I frown. "Like what?"

He looks away uncomfortably, sighing as he runs a hand through his hair. "What I'm trying to say is there might be things we don't want to talk about yet." I snort, which he ignores. "But you can trust me. I just want you to know that. I'm here if you need me."

Then he strides out the door.

#

The moment Jace sees me at the cafeteria door, humor and chagrin cross his face. He lays down his fork and leans over his tray, his weight on his forearms, as he holds my gaze. I can tell the second that Ty comes through behind me. Jace's face goes carefully blank.

"What's this?" he asks as Ty and I sit across from him. The other person at the table takes one look at our faces and picks up his tray, scooting his chair back quickly.

"I'd like you to do a favor for me," Ty says.

Jace glances at me. "Yeah?"

"I'd like to borrow an old set of catching equipment from the team."

Jace pauses, shocked, then barks a laugh. "Good luck with that," he says. "We're in our fall season now. We're using our equipment."

Ty nods coolly. "I know. I also know there are stashes of old equipment that you're not using. I need to borrow some of that, everything but the glove."

"Go ask Walker, then," Jace snaps, picking up a buttered roll and taking a big bite.

Ty crosses his arms on the table and smiles. "I'm asking you, Jace, because I'd like to keep this just between the two of us."

Jace lowers the roll, still chewing. "Why do you need it?"

Ty tilts his head toward me. "It's for River. You don't want her to not have what she needs, do you?"

Jace stops chewing and studies my face. There's a faint unease in his expression as he swallows. "Dude," he says, turning back to Ty. "I could get into so much trouble for this."

"Only if you get caught," Ty says as I lean closer until we're both in Jace's sight. Jace scowls, slouching back in his chair.

Chapter 26

"This place isn't nice, but it has lights." Ty's headlights sweep the white metal building as he pulls into the gravel parking lot. "They call it the Barn because of how it smells."

I turn from the building to narrow my eyes at him. "Seriously? Are there animals?"

"You're not scared of mice, are you?" He grins at my groan.

My foot dislodges a baseball glove on the floorboard as I get out. Bending to pick it up, I turn it over in my hand with a sinking heart. I hope this isn't what he's intending to catch with. Then he hefts a large bag out of the back and unlocks the building, flipping on florescent lights.

It's warm and humid inside, a faint odor of tire rubber and sweat. Green indoor-outdoor turf that's seen better days lines the net batting cages. I flick a relieved look at Ty, and he grins. It seems pretty clean after all. Some of the tension leaves my shoulders.

Ty switches on a radio and sits to unpack the catcher's bag. He glances at me now and then as I absorb the atmosphere of the Barn. It's bigger than where I used to take pitching lessons. I glance at the high ceiling, thinking that it would've been nice to have that much room when I'd started; I wouldn't have hit the metal beams as often. Each uncontrolled pitch had sounded like a gunshot.

"What're you smiling about?" he asks.

I laugh and gesture to the ceiling. "I learned to pitch in a building with lower ceilings. We'd bet on how many times I'd hit a beam in one lesson."

He eyes the ceiling before bending down to buckle a shin guard. "There's a learning curve." He smiles. "I started catching in machine pitch and loved it. Then we moved up to kid pitch, and I got so pissed running after every ball because the pitchers sucked. They either threw over my head or in the dirt, every time. I seriously considered becoming a third-baseman."

"Oh, wow." I chuckle. "Machine pitch days, I'd almost forgotten." I poke in buckets along the wall, touch bats leaning haphazardly. I pick up a loose baseball, turning it in my hand. "What made you stick with catching?"

He stands up and slides the chest protector over his head. "Attention problems, I guess. I had to be involved in every play or I was bored."

He picks up his helmet and lifts a net aside so I can duck into the cage as "Sweet Caroline" by Neil Diamond begins. We sing along as we warm up, growing louder and louder.

"Good song," Ty says when it's over, throwing the ball with perfect form. And to think I'd insulted him once about his lack of athletic ability.

"I'd like it more, if it weren't for the Boston Red Socks." I throw the ball back.

"Come on." He pauses. "Don't tell me you're one of those people who only like one team."

"I like other teams." I stretch my shoulder. "But not the Red Socks. There was that World Series, remember?"

"Which World Series? 2004 or 2013? Okay." He holds up a palm to stop my protest. "Okay. You're holding a grudge against a World Series. I'm sure the Cardinals appreciate your defense of their honor." He rolls his eyes, dropping his glove to stretch his triceps, elbow up by his ear. "A little petty, but okay. I'm a Reds fan myself."

I lean over to poke a finger in my mouth. He laughs.

"Seriously, I hate the Reds." I shake my head. "As any true Cardinals' fan should."

"The Cardinals," he taunts. "can't win a game until half-way through a season."

I inhale sharply. "Watch it. You're talking about my team."

He laughs again and adjusts the lacing on his glove. Intrigued, I cross to look at it.

"That's not the glove from your truck," I say. "That's a real softball catching glove."

He holds it up proudly. "I found it at a sports consignment store." He slides his left hand in, opening and closing it experimentally.

I trace a finger over the suspiciously dark leather, then examine my finger. "Umm. Do you have any Lysol?"

He scowls and pulls the glove out of my reach. "You ready to pitch?"

As I watch him grab a five-gallon bucket and sit at home plate, I hope this won't be a disaster. He used to be a catcher, I remind myself.

He can probably handle what I throw. But I can't help saying a brief prayer that he won't get hurt. He's just so confident, so gung-ho about doing this. I really hope he's as good as he thinks he is.

I pace off forty-three feet and mark the spot with an empty cup. Then I walk back to within a few feet to practice my snaps. His brown eyes are intent on my every move.

"What are your signs for pitches?" he asks, and we go over what the team uses.

When we're warm, I say, "Fastballs first. Then change-ups and drop-curves."

He nods and moves the bucket out of the way. My heart is in my throat as he drops into a half-squat, his glove out and steady. My first fastball makes a satisfying pop, despite it being a timid pitch. I can't shake my concern about his reaction time. Even if he were used to catching baseballs, everything about a softball pitch is different—the size of the ball, the wind up, the release point, the distance. Besides, he hasn't caught for a long time. That's a lot to overcome.

All he says is, "Nice."

"How's the glove?" I wipe my palm on my pants.

"Fine." He sets up again.

The next pitch is over his head, and I bite my lip.

"Riv," Ty stands. "I know how to catch." He lifts the helmet to give me an exasperated look. "The glove is great. I'm super-duper. Stop worrying and pitch."

He retrieves the ball. Before he pulls the helmet back into place, he crosses his eyes, and I laugh. He drops into a catching squat and doesn't flinch on the next pitch—I give him credit for that. Slowly, I realize that he's right. He can catch.

"Change-up," I say, and he nods, adjusting his stance up a little.

I'm kind of proud of my change-up. It took me years to get it as consistent as it is because it has to look like the same delivery as a fastball, only twenty mph slower. It needs to hang out there forever before tailing off at the plate.

Ty extends his glove and visibly flinches; gasping as the speed of the pitch throws him off. When the ball finally gets to him, he pops up with a laugh.

"That was amazing! Completely freaked me out. If I'd been batting, I'd have swung three times before it even got here. I love it! Throw it again."

He sends the ball back to me and resumes the position with a grin. Pleased, I throw another one, putting just enough spin to make it tail to the right. He snags it out of the air and gleefully lunges up to throw it back.

"That is wicked! Just... mean. And wicked!"

I can't remember when I've had this much fun. We talk about pitching and catching and decide to go through more of my pitches. I throw a screwball, and he whistles.

"Whew. If I'd been batting, I'd have swung at that and got air."

"Do you want to bat?" I shrug. "I mean, you could if you want."

"Heck, yeah." He flips the glove to land by his keys and reaches for a bat leaning against the wall. He takes some practice swings.

"So, fastballs?" I ask.

"You pick 'em. I haven't seen live pitching for a long time. This'll be great."

He does rather well, all things considered. But after a while, something changes. He's made contact with the ball a few times now, so he's started to crowd the plate. I can read in his small, confident smile, he thinks he can crush one. So, we're competing, are we?

I throw three rise balls in a row, letting the spin on the ball climb from below the strike zone to above it. After the first one, he flinches and walks in a circle, adjusting his helmet and muttering to himself. At least he stays in there for the next two, but he can't touch them. I feel his impatience; the way he wants to lean into a good pitch, but he won't say it, just gives me a withering look. So, I throw a don't-crowd-the-plate pitch nice and close on the inside by his elbow.

He twists in and away from the ball, which came in friendly enough it should've paid for dinner first. "Really?" His voice rises. He chucks the bat behind and stalks toward me, eyes narrowed.

I swallow a shriek and back pedal, losing control of my silly grin. I hold up my palms. "Okay, you made me run, and I made you flinch. We're even, right?"

He pauses, his expression unreadable. Then he shakes his head, humor lurking at the corners of his mouth. "Tried to hit me, huh?" He takes another slow step.

"What?" I gesture toward the plate. "There's no way that would've hit you unless you stepped into it."

He takes another measured step, and I laugh.

"Truce?" I ask sweetly.

I don't know how he makes walking look so intimidating, but I forget to breathe. Each deliberate step brings him closer until I have to tilt my head to see him. I barely hold my ground. I guess that's a no-go on the truce? Then he passes me, so close that I smell his soap.

He opens a cooler and pulls out two bottles of water. My breath whooshes, and he chuckles as he hands a bottle to me. We sit cross-legged on the worn floor.

"Who taught you to catch?" I watch his throat work as he swallows.

He tenses, then screws the lid back on. "Henry."

"Henry who?" Then I choke. "Shut up! Henry Fields? The backup catcher for the Cardinals?"

A faint smile crosses his face. "Thought you'd recognize him."

I collapse onto my back and stare dumbly at the ceiling.

"He—" Ty says, and I hold up a hand to stop him right there. Of course, he plows ahead. "He was the bullpen catcher before he retired. I haven't seen him in a couple of years."

"Were you close?"

Ty shrugs and picks at grass stems on the carpet. "From the time I was little, I was Henry's shadow. I wanted to be just like him. He came to my games and all of my graduations. He was the one I talked to about my first crush." Ty gives me a rueful look as I sit up.

"He sounds great," I say softly.

Ty nods then, after a pause, shifts gears. "So, I've never paid attention to softball before, but I watched some internet videos last night. There's one with that girl Lawrie pitching against a baseball player. It was obviously staged..."

I laugh. "Whatever."

"Obviously." His eyes are lit with humor. "But she was good. It was interesting."

"Wait until you see a live game. They're faster paced than baseball. You're gonna like them better."

"Let's not go crazy." He looks skeptical of my sanity.

"Hey, it could happen." I stand and hold out a hand to him. "But first, it's time for my batting practice."

"Heartless workaholic." He shakes his head woefully.

I lean back to hoist him up. "And I'll need to practice tomorrow, and the day after that, and the day after that. Maybe two-a-days? Two-a-days tomorrow, two-a-days the day after..."

He picks me up and whirls me in a circle until I squeal.

#

That evening, someone pounds on my apartment door. "River? Are you in there?"

I look up from my algebra homework, bemused. A moth buzzes the porch light when I open the door, flitting noisily above the heads of three girls. The three who put me in this apartment.

"We brought chocolate," Andy says as she passes. Katie and Dawz follow her in.

After a quick glance down the landing, I close the door. The room feels smaller with the three of them here, living and breathing, overwhelming the shadows that've been keeping me company.

"Look." Katie opens a white cardboard box. "Dark chocolate peanut clusters and chocolate-covered marshmallows."

I peer over her shoulder. "Chocolate? My favorite."

"We know." Andy settles on a dining chair, hands clasped between her thighs. She eyes my practice clothes.

Dawz sets a jug of sweet tea on the cabinet. "Where've you been?" She points inquiringly to a cabinet for cups. I gesture to the next one over.

"Pitching with Ty." I perch on the arm of the sofa and take a bite of a peanut cluster.

"You have somewhere to practice?" Katie asks, startled enough to look me in the eye. I pause, the candy halfway to my mouth and glance between them. Why are they avoiding my gaze?

"Yeah, actually." I take another bite, though my appetite has disappeared.

"With Ty?" Andy asks. "What does he know about softball?"

"More than you'd think," I murmur, then paste on a smile. "You guys should come."

Katie frowns. "It won't matter."

"We'll never play again after this," Andy says. "Might as well quit." She studies the floor, curled over herself like a question mark.

Dawz stares blindly into the open cabinet like her battery has worn down. With a sigh, I cross the room, reach over her shoulder for a glass, and hand it to her. She blinks.

"We're going to be fine. I promise," I say, but their hollow-eyed expressions send a draft through my chest. I'd felt the same just yesterday. And, while we might miss the team, maybe they hate us. I swallow and force confidence into my voice. "Bring your bats tomorrow. It'll be fun."

Dawz nods. "Okay. Cool." She puts her hands in her pockets. "Want to watch a movie?"

Later, when someone else knocks on the door, we're spread, shoeless, over the floor with pillows and cushions. Andy pauses the movie and leaps up to answer the door. She sends me a wary glance when Lily and Emma walk in.

"Hey, ya'll." Lily takes in every detail of the room. "Heard the party was here tonight."

"Too soon," Dawz says. "No party here. But you can watch the end of the movie, if you want."

They slip out of their sliders as if it's no big deal, and I stare at the growing pile of shoes—all exactly the same school-issued team footwear.

We rearrange, careful to make space for each other on the sofa and floor of my tiny space. The movie resumes and, slowly, our stiff polite-ness relaxes into a giggling, friendly comfort, like a nest of puppies. Lily leans her head on my shoulder the way I think a sister would, and for the first time in a long time, I feel peaceful. I'm so calm, in fact, that another knock at the door makes me jump.

"I'll get it," Andy says. I frown suspiciously at her eagerness. If it's from guilt, we might need to talk.

"River, it's time for a…" Fletch's voice trails off beyond the door. "You're not River." At the sound of laughter, Andy steps back and Fletch's face appears.

Emma sits up and runs a hand over her hair. "Hi, Fletch."

He nods at her, then acknowledges each fresh face until he gets to me. His unabashed grin is the look of a young boy on Christmas morn-ing.

"Time for what?" I ask.

He tucks his hands in his front pockets. "Well, I thought it was time for a smoothie, knowing how much you love them, but—" He scans the candy wrappers and water bottles. "It looks like you're busy."

In a flash, we're off the floor, bumping, and shoving, and digging through the shoe pile. Emma is ready first and winks at Fletch, and I swear he blushes. He watches, amused, as we pour out of the room. When I bring up the rear, he leans close.

"You are my favorite sister, you know that?" he says.

Chapter 27

On the day of our scrimmage, I can't sit still. It's maddening not to be on the field with my team. Cruel not to be allowed to watch in person. The radio, though. It has wrung me out to listen to the play-by-play. Won one and lost one. By the time Ty returns, I'm a ball of nerves, tethered to the apartment like a pet on a leash waiting for its owner to come home.

His window is down as he pulls into the parking lot and he zeros in on me immediately. "Hey," he says as he parks. "You listened?"

"Did we look good?" I open his door.

His pause is so brief as he steps out, he probably didn't notice, but I see it. His every word and gesture a lifeline to me. "The first game they seemed scattered, but they had it together for the second." He closes his door.

"Did anyone else warm up while Zoe and Abbey played?"

Ty shakes his head and takes the apartment steps as well as he can with me glued to his side. "I know you said they were letting other girls practice pitching, but the coach must've been testing Abbey and Zoe."

He opens his apartment door and walks in, leaving me standing on the threshold. He comes back in an instant and holds up his catching glove. I nod with relief.

The metal barn is warm with pent-up sunshine when we get there. As I pitch, the sweat eases the knot in my stomach. Ty doesn't falter. Catch after catch, he's right with me.

When we take a break, I lower the water bottle and wipe my lip. "Do you think my screwball is working? Am I falling off too much?"

Ty opens his mouth, then closes it. Finally, he half-smiles and says, "It's hard to say. I wasn't watching you. Kind of had my eye on the ball. Show me again, and I'll see if I can tell."

I throw a few more, conscious of where his glove has to move to catch them. He sits back on his heels. "If you were falling off, you've fixed it. You're hitting your spots. Zoe had a few wild pitches today."

I nod and go back to the pitching mat, already turning the ball in my hand for a fastball.

A couple of pitches later, I ask, "Is that faster than it was?"

"Yeah. It had a good pop."

If my pitches are doing what they're supposed to, what else should I work on? The answer is automatic. Speed. I re-tighten my ponytail. But what if I just think my pitches are working today? For sure doesn't mean they'll work tomorrow. If they aren't perfect at the right time, Coach won't give me another chance.

After several more pitches, I ask, "Do you think I can earn a spot on the team again?"

Ty stands up and walks toward me, his shin guards clapping against his cleats. He holds the ball out but doesn't let go when I reach for it. "How did you get here, Riv? How did you become a college pitcher?"

"What? I don't know." I dismiss his question with a flip of my hand.

But I can't escape the fears I've caught from Dawz and Katie. What if I never get to play again? "What if they don't play me because they don't like me?"

"Who doesn't like you?" Ty frowns, letting go of the ball.

"The coaches." I swallow and lift one shoulder. "The girls. Some girls." I've had hours to think while the rest of the team scrimmaged. I've cataloged the problems between us: the quiet snubs, the dismissive glances, the broken bonds—worse than we felt about Chelsey. Especially from those who think Zoe should be our pitcher, not a troublemaker like me.

"What have they done to you?" He's suddenly very still. "Has something happened?"

I shake my head. "But I might get benched. If they let me back on the team at all. And if I walk a batter, then I'm... I'm through." Because the team won't trust me any more than Coach does.

Ty pulls the catching helmet off by the face guard—the better to see me with—and lets it hang from his fingers. "So, you're worried about walking a batter?" Ty asks quizzically.

"No!" I snap. "If a batter gets up in the count, I can get out of it. I know that. But if Coach pulls me after one mistake, I'll never get the chance to prove it. And that gets in my head, you know?"

He opens his mouth, but I narrow my eyes in warning. He waits.

"She didn't pull Zoe, did she?" I ask, my chest tightening. "Even though they lost, Coach Bosswood didn't pull her. You watch, she'll pull me if I throw three balls in a row."

"Who else were they going to put in? You haven't even played for Coach Bosswood yet. Why are you so worried?" He starts to laugh but sees my face and sobers. "She's a good pitching coach. When she suspended you, she was trying to make a point and not leave room for criticism. She knows what you can do as a pitcher."

He doesn't know. Why would he suspect that she didn't want me?

"She didn't recruit me, Ty. She doesn't know what I can do. O'Daniel liked me, not her. She never lets Abbey catch for me. Every time we inter-squad scrimmage, I'm on the B team."

"You're a freshman, River," Ty says logically. "You have time to work up to varsity."

I shrug impatiently. "I've pitched against the best Gold ball batters in the country. I can handle varsity. I just don't know if I'll ever get the chance."

Ty studies me. I wait, almost breathless with hope that he understands my clumsy words. Understands the difference of knowing that someone believes in you.

"What's this really about?" he finally asks. "I watched you all summer. You practiced, conditioned, worked on technique—you're not afraid of hard work. But now you're flipping out over playing time?"

I nudge a curious beetle who's gotten too close. "It's not just playing time. All I've ever wanted to do is play softball. But I can't do it if a coach doesn't let me." My eyes burn. "And there's nothing else for me to do. I can't help Coach O'Daniel fight for his life. If I don't play—if I'm not on this team—what good am I to anyone?"

He's thoughtful, his brows drawn in concentration, but he knows me. He gets it, I think. Teams are woven together with respect and trust. If I don't have either from my team or coaches, then I can't shoulder my corner of the load.

"Are you trying to make excuses, so if you get pulled, you'll have someone to blame?"

What? I toss my glove and scowl. "Forget it."

"No." He steps in front of me. "You're upset about something that hasn't happened yet, so tell me why. You're tougher than this. I mean, come on, you're River Harte, Girl Wonder. You toss fifty-pound bags of feed after pitching five games, make world peace, and feed the hungry."

"That's not funny," I say hoarsely, despite his joking look.

The smile leaves his face. "I'm dead serious. No matter what happens with the coach, which you can't control anyway, you're still going to be amazing. A stubborn, hard-working, amazing girl, whose dad would be proud. You know yourself. Don't let softball take that away. Either enjoy it, work your butt off more than anyone else, or get out. Either stay or quit, but don't lie to yourself about who you are because of a sport."

I want to strike back, swear that I'll quit. But the words won't come. Even as bad as everything looks, it panics me not to have softball. No matter how many times I've asked myself whether all of this was worth it, I still want to play.

I crumple to the ground, head drooping. Ty looks at me for a minute, then sighs. He unbuckles the chest protector and unsnaps the shin guards. With his equipment in a pile, he groans as he sits beside me.

"One of your drop balls got my knee." He rubs his kneecap gingerly.

"I'm sorry. You didn't tell me."

"I haven't noticed that complaining makes it feel any better." He looks at me crossly. "You'd probably just laugh, anyway."

"I wouldn't." But a smile threatens at his frown. "It's not funny."

He shakes his head mournfully. "It's-snot-funny."

"Eww!" I groan.

He bends his knee, examining it. "It's already bruising. Look." He tilts his knee to me.

"Yeah," I say, then look again. "Is that the imprint of the stitches on your bruise?" I raise my eyebrows and admire my work. "How did that happen?"

He smiles. "Your ball broke like crazy—right above the shin protectors."

#

Andy, Katie, and Dawz show up at five-thirty the next morning to run. Their dedication warms my heart, but not my ears, so I pull on ear warmers. Sharing the work is not exactly fun, but it's easier. I lead the way to the cold, dark trail where we jog and laugh about who hates running the most.

When we meet again that evening at the barn for batting practice, I realize it's the first day I haven't been in a dark funk since being suspended.

"Keep your head in," I tell Andy.

Sweat glistens on her forehead as she nods and swings again. The ball blasts toward the netted ceiling at the end of the cage. She sets up and sends out another home run and another. I shake my head, glad that I didn't know she was this lethal a batter when I faced her at the State tournament. I'd have been too intimidated to pitch. In the other cage, Katie and Dawz are working with Ty.

The door opens with a draft of cool air. Lily, Emma, and Rachel appear with softball bags over their shoulders. We stare at them.

I stand... because it feels like I should. "What're ya'll doing?"

Emma drops her bag and crosses her arms. "We wanna play, too."

"Got room for a few more?" Lily tucks one hand in her pocket; the other has a death-grip on her bag. I glance at Dawz, and she gives a small shrug.

"What're you looking at?" Rachel tosses her bag and pulls her sweatshirt off her practice t-shirt. "Take a picture. It'll be worth more when I'm famous."

"Yeah, or infamous," Dawz says. Rachel grins and kicks off her slip-ons.

After that, it's loud, the little barn shrinking under our assault. And it is an assault. Balls pinging against nets, bats whistling through air, and somewhere between Dawz and Andy starting a water war and Rachel flipping the net up, yelling as she marches over to rescue her damp bag, my heart melts. We're still a team. Man, I didn't know how badly I still wanted that. Yearned for it.

Then Emma pours water down my neck.

#

The last day of my suspension, I'm at the bench in the park. It's a habit now to drive by and look at it from a distance. But today, the homeless guy is hunched there, and I've got a stash of drinks and snacks for him.

He glances toward the parking lot at the sound of my engine, then turns back, leaning forward with his elbows on his knees. Not sure if this is a sign of disinterest or unhappiness at having his peace interrupted, I approach him cautiously.

"Mind if I share your bench?" I ask.

He motions for me to sit. The drinks and snacks clank as the bag settles beside me.

"Do you remember me?" I scoot the bag closer to him. "I've brought you some food."

He looks at me through a fringe of gray hair but doesn't take the sack. "Thank you."

Sparrows dip and rise in a small cluster before disappearing over our heads. A few cars pass on the road behind us. Still, we sit in silence, like the childless fields we're studying.

"Have you ever played softball?" I ask. I can't see his face well, but he's sitting easier. Maybe he feels better than he did the first time. With a start, I realize he was probably tall before life wore him down into this shadow of himself.

His shoulders relax under his faded clothes. "Yes," he says. "I was a catcher." He peeks at me. "Where did you play?"

So, he remembered... I lean back with a smile, pulling one foot up on the bench and loosely hugging my leg. An actual conversation. "I'm still a pitcher."

"I bet you're a good one." His voice is low and rusty.

We continue looking over the fields, but now we're doing it together. "We have a game tomorrow," I say.

He nods as if we're talking about the weather. "Are you excited?"

"I'm nervous, actually." When he glances at me, I drop my foot from the bench and lean forward, mirroring him. "I've kind of been in trouble, and tomorrow is my first day back."

He reaches down and picks a tall grass stem and smooths it between dirty fingers. Burn-scars wrap his wrists under his sleeves. "Trouble comes and goes. You learn from it. But first days are firsts—you only get one."

I purse my lips. "That's profound... sorry, I don't know your name..."

He swallows and looks at me. "Ian."

"I'm River." I inspect my clasped hands. "You're right, Ian. Really. I shouldn't keep feeling bad about what happened, and I've learned a lot from it, believe me. It's just... it's not a real first day. Everyone knows me. I can't start over."

"It's the first day of your second chance, right?" He studies me, twirling the grass stem. "Why aren't you happy?"

Surprised, I think about it. "I am. I can't wait to be back on the team—to play." I sit back, crossing my arms. "But I think it's going to be awkward. They punished me for helping some teammates. The rest of the girls have carried on without us. I'll have to earn my spot again."

After a pause, he sighs. "The last time I got in trouble at home, I was fifteen." He runs his fingers down the grass stem, over and over. "I was supposed to go to a concert with some friends, but I ditched school to get ready. Dad heard about it, and I knew I'd be punished." The corners of his eyes crinkle with his smile.

"I was getting big, so Dad asked first, did I want a thrashin' or a groundin'? It didn't take a minute to decide I could handle a few swats, but I sure didn't want to miss going with my friends. I told him I'd have a thrashin'. He said I'd have a groundin' and that I'd just told him everything he needed to know. My friends would be goin' without me."

That sounds like my brothers, and I laugh.

Ian's shoulders shake with a silent chuckle. "They went, and I had a terrible time by myself until my little sister brought home a new friend from school. They shared their pizza and a board game with me."

He tosses the blade of grass down and sits back. When he glances at me, the wind moves his hair enough that I glimpse a long, jagged scar across his forehead that just misses his left eye.

"I married that girl," he says. "So, just go and do your best. And eat pizza every time you get the chance."

Chapter 28

The next day, I arrive at the practice facility fifteen minutes early with a stomach empty of everything except hope, courtesy of the anxiety of meeting with Coach Bosswood, since the last time had been such a complete fail. But a few steps in, I stop cold, all the breath knocked out of me.

Andy, Katie, and Dawz clatter to a halt a few seconds later, transfixed by Coach O'Daniel's large-as-life picture hanging in the lobby. He looks healthy and amused. The fresh flowers on the table beneath sweeten the air, not like the sickly aroma the flowers assume at the hospital. We've visited him there, at odd times to avoid the crowds, and he's just a shadow of this photo. But I know as I look at him, if he were here, he'd tuck his hands in his pockets and ask what we're waiting for with that knowing blue gaze. It gives me the courage to face Bosswood.

She doesn't stand, just motions us to the chairs across from her desk and steeples her fingers. "It's against my beliefs to let you four back on the team. What do you have to say for yourselves?"

"We're so sorry," Dawz says quickly.

Bosswood shrugs that off impatiently.

The silence grows uncomfortable. Katie shifts in her seat. "I've never seen someone run over before." She looks up, twisting her fingers in her lap. "I couldn't get it out of my head. It's no excuse, but that's why I went to the party."

As if that's what she was waiting for, Coach leans forward. "Why didn't you talk to the counselors we brought in?"

Katie glances at Dawz. "We didn't want to talk to a stranger. We just wanted to be together."

Coach snorts. "Well, had enough of that yet?"

I lower my eyes, but my cheeks warm. Dawz's heel staccato-taps the floor and her shoulders rise, as if she'd like to say something, then thinks better of it.

Andy fiddles with a thin gold band on her finger. "You should know that River was only there to pick us up, Coach." I turn to stare at her. "I knew she'd come if I called."

Coach studies me for a moment, then moves to the others. "Have you stayed in shape?"

Dawz straightens. "We run in the mornings and practice batting and fielding in the evenings. We didn't have weights, but we did body weight stuff." She clasps her hands between her knees. "No days off."

"And you?" Coach asks me. "Have you pitched?"

I nod. "I run your drills and pitch live to these guys."

"Just the four of you?" she asks. I cringe, because last night a lot of the team had been hanging out in the barn with us.

When we don't respond, she stands. "I've heard about the others."

My face flushes. I can only imagine who ratted us out and why.

She perches on the front of her desk with arms crossed. "So, I've discussed this with the A.D., and I've actually taken the advice of the counselors—whom you didn't visit."

I squeeze my fingers until the tips are white. The weight of my backpack and the uniform inside is heavy against my foot.

"Under these unusual circumstances, I'm giving you a second chance." She levels a slim finger at each of us. "But if you break one more team rule, you're off—for good. Understood?" When we nod and start breathing again, she says, "Now get out of here and dress out."

Chairs scoot across the floor as we stand. "River," Coach says. "Stay for a moment."

The others give me reassuring looks and close the door behind them. I sit down again.

"How're your pitches?"

"They're good," I say firmly, because nothing could be worse than the past few weeks.

"Liz had surgery on her ankle, in case you didn't know." She pins me in her gaze. "I've only got Zoe. Which means you're pitching one scrimmage today, sight unseen. I need to know where you stand in live pitching. If it doesn't go well, Zoe will take over. Understood?"

"Yes, Coach."

She nods. "We'll see." She motions with her chin. "Get suited up."

Later, it feels like every eye is on me when I cross to the third base line with the rest of the team. I peek over my shoulder to find my family and Fletch in the stands, but it's Ty who lifts his fingers in the wave I taught him. He's leaning forward, elbows on his knees, baseball hat low over his eyes. His smile warms me. The feeling cools when I take my place next to Lily on the baseline and glance at the girls beyond her, who avoid my gaze. They know Coach doubts me. When I straighten, my elbow bumps Andy on my other side. She's wide eyed, and so close she's in my shadow.

Her expression mirrors everything roiling inside of me at being with the team again. The joy. The tension. The wariness. I take a deep breath, reminding myself this is like a hundred other games. All we have to do is play ball. But we both keep the contact at our elbows.

Zoe pitches a two-hitter in the first game. When I take the field in the second game, Coach Bosswood stands at the fence, scrutinizing my warm up. Even though I want to be here, and I'd do anything to stay in this game all seven innings, the circle is lonely today. For the first time I feel vulnerable and unprotected.

Even after Lily catches my last warm up pitch, I feel the fans scrutinize my every move, and I know at the hospital, the radio relays each throw for O'Daniel. But they're nothing compared to the weight of Bosswood's cold stare.

Then my nightmares come true—my first two pitches are balls.

"Let's go!" Bosswood yells, "Throw strikes."

This coach. She thinks I'm going to fail. And I'm proving her right. Aiming pitches, playing it safe. But I can't stop. The ball is foreign in my hand. The spins suck. The snaps reek. I'm dying out here... and she's going to pull me.

Lily calls time and jogs over. "So, I loved that chocolate cake for lunch, didn't you?" Her glove hides her mouth, but her eyes sparkle with mischief.

I squint in confusion. "What?"

"I'm going to see if we can have another piece or two after the game." She puts two fingers against her glove where only I can see it. "You in?"

"Lily?" I lean closer, hiding my mouth, too. "What're you doing?"

"I want them to worry about what we're planning." She glances at the batter. "So, more chocolate cake?"

My brows rise. "Okay." The word drags out. "If it's chocolate. Fine."

"Gotta say it, Harte."

I roll my eyes. "Yes, Lily. I'll take two pieces, and I'm not sharing." She smiles. I find myself smiling back. "You're crazy, even for a catcher. You know that?"

She dips her chin, her gaze steady. "Let's get this girl out, just you and me. Spin the ball, Riv." And she jogs back to home plate.

I sweep my cleat up the lane, studying the marks left by the pitchers before me. I turn at the rubber and wipe my palm on my pants. With a deep breath, I face the batter's box. And there he is. Ty, feet wide and braced, stands between the bleachers beyond home plate.

Arms crossed, he looks like an immovable mountain. Even with his dark sunglasses, I feel his gaze. All of that strength, that no-nonsense confidence, extended to me. My eyes sting and my throat closes. But something inside of me shifts.

I rub the ball on my hip as the batter sets up, and almost laugh when she points her bat at me before pulling it up high and loose. If she thinks that's intimidating, she hasn't seen the year I've had. Then I launch off the rubber and it's smooth. Powerful. The batter dinks it up and is out with an easy throw from Dawz. I finally exhale. Now we're playing ball.

We win the scrimmages as if we'd never had a break as a team, but the tension in the dugout is a different story. I don't know how long the hidden rifts will take to heal.

My family waits for me behind the dugout in their Northbridge softball t-shirts. Mom's camera digs into my stomach when she hugs me.

I gesture Andy closer. "Mom, do you remember Andy from the State tournament?"

"Sure," Mom says and, to Andy's surprise, hugs her, too. "Nice home run tonight."

Andy glows, a far cry from the look she'd worn before the game.

Zoe's parents join us, waiting on their daughter, and I cringe as Zeph glances toward the dugout with barely concealed interest. Is it my place to tell him what she's really like? Would it make a difference?

She emerges, her shoulder wrapped in ice, with a smile for her parents. At least it better have been for her parents. I'm not sure about that when she introduces my brothers to them and skips me altogether.

Just as I think my shoulders might crack from tension, Ty presses close and my thoughts scatter. He's so big, like an infrared heater at my shoulder. And how does he always smell good?

Zoe's mother turns to Kody. "Are you in school at Northbridge?"

"No, ma'am," he says. "We—"

"We've graduated." Zeph interrupts with a quick glance at Zoe.

"You did?" Zoe smiles. "What was your major?"

"Geography, for me," Zeph says. "With a minor in cartography. Engineering for Kody." Zoe's parents seemed stunned.

Ty's chest vibrates with a silent chuckle. He leans down, his breath on my ear. "It's so hard to take them seriously, and they're probably geniuses."

I look at my brothers, so alike and, yet, so different. "Yep. Part of their charm," I whisper back. "Hard to imagine them studying, isn't it?"

He makes an affirmative noise. "But why..." A pucker appears between his brows. "If they've got their degrees, why are they still at the farm?"

Then realization dawns on his face. I guess he hadn't really considered the cost of my brothers' dedication to finding Dad.

#

Sunday night, my apartment is quiet, which is saying something with seven girls and their homework spread out. Only the occasional shift of a pizza box or slap of a closing book breaks the silence.

Lily clears her throat. "How many wins did Jace say Coach O'Daniel needed to break the school record?"

I look up and blink. "I think he needed sixty to break twelve hundred, right?"

"Why do you want to know?" Rachel closes her computer.

Lily leans back in her chair. "I just checked. We have fifty-five scheduled games this spring. There's the possibility of three or four more at regionals, three at Super-regionals, and three during the bracket play of the WCWS. The championship finals are always best two out of three. So, all together, if we win sixty of those, we earn Coach's record for him."

"Really?" Andy sits up. "He'd get the credit even if he isn't there?"

"Well," Lily says. "He hasn't lost his job, so he's still technically the head coach this season. And we don't know, maybe he'll be back for part of it."

"Wow." Emma looks awestruck.

"Let's do it." Dawz pops her knuckles.

"You know that means we can only lose, maybe, five games all year." I raise my eyebrows. "Assuming we get into the super-regional, let alone the championship tournaments."

"True. But winning fifty-nine won't matter either," Lily says. "It's sixty or nothing."

I picture the end of the year and Coach accepting the plaque, his name in the school's hall of fame, and it makes my eyes sting. Then I remember how half of the team won't look at me at lunch. The way we are now, winning at all will be raw talent. With our competitive conference, if the miraculous happened and we pulled our splintered selves together and forgave each other, we'd still be long shots. Five losses in a season? When we've always been more of a qualifier team than a championship-winning team?

"I've been thinking," Andy says. "We need a better tribute for Coach than patches on our jerseys. He deserves more. We need something shareable to keep him on everyone's mind."

"You're right." Lily turns, as if she'd been watching me, and pulls her computer close. "Any ideas?"

"He's been a coach for thirty-four years," Katie adds. "Maybe use that number?"

"Gotcha." Lily scrolls through screens.

"I know." Emma holds up three fingers. "We can do the power of three sign."

"It's been done," Katie says.

"Or like one finger over your heart before you bat?" Dawz says.

"I always loved that the sun made his white hair and mustache glow," Rachel says.

We all seem to freeze at that. If you asked us, the image of Coach in the sun would be all of our favorite, even if he was making us run triangles. Even if he was pulling us from the game. If only we could see him like that again.

Lily leans back. "So, maybe a white game-day bow for our hair?"

"Yeah," Emma says. "And we could make a board to put a ribbon on for each win."

"When he smiled," I say, embarrassed. "I always thought of bird wings. Is that weird?"

"I did too," Katie says, grinning at me.

Andy's eyes widen. "Maybe we should add white feathers to the ribbons."

"Whoa," Dawz says. "I appreciate the idea, but I'm not wearing ribbons, and definitely not feathers."

"Oh, come on, Dawz," I say. "You'd look so cute." I laugh, ducking as she throws a pillow. "What are we going to do, then?"

"Let me see," Lily says, typing again.

Something grabs my attention as Dawz takes the pillow back. I frown, reaching forward to tug her wrist up for a better look, and she's so surprised she doesn't slap me. "Do you like these rubber band bracelets?"

She looks from the band to me. "I'm wearing it, aren't I?" Then she makes a small oh with her mouth and pulls her wrist back. She scrambles to her knees, holding it up to the group. "Hey, I know how to order these bracelets."

"I like bracelets," Rachel says, watching all of us fawn over Dawz's wrist. She leans back in her chair, crossing her arms. "But they're going to have to be light green."

When we all frown at her, she nods. "Yeah. My aunt, who owns a flower shop, says that green means rebirth, new life, good health, all the good new things."

"Why can't they be red or blue, like our uniforms?" Dawz asks, baffled.

"Or pink," Katie asks, and Dawz's frown turns into a scowl.

"Green." Rachel shakes her head.

"Homecoming is next weekend," Lily says. "We're supposed to

have that pitching booth for our charity fundraiser. Let's see if the team wants to do the bands, probably green," she adds to a few groans. "We can start the white bows that night, too."

"Will we have them for the last scrimmage?" Andy closes her book.

"Better question. Are we going to be the only ones with bands?" Emma asks.

"You mean, should we sell them?" Dawz asks.

"We need to ask the school first," I say. "So, who's calling Boss-wood?"

Lily glances between us and shrugs. "I think we should go as a team." She picks up her phone and starts typing. "Is it okay if we have a team meeting here, Riv?"

I huff a laugh, looking at the small space. "Whatever." Although, the barracks may never be the same after this.

Chapter 29

On homecoming Friday, excitement is like a drug in the air.

"Stay close," I say over my shoulder to Lily. "Or I'll never find you."

We skirt traffic barriers to enter the east end of campus, trading vehicular congestion for a solid pedestrian wall. But safety is relative as, right away, a stroller bounces off my shin. The harried mother doesn't make eye contact, and I back into a big student on my other side who glances over, interested. Lily all but disappears in the crush, and I reach back to tug at her shirt. She bats at my braid.

"Your ribbon is in my face," she yells, but she stays close in my wake.

The darkening blue skies and the gold evening twilight are magical, making our ordinary campus exciting, like an exotic carnival.

"Do you smell that?" Lily taps my back with each word. "That's barbeque."

"Ty first," I say over my shoulder. "Then food."

We round the corner to find a band set up on the front lawn of a fraternity and have to burrow through the crowd like a needle through fabric. At the end of the block, the Walking Rally displays begin. I squint against a fraternity's floodlights over their lawn and duck around a group of high school boys. A stationary float obscures the frat house with a yard full of chicken wire and colored paper.

"They're taking donations." Lily points to a table.

"Is that how they make money for their charity?" I wave off a swarm of insects, exposing the two green rubber bracelets bright against my skin.

It had taken a while for us to agree on what the bracelets would say, although the feathered mustache was unanimous. In the end, we'd stayed simple. *Hold the Hope.* I think Coach would've liked that his words had become our mantra. He'd said once that it took something exceptional to pick yourself up when you were knocked down, when your talent wasn't enough, when your fears took over, and every practice throw and drill was all you had left in the tank. That was when it mattered what you hoped in. And he'd quoted Hebrews, which said to hold on to the hope of our beliefs, because we weren't in this alone. His eyes had shone when he said all that remained was heart.

"Is this what most homecomings are like?" I ask.

"I don't know, but hurry, Riv." Lily pushes me. "We have to be back in thirty minutes. Bosswood is scary when she makes that face."

I flip my hand like it's no big deal.

Lily gives me a crabby look. "Yeah, it's all fun and games for you, but I'll be running poles right beside you if Bossbaby's not happy."

Out of all the things to worry about, the booth is low on my list at the moment. Way down there behind algebra.

"There they are." I point ahead to a two-level wooden platform covered on the front with chicken wire. Eight guys, in matching neon t-shirts, jeans, and goggles, pose behind the wire, four on the upper level and four below.

Ty, the tallest guy there, looks like a lightning rod on the top. He slants a rueful gaze my way, and I laugh. At least he'll avoid the worst of the eggs up there.

"Six eggs for twenty dollars," a guy calls. "Come on up, ladies."

I shake my head. "We just want to watch."

"Try one egg?" he cajoles. "The five dollars is for a great cause."

Another neon-shirted worker, loaded down with cases of eggs, steps closer. "Our Father's Shelter needs paint and new bedding. Have you seen it?" He gestures with full arms. "Across from the city park."

In front of the platform, a young father crouches behind his pre-school-aged daughter and hands her an egg. Her little arm rears back, but the egg doesn't reach the wire.

"Hey, try again!" a guy encourages from the lower level. "You can do it!"

She backs into her dad's arms with a shy tuck of her chin. She notices me watching and my heart twists. She reminds me so much of myself as a four-year-old. Except, I'd been wearing a princess dress when Dad taught me how to throw. Did he regret what he'd gotten himself into when my little team showed up in royal hero dresses? I smile softly. If only he could see me now.

I splurge for an egg, then crouch to hold it out to the child.

"Know what? They forgot to tell you to move up to the magic line." I point to a spot in front of the painted line, aware that Kody would be smugly proud. "That's where a big girl like you throws from."

She measures me with a serious blue gaze, so I slip off one of my green bands and hand it to her. "And take this special bracelet. It helps me when I throw."

To my amusement, she slides it above her elbow, then watches it sway as she takes the egg. Her dad smiles gratefully. She resolutely steps up to the new line, rears back, and throws. The egg breaks low on the fence and drips onto the grass.

I raise my hands with a grin. "Yeah! What a throw! Give me five." She smiles but runs into her dad's arms and peeks at me from against his chest.

Lily's gaze is on the girl when I stand. "You've got to do it, Riv. I'll pay if you'll play."

"Do it yourself," I murmur.

A high school girl takes her eggs to the line. People pause in the street and laugh at the spectacle, just the way the guys had planned. The little girl watches from the shelter of her father's arms, her blue eyes missing nothing.

The high schooler's egg splatters someone on the lower level, earning cheers from the passing crowd. The guys, encouraged by the attention, promptly start dancing around and playing the crowd.

Then Fletch shows up with another box of eggs and his face lights up. "You made it." His neon t-shirt is snug over his muscles as he pretends to check his watch. "About time."

I sigh, and Lily cheerfully buys six eggs.

A guy on the upper level with chestnut hair whistles when it's my turn. "Hey, sweet thing, love your uniform." He gives a thumbs up. "Hit me. You can do it. Easy-peazy."

As people stop and chuckle, I give Lily a sour look. Even Ty laughs. So, my first throw hits chestnut-hair squarely in the chest, just like he asked. He tucks his hands under his armpits and crows triumphantly to more good-natured cheers.

I pick up the next egg and splatter the shirt of another guy on the top level. The others hoot at his yelp.

"Lucky shot," calls chestnut-hair. But I seem to have all of their attention now.

"Here," a guy on the lower level says. "Hit my hand, if you can." He lifts it in front of the dude next to him. "I'm such a poet."

I aim at his own t-shirt rather than his hand, and he doesn't move in time to avoid the slime. "Ugh." He laughs. "I said hit my hand."

Although everyone is having fun, the eggs start to feel like balls of lava to be rid of. Chestnut-hair flinches at my next throw, dramatic as a baseball player avoiding an inside pitch.

"Oww." He rubs his neck. "She cut me with that eggshell, man!" When someone calls him a wimp, he warns, "You wait. She's throwing hard!"

I toss an egg gently in my hand, deliberating. Ty's expression is half hidden by goggles, but his head tilts, and I know what he's thinking.

Fletch bellows from the side, "Don't let him off that easy."

Ty shakes with laughter, and he'd make an excellent target, but... I look back at chestnut-hair.

At the direct hit to his goggles, the guy beside him takes a nervous step back, saying, "The uniform is no joke, man."

Chestnut-hair takes the next egg in the chest, yolk blending into the neon lime shirt. The last egg peppers him as he raises both hands to protect his face. With my stash exhausted, he flips his goggles up, pinkie in the air, and studies me amid the others' glee.

"What'd you do to piss her off?" the guy next to him asks.

"I don't even know her," he says, causing more laughter.

"She's hot," one of them says.

I glance at Ty and he shrugs as if he agrees. Then he lifts two fingers and tilts his chin toward my side of the campus. I smile, turn to go...

...And halt mid step. The jostling crowd has swelled, overtaking the street. Between amused groups, people line up to buy eggs, eyeing me speculatively.

Never one to miss an opportunity, Lily raises my arm, pointing at the bracelet. "We're having a pitching booth. If anyone's interested, come try your luck."

A neon-shirted mom moves a stack of empty egg cartons at the congested sign-up table. She gestures to my softball pants. "You play softball?"

Fletch appears and slings his arm over my shoulders. "All-State high school pitcher, right here."

She glances down the line of waiting customers. "I thought so." She winks. "Good job, honey."

"You're famous." Lily laughs, tugging me away. "But hurry! We're almost late."

By the time I'm warmed up, I expect Zoe to be ready to relinquish the mound. But she's still shifting dirt by the rubber when I stride out. She glances up as I near, and I stiffen. Instead of impatient, she looks strangely friendly. Would she try something with all these witnesses? No, she'll probably just drop the ball when I reach for it—anything to make me look like a bungling giant.

"River." She tucks the ball in her glove instead of handing it to me, and I brace myself. "I've been thinking."

"Okay." I peek over my shoulder, hoping the coaches are watching. Nope.

"I really want to win the record for Coach O'Daniel."

"Me, too." I shift to afford the staff an unobstructed view, just in case.

"The thing is, we're in a position to uniquely help each other." She steps closer and I almost raise my hands in self-defense. "I don't know if you realize how different this season is going to be. Normally, we play hard, then accept the result. But, this year, we *have* to win. Everyone is watching. Do you know what that expectation could do to us? It'll make each game less a game and more terrifying, where Coach's record lives or dies. I don't see how we can pull that off without—"

"A miracle," I say, and she looks pleased. It doesn't make me feel better. Not when I'm waiting to be her punchline.

"We need to be there for each other," she says. "We can't let each other get down over bad pitches or off days."

A large part of me knows it would be stupid to fall for this. Still, I study her. "You want us to keep each other from being too mental?"

"It's smart, right?" She shrugs, matter-of-fact. "Who else knows exactly how we feel?"

"Well," I say slowly. "I don't..." But my mind draws blanks. What am I missing?

"I've never seen you be mean," Zoe admits soberly. She maintains eye contact, and I notice dark rims around her light blue eyes. I guess they're kind of pretty. "No matter what anyone does or says to you, you just keep going. You work hard, even when you think no one's watching. You're crazy, but it's a good crazy."

Now Coach is glaring, and I don't need her irritated. But I have the weirdest urge to duck my head and shuffle my feet. "Thanks, I guess. It's a great idea, Zoe."

She hands me the ball with a satisfied smile and leaves. A small part of me wonders if, maybe, leaving me dazed was her plan.

Over the next hour, I face a lot of different batters. Most are just having fun. A few, like the current one, are baseball players. Strong and quick, this guy is totally comfortable with the bat in his hands. His friends hoot from the fence as he takes a practice swing and weighs my merit with a narrowed gaze. Coach gives Lily the sign, then relaxes into her perfect expressionless mode.

The batter misses my curve and my change-up. When I throw a rise ball, I know he'll be upset, unless he's hit off a submarine pitcher before. He swings under it and shakes his head, confirming my guess. Yup. Baseball really is missing out on the equivalent of a rising pitch.

Over the sounds of his friends' jeers, or maybe because of them, he adjusts his hat and growls, "Send me the heat. Come on, just send me your heat."

So, I do, and it blows past his bat.

Katie, who's manning the gate, says sweetly, "Forty-three feet. Wow, so different from sixty, isn't it?"

Chapter 30

Later that night at the barn, Ty shifts up to his knees to throw the ball. After feeling some glitches while pitching earlier in the evening, I'd intended to practice anyway, but that smile glinting through the grill on his helmet, well that's reason enough for me to say yes to more pitching, despite being back on the team.

"How many did you strike out?" he asks over a rap song from his playlist.

I grin. "Enough to make Coach happy."

I throw another change-up. Ty frames it in the strike zone.

"Good one." He tosses it back. "Hey, wanna go fishing after your game tomorrow? I bought a new lure."

I laugh. The fishing competition had been fierce between us last summer, to no one's surprise. There was plenty of smack talk, of course. But it was the times with only the whisper of water and birdsong karaoke, that... wow. It explained a lot about why Dad loved fishing with Mom.

Gross.

"Still trying to beat my dad's old favorite?"

"That lure's luck can't last forever—"

"Luck? You mean skill..."

Suddenly, the door swings open behind him, and I flinch back, eyes wide. Ty whips around, rising to face the threat.

Coach Walker, cold as an early winter, steps in.

He doesn't say a word as he closes the door behind him. Music thumps through the building.

He reaches down and shuts it off.

In the silence, his gaze catalogs every object in front of him until it lands on the Northbridge baseball team's equipment bag sprawled on the floor where Ty had dropped it. He compresses his lips and nudges it with a toe, his face turning decidedly red. Then he looks up to glare at the matching helmet on Ty's head. My heart sinks.

He pins Ty with his gaze. "I expect this equipment in my office in the morning, along with an explanation. Is that clear?" It's not a question.

"Yes, sir," Ty says. I hear him swallow.

Coach Walker scans the room again, letting the weight of his presence settle good and heavy over us. Then he acknowledges me with a chilly dip of his chin and leaves. My stomach churns as I cross the lane to stand by Ty. He takes the offending helmet off and taps it against his leg, still facing the door. I wish saying I'm sorry would help, because I'd say it a hundred times, a thousand times.

"Well," Ty says grimly. "That wasn't too bad."

#

The next day, music plays over the speakers at the softball field during the pre-game—because everyone knows you need a melody with a beat faster than your heart to warm up.

Except, my heart rate is already off to the races. In fact, the only thing that'll keep me from a full cardiac infarction will be seeing Ty's serene face after his meeting with Coach Walker.

"There he is." Lily points to the brick arches at the entrance of the complex.

I catch his eye.

"I'll be back." I lift the netting and leave the cage. My cleats crackle on the concrete as I scoot around Sarah and Mia dancing and laughing.

Fans pour in for the ceremony honoring Coach O'Daniel as Ty meets me at the brick half-wall separating the field from spectators. He doesn't look noticeably different, but I've known him long enough to recognize the strain of his smile, the stress bracketing his eyes. The stiff jerk as he adjusts his baseball hat.

"Have you been with him all this time? Are you in trouble?" I ask quietly.

He scans the bleachers rising at our side, his brown gaze tripping over the rows. "Not the kind you mean," he says. He stills suddenly, finding whatever he'd been searching for. "But I'm in trouble all right."

I follow his gaze as Jace glances at us over his shoulder. I clench my fists. "Do you think he turned us in?"

Ty's gaze hardens. "Oh, he turned us in, but the joke's on him." He looks down at me. "Coach Walker wants me to walk-on for the team."

I cover my mouth. "No!" I move my hand. "How would he even know you could play?"

His jaw tightens. "He tried to recruit me out of high school."

I stare at him.

"Close your mouth, Riv." But he's pale, and it's so unlike him that my emotions rise.

"Only you, Ty." I half turn, not knowing what to do. "Only you would go out of your way to not play and end up on a team anyway."

He scowls, but behind it, there's vulnerability. And shell-shocked stress. It puts things back in perspective. "How do you feel?" I step closer. "Are you excited?"

"I don't know yet. I walked out of the baseball offices and hurled in the bushes."

"That bad, huh?" But I imagine it was that bad and more. "What does he want from you? I know what a walk-on is, but what does that mean for you?"

"I'm trying out for the team without a scholarship for this year—if I make it."

"Yeah." I nod like a bobblehead and look away. "That's what I thought. So, you'll travel with them?" I tuck loose hair behind my ear.

He shrugs, as if his shirt is tight. "He promised to keep it all under the radar as much as he can at first, so…"

"Why? Oh. The publicity? Will your dad hear?"

He makes a noncommittal grunt and adjusts his hat again. My heart aches at the sight of his stiff shoulders and clenched jaw.

I glance to where Jace reclines casually in his seat. "Why did he turn you in?"

Ty follows my gaze. "Coach Walker won't say when he found out the equipment was missing. What he said was he overheard Jace, so he grilled the team." He looks at me. "He was going to see how far they'd take it, but when he told them to run and not stop until someone talked, the guys turned on Jace."

"Him and his big mouth." I cross my arms.

"Yup." Ty rubs his jaw, the sound of whiskers barely audible.

I frown. "But why did you ask Jace to get the equipment if you knew Coach Walker and could've asked him yourself?"

He shrugs impatiently. "Look what happened, River. Besides, you're not the first girl I've heard that Jace jerked around. He owed you." He glances over my head to my team. "They're almost ready." I turn to go, but pause at his touch on my elbow. His voice is low. "Nothing's changed. I'm still going to help you."

"I wasn't worried." Because that's not what worries me.

His lips tilt to the side. "Right. I know you, remember?"

When I take my place on the baseline, I glance back and he lifts his chin in a silent assurance. He thinks I'm only concerned about needing his help. What would he do if he knew the truth? That I'm afraid everything about us will change. The quiet talks, the teasing, the way he drops what he's doing if I need him. The look in his eyes.

Behind my back, my fingers twist anxiously. It's obvious Ty is a baseball phenomenon. He could make it all the way to the pros. If I can see it, anyone can. So, I'll be the one who'll have to change. I'll have to let him go. His reality is something I can't compete with.

I'd run back and tell him that, of course, everything will be fine for us, but how many famous people do I know? None. Because they don't stick around. My throat aches at the magnitude of change that's coming now that he's a shooting star.

If only he was still just a freaking math tutor.

Then the program starts, and we all shift our attention. The athletic director takes the microphone. As he talks about Coach O'Daniel, my eyes stray to the dugout, to the spot where O'Daniel usually stood with his all-encompassing gaze. He could make me run faster and push harder with one barked word. My confidence soared with one nod of his white head. And, most amazing of all, he'd somehow pulled me in from the outside and tucked me under his protection with a calm assurance. Now, I'm unanchored, tossed around, black and blue.

The A.D. calls for a moment of silence. Despite not much progress yet, the medical staff seems optimistic when I visit the hospital. Behind closed eyelids, I see all the good wishes and prayers rushing across the sky to his room and imagine them settling around his bed like a hedge, bringing the breakthroughs that have eluded him so far. But honestly, after the prayers are said, there's nothing I can do to make a difference. Just like there's nothing I can do to keep Ty near.

Then I remember how Coach urged me to get out there and live. He'd been encouraging me for my dad. He didn't know I'd have to put that into practice to have something to show *him* when he gets back. My ribs threaten to crack under the pressure of unshed tears.

The moment ends and music blasts. We break our huddle. And I see it then, what we can do. What we have to offer. It's such a relief to know how to contribute.

But in the back of my mind, spring looms. Our real season. When we'll find out if our strengths as a team are enough on the softball field. Or if we can break a record.

Chapter 31

February.

"Are you done with that ribbon?" I hold my hand out.

But when I look back at Rachel bent over the locker room bench, lip caught in her teeth, she's still coloring the large navy number five on the white satin. The other four ribbons flutter against their staples on our poster board, neatly numbered in her handwriting.

Sarah stops to watch, backpack on her shoulder. "You heard the alumni want to make an official banner, right?"

Rachel glances up mid-stroke. "What's wrong with our board? It's our season."

Sarah shrugs. "They like the idea of a visible win-tracker. They want everyone to see it, not just us, kind of like our bracelets that they're selling now." Her expression hardens. "Rumor is, the banner will hang down the press box wall by the bleachers. After every win, they want us to walk out as a team and attach a preprinted number."

"Like Oklahoma does?"

"OU's panel is for appearances at the WCWS, and it's on the outfield fence. Not the same thing. They hope we'll be adding to our banner every game, instead of once a year."

Rachel and I share a glance. "No," I say, as she says, "Not going to happen." Mia and Dawz join us, looking concerned.

"That's a terrible idea," I say. Those of us on the field will have the banner and what it represents shoved in our faces daily at games and practices. As if we won't already be thinking about it. "You told Jace that we don't talk about things like this. That we just play the game."

Dawz's eyes widen. "That would be bad, so bad. We can't let this go public." She puts her arm protectively over the board. "This is just for us. They'll bring us bad luck if they put it out in the open." She turns to Sarah. "I'm not kidding. Don't let this happen."

The others crowd around. As their grumbles grow, Sarah holds up a hand.

"I only said they wanted to make a banner. Coach Bosswood nipped it in the bud. She said she couldn't confirm there was such a goal, and that they needed to remember this was a D1 program, not a United Way campaign."

A smile spreads across Dawz's face, and her shoulders relax. "A-plus comeback, Coach."

Rachel thrusts the ribbon up, and I staple it on as everyone watches. Maybe the fans would like to share in the glory of what we're trying to do. I understand that. But will they carry the pain of failure, too, if we fall short?

I swing my backpack over my shoulder and tap the board. Quietly, the rest of the team gathers behind to tap it on their way out. This is what the board is for us, much more than numbers, more than single games. It is what we've done together, for another one of us who can't be here.

Lily zips her coat and falls into step beside me. Ducking our heads against a winter wind, we walk to the bus to catch a plane to Florida. This is a big weekend. Not only ranked teams will be in the five-game series, but number one seated Michigan. I hope a single tap on the board is enough mojo to last the entire weekend.

The next day on the bus from the hotel to the softball complex, I'm deep in online research for a paper due Monday, when Dawz's and Rachel's voices intrude.

"The best softball camp was at OU," Dawz says.

"You don't know," Rachel says. "How many camps did you go to?"

"She's only been to one," Kim says. "Haven't you, Dawz? That's what you said when I told you about IUPUI's camp in Indianapolis and how the overhead tunnels kept you from having to walk through snow."

Sarah's head pops over the seat. "That's nothing. The prettiest camp I ever went to was Texas A&M Corpus Christi. It's right on the Gulf."

Over the merits of Iowa State's indoor facility and Kansas University's nice field, I lose interest in my research. Most of the team perks up, voicing their opinions on San Diego State's view versus Florida Atlantic's, or the University of Georgia's hills to Oklahoma State's wide-open spaces. Andy asks me what camps I've been to.

"I've only been to one." I sit up and put my computer away. "When I met Coach O'Daniel at Northbridge."

It grows quiet, and there are a few nods. "I went to that one, too," Andy says.

Mia drums her fingers on the headrest. "I never went to our camp, but I've helped run it. Coach O'Daniel makes it fun, no matter how much work it takes."

"I always felt like I was missing out when I wasn't wherever he was," Sarah says.

"Have you seen him jamming in his office?" Emma asks with a glance at me. "He had the door open once when we were practicing, and he was having a good time with the music." The chuckles die off as we imagine all of that life confined by tubes and tape.

"He tried to coach me using hockey lingo because he knew I liked the sport," I say. "And sometimes, I didn't even know what he was trying to say—just why. I love him for that."

"He did that for me, too," Sarah says. "Only he referenced *Karate Kid.*"

Everyone talks at once, then, recalling all the weird, sweet ways he had sought to connect with his team.

"Hey." Bree raises her voice above the others. "I don't know if you remember what last year was like for me?" she says, and by the way some girls turn to her, it's obvious they do. "Coach was there for me." She leans back against the bus wall, arms spread over the headrests on either side. "He'd ask how my dad was handling the cancer treatments, how my family was doing. How I was doing. He didn't even talk about softball—just sat there like a bucket jockey and gave me someone to talk to."

I have to look out the window at that—too much emotion roiling through the bus to handle safely. Nothing's the same now. Even Mrs. O'Daniel looks different, like she's wilted without Coach's thoughtfulness every day. When the bus stops, it's not only the bright Florida sun or the sixty-five-degree weather drifting between palm trees that makes me blink quickly.

I pull my bag from the storage compartment and turn, almost running into Dawz. She rocks up on her toes, craning her neck to see what's causing the bottleneck.

"Someone's talking to Coach Bosswood," I say.

Dawz scowls at my feet, flat on the ground.

"Everyone," Coach says above the noise. "This is Dr. Dot Richardson's assistant. She'd like to say a few words."

A ripple of excitement runs through our group. If her assistant is here, maybe we'll get to meet Dot Richardson herself this weekend. I scan the area. I wish I had something for her to autograph. Would the school be too mad if she signed my jersey? I couldn't care less about seeing a movie star, but if I could meet someone like Dot, I'd wait in line all day.

"Welcome, Northbridge University." She scans our faces, and the fidgeting and whispers fade away. "I'm so sorry for your tragedy. Coach O'Daniel is a good man. I have the pleasure of knowing him, and we all miss him today."

Her simple sincerity holds us riveted as she continues. "I know you're all probably close, but you will likely be even closer before this season is over. You need to lean on each other and be strong for each other. This isn't how you saw your year going back in August, but what you're doing, playing ball and honoring your coach, is bigger than you think. You're getting a chance to be the team you want to be and to elevate a great man. A lot of people are watching and pulling for you. You have our support. Believe in yourselves and don't quit."

She smiles and moves through our group with comments and fist bumps. When she gets to me, she says, "So, you're a pitcher?" Gripping my arm, she leans close. "Go get 'em."

"Thank you." I return her contagious smile.

"Stay positive." Her eyes shine with energy. "Your team needs you."

She pats my shoulder and moves on as I hitch my backpack a little higher. Stay positive. *Believe.* I pick up the pace, suddenly eager to get on the field.

Two days and three triumphant games later, the novelty has worn off. I'm ready to pitch our last, but toughest, game against Big Ten's number one ranked Michigan University. With the Big Twelve emblem on my backpack, I know we belong here, but my gaze keeps straying to the Wolverines as they warm up. They seem relaxed as they laugh with their coaches and barely spare us a glance. Emblem or not, it's a reminder that we're not on anyone's radar. To everyone else, this is a simple David and Goliath game. Except, Goliath is so big, how could we miss?

The first batter, number thirty-two, adjusts her batting glove outside the box. While we wait, Abbey gives me the salute north—our school's rally symbol—and I turn and pass it to the outfield. The music stops.

By the fifth inning, we're still zero to zero. Another team warms up in the humid heat beyond our outfield fence with pings of bats and pops of leather. Michigan's lead-off batter is up again, her jersey not as white as it once was. Thirty-two watches my change-up for a strike as her team spills over their dugout wall to cheer and clap.

She crushes my inside rise ball.

I tilt my head and follow it across the sky. Shoot, I'd planned on her waiting for the drop curve.

Before it passes the left fielder, I know it's gone, and it's all I can do to keep from stomping my foot in frustration. The team warming up behind the fence shrieks as it lands in their midst.

While the batter runs the bases, and their fans celebrate, my infield jogs over.

"Sorry," I say immediately. The batter punches the air as she runs.

"Don't worry about it," Bree says.

"That's all they're going to get." Dawz creases her mitt. "Hope they enjoy that lucky dinger."

"Yeah. You're right." But instead of glancing at home plate, I watch Coach Bosswood scribble on her clipboard, then lean past the fence and yell. Zoe's head snaps up. She picks up her glove. I turn away, wiping my palm on my pants. Coach's lack of confidence is a hard blow. A reminder that I'm on probation.

Abbey plants herself in front of me. "River, it was a hit. That's all. We'll get that run back. Go finish this. I believe in you."

"Right." Sarah wipes her chin on her shoulder. "Shake it off. We've got your back."

"You can do it." Bree squeezes my arm.

I keep my head up as they run back to their bases, but that wasn't an ordinary hit. That home run could cost us the game. And I did nothing but watch it happen. I take a deep breath, willing myself to let it go and reset. Abbey gives me a thumbs up. I spin the ball into my glove and nod back. It takes a lot of energy to ignore whatever is happening in the dugout. If Coach is going to replace me, then she will, no matter what I do.

She leaves me in. But every remaining pitch is torture. And every swing we take over the next two innings proves to be merely counting down to the end, ticking away each possibility. Not even a two-out rally saves us. When the last out is called, despite jaw-clenching, steely-eyed good intentions, the score is 0-1. We lose.

Our team is quiet as we line up to congratulate the Wolverines. I'd never been foolish enough to believe we wouldn't lose a game, but I hadn't expected the loss to feel so ominous. My hands shake under the weight of responsibility. The door to defeat has opened. In the hospital, Coach O'Daniel fights for his life, and I can't even prevent a home run.

With each fist bump down the Wolverine line, I force myself to face the triumph in their eyes. Their joyful satisfaction. They deserve this, and I deserve to let it shred me. I let Coach down.

Maybe in a normal season, this loss would've been just a bump in the road. But this year, I realize it won't matter how many wins we have. Every loss I allow will crush me.

I won't... can't... feel like this again. I will *not* be the weakest link that kills our desperate vision. What a sucky way to end the weekend.

When we're ready to leave, I hoist my backpack over a shoulder and duck my head, intent on avoiding the disappointment etched on my teammates' faces. I don't notice Zoe until she grabs my arms. Her blue eyes are direct and filled with empathy. It's more dangerous to my emotions than if she'd been self-righteous.

"You did not lose by yourself," she says fiercely. "Don't you dare believe that."

I hold my breath to keep tears at bay as the others give us a wide berth. She pulls my head down to her shoulder and whispers, "You did your job. We can't win if we don't score. This loss is on all of us. Keep your head up, girl."

I clench the sides of her jersey. "I never want to lose another game." My voice breaks, harsh and jerky.

"I know. We have four left for the season, Riv. Four that we can lose and still win the sixty. This doesn't hurt us." She pulls back and waits until I nod through stupid tears. "Hey, if it'll make you feel better, when we get back, let's go through some drills after watching the films. Come on, we can do it together."

More tears spring up at her unexpected support. "Thanks." I sniff, running my knuckle under my nose. "But..." I huff, half sob and half laugh. "Stop already. You're killing me, girl."

She chuckles, slinging her arm around my shoulder as we walk out of the dugout. "The season's just starting, Riv. Don't you leave me here alone."

Later, in the airport, I sit on the floor in a quiet corner and call Zeph.

"You're leaving today?" I say evenly when he answers, glad he can't see how bruised and worn I feel. A few rows away, Emma and Dawz argue over homework spread in front of them.

"In about an hour, hopefully."

"And this rumor is trustworthy?" I twist the green band around my wrist and wonder how long they'll be gone.

"It's coming from a canton that we haven't visited yet. That'll mean a lot of new districts to explore if nothing else. We'll do like we always do: make friends, touch base with the contacts they have, follow the rumors. We don't want to rock any boats that might hurt Dad."

I lean my head back and close my eyes. "Are you bothered by the flight?"

He sighs, dolefully. "No. I'm used to it. You?"

"It's easier since it's a big plane." I glance out the window at the commercial planes. "But I don't want to fly in a helicopter again unless Dad's the pilot."

"No kidding. I didn't enjoy my last helicopter flight," he says wryly.

"Well, you'd have to be a little sick to have enjoyed that one. You said you were flying close enough to the treetops to grab a branch and could still barely see under them."

He hesitates, and I wonder if he's rubbing his face. "I don't know how many more trips we can make, Riv." His voice is a whisper.

Dad's wreckage had been easy to find, but that's all that's been easy. Every turn since then, there's been another wall, whether it's a lack of information, lack of leads, or lack of resources. We've mortgaged every-thing we can, dredged every penny. We all feel it coming—the day when we'll have to decide how to keep searching.

"Be safe, Zeph." I rub my eyes wearily. "Just promise me you'll come back."

"Don't be morbid, kid." But he sounds more like himself. "And you didn't say how the games went today."

"We lost one." And knowing the two of them will be gone when I get back has made the day that much harder.

Chapter 32

It's a wonder we don't get motion sick with the way the season goes after that. Up and down and sideways, like today. We don't need help to sabotage the season. It just shows up.

Coach Bosswood calls time and marches across the windswept field to home as Brigham Young's batter drops her bat and jogs to first in the last inning of the game. The umpire clears his clicker, removes his face guard, and strolls to meet Coach. My fingers ache with cold as I watch them. It may be forty degrees now with flashes of sunlight, but Coach isn't thinking about that. She's too riled about the umping that seems suspiciously one-sided.

"I didn't see you crow-hop," Sarah says from my left.

"I've never had an illegal pitch called since they allowed the leap." I drag my toe over the rut in the pitching lane and look up to see if an ump is watching. Here's the proof that I don't crow-hop.

"It's because they can't score," Dawz says, wiping a knuckle under her running nose. "So, the umps have to help them out."

"Hey." Sarah turns on her. "Don't stoop to that level. We haven't scored either."

The CU emblem on Coach's head warmer perfectly aligns on the middle of her forehead and her puffy jacket doesn't dare sag as she marches toward us.

"He said you replanted," she says with no preamble. "Keep it down and keep doing what you're doing."

"She didn't—" Dawz starts.

Coach pins her with a stare. "I know, but we'll play along. I'm watching them and you. I've got this handled. Don't let this girl on base, got it?"

After we break huddle, I'm super conscious of every mechanic of the next pitch. The batter watches the strike, then backs out of the box and glances at the ump. But it's her fault, not his, that she missed that one.

"You've got this," Bree yells from shortstop. I nod and turn, giving the outfield the two-finger peace sign for the two outs.

I throw a drop curve next.

"Illegal pitch," the ump behind me yells.

I turn. Heat, that's not windburn, spreads over my face. The batter steps out and takes a practice swing. I nearly rip off my headband and throw it across the field.

"Where is he looking?" Coach Bosswood bursts from the dugout, louder than I've ever heard her. She marches toward the home ump, a gloved finger aimed at the offending ump. "Come on, Blue." She stomps her foot, arm still raised. "What's illegal about that pitch? He's not paying attention. Probably has a date later, as much as he keeps messing with his hair."

"That's enough." The home plate ump points to the dugout and stares her down. She drops her arm and mutters all the way back.

Some of my frustration dissolves at the sight of Bosswood coming unglued on someone else. It's a new feeling to see her perfectly composed self mad *for* me instead of *at* me.

The batter, who I've struck out twice today, returns to the plate. Within minutes, she's got a full count. I make promises to myself as I set up on the mound. When she's out, I'll find a spot on the bench out of the wind, treat my hands to a warm towel, and watch our team rack up the runs. I get the signs from Abbey, check the code on my wristband, and throw a changeup.

"Illegal pitch!"

Loud boos erupt from our little huddle of fans with more volume than I would've thought possible.

The ump gives the batter first base. She unfastens her batting glove as she goes, surely knowing she'd never have gotten on base without help. The lead runner also advances to scoring position on second. I stare at the home ump and dare him to read my mind.

"Are you kidding me?" Coach Bosswood throws her clipboard down and kicks it.

The home ump draws himself up and points out of the field. "You're out of here." Coach marches toward him like a ballistic missile, but he isn't daunted. "Now!" he bellows.

She turns to me, eyes flashing. "There's nothing wrong with your pitching, River. Don't let these guys get to you. Let 'em have it." Then she stalks off the field.

I stare after her, not even blinking despite the cold. Now what?

Zoe, Coach CJ, and Liz gather in the dugout over Coach Bosswood's pitching stat book. Liz finally sits on Bosswood's bucket, with Zoe close beside her, and flashes signs to Abbey.

There are runners on first and second, both unearned. Dawz glares at the girl on second, then turns, kicking dirt on the way back to her spot.

"You've got this, Harte," Sarah yells, clapping her glove.

"Take it to one," Bree calls. "Let's get the out."

Our dugout fires up, chanting and cheering, until I can't hear anything else. The fans stomp their feet inside their sleeping bags and blankets, their beanies pulled low. They clap gloved hands as Brigham's leadoff batter steps into the batter's box.

She swings low and whiffs my rise ball. The crowds grow louder.

Painfully conscious of my feet, I throw a change-up low and outside. The batter slap bunts, and I lunge to scoop the ball and fire it to Sarah. As she stretches to catch it, the runner purposely bumps the ball loose.

That runner is safe on first, but Sarah recovers the ball and throws to Callie at third to try to get the lead runner out. The throw is a little off, and the runner speeds past. Behind Callie, Rachel digs out the ball and throws it to Abbey at home.

It's not Abbey's fault that the run scores.

The rest of the game is like trying to straighten saran wrap. We finally ball it up and get off the field.

On paper, this second loss looks like a bunch of errors. Which stings even more.

Chapter 33

March

"Large chocolate-chip Frappuccino with extra shot of espresso." Ty sets the drink in front of me. Lazy Sunday afternoon sunshine stretches across the coffee house floor. I cradle the mug in both hands as I look him over, noting every change since the last time we saw each other. Between his games and mine, it's been a while.

"Let me see," I say.

Ty gives me a crooked smirk and pulls up his gray thermal sleeve to reveal a purple circle above his elbow. I lean closer. "Hmmm. Good one. Fastball?"

He tugs the sleeve down. "Eighty-five mile per hour screwball." He gestures toward me.

I pull up my legging to reveal the bruise on my shin. "Coach Bosswood's infield practice."

Ty raises his eyebrows and runs his finger over the knotted bruise. "Nice."

"I don't know how fast it was, but it bounced off the ground like a gunshot."

He laughs as I fix my leggings and sit back. "Your mom's going to love that one. Are you going home this month?"

"I can't. Every weekend is booked. I'll go in April. Besides, my brothers just got back, and they'll be busy now."

"Oh yeah? Where'd they go?"

The door opens, and my attention shifts to the slight, dark-haired girl who enters and scans the room. Her gaze lands on us, and Ty turns to see what's wrong. He sets his coffee down slowly.

"Lexi?"

She holds up a finger and moves to place an order.

"Who's that?" I ask.

"My sister." His forehead creases as he studies her.

I draw back in surprise. "How did she know you were here?"

Now that I look, the resemblance is there, though she's petite to his extra-large. They share similar coloring. He'd once said she was nice.

"Who knows?" he says absently and follows her to the counter.

Ty towers over her, but when they hug, it triggers a memory. I've seen him do that before—at the football game last fall. Could it have been Lexi that night?

When Ty ushers her to our table, she doesn't stroll. It's not marching either, but it's purposeful, no-nonsense, and intimidatingly graceful. Despite her lack of height, her body language is strong and sure. I wonder enviously what that would feel like. And how she does it by just walking across the room?

"This is River Harte." Ty takes his seat beside me as Lexi removes her coat.

"It's so nice to meet you! I've heard a lot about you." Her eyes twinkle like we're co-conspirators as she sits, and I instantly like her.

"Me too," I say, and we both look at Ty.

"What?" He shrugs. "It wasn't gossip; it's all true!" His brown eyes fill with an innocent mischief, and my heart skips a beat.

How did his mother endure raising a boy with on-demand angel eyes? They must've been lethal to her resolve.

As though she can't help it, Lexi leans forward to lay a hand on Ty's crossed arms. "It's so good to see you."

"You were just passing through, right?" he asks mildly. But I notice he's tightened his grip on his coffee cup.

She rolls her eyes. "You know I came just to see you since you never visit me. When are you coming home, anyway?"

"I haven't decided," he says, but her face lights up. Before she can comment, he asks curtly, "What's really going on, Lex?"

"What? We're skipping the niceties?" She holds up a palm to ward off his frown. "All right. There's been a rumor. I came to see if it's true."

His leg bumps mine as he watches her. "It's not a rumor."

She glances at me briefly and seems to measure her words. "I know."

Ty gives me a wry smile. He'd predicted this moment since his first at-bat with the team. "It's River's fault that I'm playing."

She eyes me, then cocks a brow at Ty. "I'd love to hear all about that but first, you should know I didn't come alone."

Ty straightens, releasing his cup. "You didn't! How could you bring them here?"

"Oh, no! Not them." She reaches for his arm, but he pulls away. "I brought Henry!"

My pulse jumps. Henry is the mentor and friend from Ty's youth, the Cardinal's bull pen catcher. He loves Henry.

But instead of joy, his jaw tightens. "Lexi, I trusted you."

"I didn't do it to hurt you." Her blue eyes are earnest. "It's time, Ty. You know it is."

"That's for me to decide. You don't have that right." His voice hardens. "I can't believe this."

The rawness in his words breaks my heart. I look down at my folded hands.

"It wasn't her fault." A deep voice says from behind, and I whirl around. A large man with a grief-stricken face looks cautious as Ty lunges from his chair. "It wasn't her fault," Henry repeats. "I insisted. I wanted to see you for myself."

The two men eye each other, a tense current between them.

"Were you really thinking of coming home?" Henry asks.

"I'd gotten as far as making the decision," Ty says stiffly.

"Oh, slugger. I've missed you." Then Henry's big, weather-worn face crumples to all of our shock. In one step, he wraps massive arms around Ty and holds on for dear life.

There's too much emotion in that hug to witness comfortably. Both their shoulders heave, and Ty clenches Henry's shirt in his fist. It takes a second before I realize that Ty probably can't see through his own tears. Henry's voice is an indistinct rumble that Ty must interpret because he chokes out a laugh. I swipe under my eyes. Lexi covers her mouth with a trembling hand, her face crimson and streaked.

When they separate, Ty looks younger, but Henry looks altogether different. He sniffs, and his features rearrange into joyous relief. They slap each other's backs as they laugh, then sit at our table, which is so small that Henry's legs barely fit.

"Look at you!" Henry croons, swiping a large finger under his nose. "You're even bigger than you were in high school. You've been lifting!"

"I've been working," Ty corrects, flushed, one heel bouncing on the floor. "Ever hauled hay?"

Henry's deep belly laugh is free and happy.

As I watch the three of them reconnect, I feel like a voyeur, peeking in where I don't belong. I should leave them to this private reunion. But just as I get the nerve to stand, Ty reaches an arm around the back of my chair, including me in their circle, as if he really can read my mind. He introduces me, and Henry gives me a generous smile. I feel the impact of his acceptance through my whole body when he shakes my hand. But he gazes at Ty and Lexi with such love and affection that it's hard to bear.

They say you can't choose your family but, wow, sometimes you get so lucky with your friends.

Chapter 34

Texas University holds a one run lead in the seventh inning on their home field. Zoe smooths her blonde ponytail and faces her last batter. It's been a tough game. Even the Lone Star state's sunshine has attacked Zoe today, leaving a smattering of freckles across her nose.

Her final strike lands in Abbey's glove, and she jogs in, returning high fives, and revving the huddle. Mia pushes past to grab her helmet and bat and circles out to the plate. Zoe watches her go, face pale. After the huddle breaks, I tug her to the side by her damp jersey.

"You did good." I squeeze her shoulder. "You can't help the errors."

"We have to score." Her muscles knot under my fingers as she shrugs impatiently.

"We will." I pull her to the fence to watch the batters. "Mia's up. She always gets on base. It's what she does."

When she knocks the ball to the outfield and is unhooking her arm guard on first, I lean close to say, "I told you."

But Sarah strikes out and talks to herself all the way back to the dugout. And Zoe starts chanting a prayer under her breath.

Rachel's normally tight black curls are smooth under the back of her helmet, swaying with each step to the batter's box. She drives the ball deep into right field, and Zoe punches the air. Then the outfielder catches the fly, and Zoe sags. Rachel trots in impatiently.

"We've scored with two outs before. A two-out rally? It's our thing," I say. "Look. Mia's on first. And Dawz is ready." But I close my eyes for a second. Witnessing our possible third loss with Zoe is almost more painful than if it was my own responsibility.

Dawz watches the first two balls with a professional eye, then steps out for a practice swing. The next pitch is a strike. She nods at some internal conversation and rolls her shoulder. She taps her bat on the plate, pulls it up to stare steely-eyed at the pitcher, and checks her swing on a rise ball just in time.

Zoe bumps into me as she jumps and cheers, but Dawz is undaunted. She's cold as a metal fence post in January when she swings hard through the next pitch. The crowd cheers at the foul ball.

"Straighten it out," I yell. "Fight here!"

And she is fighting. She's fearless. But the next pitch even fools me. It looks like a fastball. Dawz doesn't realize it's off-speed until too late, and she's already swung with all her might—too early. The ball smacks the catcher's glove, and Dawz turns in disbelief.

Texas reacts before we do, leaping and celebrating. As the score board clicks the final out, I try to decide what to do after a three-out-of-five kind of loss. Zoe sags onto the bench and covers her face with her glove.

"No." I drop in front of her and shake her shoulders. "Stop. We did this together, remember?"

She lowers her glove to reveal tear-filled eyes. "But that's already three, River. They've come too early. At this rate, we'll never make it."

"I know." I grip her cold hand. "But we've won together. We'll take the loss together. We're okay." And I mean it. I mean it with all my heart. I duck to catch her eye. "Look, we've got two more games this weekend. You aren't the only one who needs to put this behind them."

Zoe bites her lip and nods. She pushes off the bench and wipes her face. As we line up to greet the other team, I marvel at the sheer guts holding her up.

The next day, she pitches the first game of the morning with the echoes of our fired-up team ringing in her ears, and we win together. One game to go.

In the fifth inning of the last game, a nasty north wind blasts through my jersey as I drop the ball on the mound. We're up by one run. I turn right around and head to the batter's box, with no outs and no one on base. I raise the bat and squint at the pitcher, all business and focus. Sand stings my cheeks and chaps my lips. I've played in worse.

But as the ball leaves the pitcher's hand, I barely have time to think *this* is going to hurt. I twist to protect my arm and chest. Pain explodes on the back of my neck. The bat drops from my numb fingers.

Initially, I wonder why Coach Bosswood and Coach CJ are on the field. Hit by pitch means I get to take first base, and I mean to do just that, although first base seems so far away. The coaches say things, but... what did I do with my bat? Never mind. Go to first base.

Then Bosswood grabs my arms, and I realize my head is killing me, and my neck throbs. The home plate ump examines me, his face guard in his hand. Behind him, Coach Bosswood gestures to Emma to check in to run. By the time they've sat me on the bench, I can't turn my head, and Zoe is warming up.

The athletic trainer parks himself at my knees and starts the concussion protocol. Beyond his shoulder, Bree, who batted after me, comes into the dugout too quickly, followed by Mia. I'm injured, not comatose. If they're out, we're in danger of losing our lead.

The trainer's ice, like fire on my neck, only makes me edgier. The others grimace-smile when they pass to grab gloves or get a drink. Zoe takes the mound, and my teammates line up on the fence, blocking my view. I realize, uneasily, Zoe's warm up was rushed because of me.

"Andy," I say, and she turns quickly, ready to help. I wave my hand. "Move over."

They scoot to the side in time for the four-hole batter to send Zoe's first pitch over the fence. I close my eyes as the Texas cheers go on and on. To her credit, Zoe doesn't let it get to her. She strikes out the next three to get us out of the inning.

As my team leaves the field, the unfairness of it all hits me. We've pulled together, done what it takes, stayed out of trouble. When will it be our turn to catch a break? Haven't we paid our dues? The freak accidents, the unending road blocks—I mean, is it asking too much for a breather? But even as I think it, I know it's the pain talking. There's no mercy in competition.

The next time Texas's lead-off batter is up, the lead-off from last summer's Nationals is on second. The batter is a slapper and good at her job. She sets up at the back of the box, but instead of tapping it down, she swings through the ball and catches us off guard. I drop the ice on the floor and gingerly lean back against the wall as one hit turns into two runs. We've lost our fourth game.

It's unnaturally quiet on the bus as we stow bags and find our seats. With four losses, this weekend cost us more than we can afford. One more loss, and we're belly up.

I tell myself it's because of the headache that I keep my eyes closed.

But I keep seeing our naïve faces back when we came up with this idea in my apartment. We'd been such babies then. Only giving up four or five losses had seemed hard, but we had righteous motivation. We were gonna get it done, win the record, and celebrate with Coach when he woke up. It's laughable. At this rate, we'll need playoff games.

And we all know everyone in the playoffs are good.

One bad game, and Coach O'Daniel's record will disappear in the cracks of a Super Regional tournament like water down a drain. Our motivation hasn't changed, but our discipline has to.

I shift, then hiss at the pain in my neck.

"You okay?" Lilly asks, her red hair dulled in the dim light.

If she's wondering if it's my body that hurts, it doesn't compare to the feeling of letting Coach O'Daniel down and erasing any chance of his name ending up on that plaque.

Across the aisle, Abbey's nostrils flare when I meet her gaze. Beside her, Sarah hesitates, then nods in understanding. She leans back, hands white on the armrest.

So, it's not just me. Something has shifted. The goal isn't just O'Daniel's record, but a quest, a mountain to scale, an ocean to cross. As the bus doors close, I make a mental list of things I need to do better before falling into a troubled sleep.

A week later, our games are cancelled as storm sirens assault the campus. The sky is dark and heavy, shredded by lightning in every direction. I park in front of my old dorm and make the mistake of stopping to watch the light show when I get out. Then the sound of rain hammering the far parking lot sends me running.

Of course, I don't outrun it, but dive into the building soaking wet. I cross the lobby and pull open the stairwell door. The official storm shelter is full. Curious faces turn as I squelch up the crowded steps. When I reach Emma, I squeeze, shivering, onto the concrete step and take the pillow she offers to shove against the icy wall.

"I'd rather be playing softball," I say. "Hide and seek with a tornado isn't my favorite."

Lily laughs. "I love storms. The louder, the better."

"I do too." I wipe the rain from my forehead. "But this is crazy. The drive over freaks me out."

"And I'm not feeling the beige walls here." Emma's pink-striped socks show under the edge of her blanket. "I'm with River. The game would've been more interesting."

My phone buzzes, and I laugh when I see the picture.

"What?" Lily pushes Andy aside to see. "Is that Fletch?"

"Hmm?" Emma leans her chin on my shoulder and tilts the phone for a better view. "Yes. Yes, it is. Tell him we'd love to play football with him in the stadium shelter."

Lily and I share a look, but Andy pulls the phone toward her. "Is that Jace behind him?" She looks up. "Do you still like him?"

"Nope." I put my phone away.

"Oh," she says in a way that makes me pause.

"Andy, you don't like him, do you?"

She shrugs and tugs her sleeves over her hands. A smile plays on her lips.

"Are you nuts? He's not worth it." I frown. "Jace is toxic. Don't trust his smile or his invitations. Don't look into his lying eyes. He's a dog. No, I won't do that to dogs. He's a snake."

There's an "amen" from somewhere above us. Girls below glance over their shoulders. I probably shouldn't raise my voice, but I can't help it.

"Preach it, River," Emma says.

"I'm serious. Andy." I take her hand. "Promise you'll stay away from him."

"Okay," Andy says. "I believe you."

Then someone higher on the stairs says, "Hey, Softball. You've moved up in the rankings."

"What?" Lily turns.

"Looks like you're ranked tenth now," the girl says.

"It's just been a month," I say.

Emma leans forward. "If we… sorry—" She waves that away. "*When* we win sixty games, we could be in the top eight."

"We could go all the way to Oklahoma City for the World Series." Lily bumps fists with Emma.

Andy nudges my leg. "That's where we met, remember?"

I huff a laugh. "It's seared in my brain." And that's also where I met Coach.

"I've never played at that stadium," Emma muses. "I've just seen it on TV."

"Wait until you see Bricktown and the canal," I say.

But I don't say this all sounds great, except none of it matters if we're not still playing ball.

Chapter 35

April

"What time will you get to Lawrence?" Ty watches me, a grass stem twirling between two fingers.

"Just after noon." I adjust my softball backpack on the ground beside him and lean on it. The indoor facility's gray shadow hugs the building as if shy in the morning light.

"We'll get to Atlanta about then to catch our bus. Text me after you play." He says it like a question, his baseball bag beside him ready for his own road trip today. His hair is shorter now, more team standard. But, as usual, it's the ways he's the same that makes me happy in these rare moments together.

"Are you still the designated hitter?" I ask.

He glances at the cars winding into the parking lot and filling the spaces around our vehicles. "Yeah. I might catch a game or two this weekend, though." He stretches one leg slowly in front of him. "This knee's a little sore."

"What did Henry do for sore knees?" I rest my chin on my palm and comb the grass with the other hand.

"That's a need-to-know basis." Ty smirks. "Did I tell you he hasn't missed any of my games?"

"You mentioned that last week."

He reaches over and stills my fingers. "How was the algebra test?"

"I got my grade Wednesday." I smile. "A freaking 91."

He punches the air. "I knew you could do it." Then his smile fades into something wistful. "You know, it's so weird to live next door to you and never see you. I miss you."

"Miss you, too," I say softly. I look away and shift casually back on one hand. "Are you going to work on the farm this summer?"

"I don't know yet." He rubs his nose absently. "Coach was talking about having me stick around and work out this summer."

Lines form at the buses and I stand, reaching for my bag.

Ty props an arm on it to hold it in place. "River." He tilts his head. "Will you visit me if I stay here this summer?"

For those brown eyes? I shake my head. "Not a chance."

Ty grins knowingly. "Liar."

#

Early the next morning in our hotel's private breakfast room, a stranger approaches me. I pause, fork halfway to my mouth, and glance from him over to Lily and Emma waiting at the waffle maker. The hotel staff don't usually sit at our tables like this.

The guy smiles, but there's a glint in his eyes. "So, your team is aiming for Coach O'Daniel's record."

It's not really a question, so I watch him warily and take a bite.

"Are you River Harte, the pitcher?"

"Yes." I take another bite.

"We have an enthusiastic sports fan group here. I'm sure you'll notice us at the game." He leans closer. "We wanted to know if it's true your father is missing in action?"

The eggs lodge in my throat as my fork drops to the floor. "What?" I manage between coughs. He looks oddly satisfied.

The morning news on a television high in the corner sends a familiar terror through me. For four years, we've been told too much publicity about Dad might draw unwanted attention from his captors. The thought of putting him in danger is unbearable, even by a stranger in a strange town.

Then it sinks in that he isn't here out of concern, and I feel cold. He's trying to get in my head. Because of a game. Personal information is merely easy artillery. And I haven't done anything to deserve this except play for the competition. The maliciousness of the attack, and it is an attack, takes my breath. Why would someone I don't know want to hurt me so badly?

"Have you heard the news about him?" he presses.

"Shut up." I surge to my feet, glaring. "Just shut up."

He pushes up from the table, hands raised in mock surrender. But it's his chuckle that unnerves me.

My appetite evaporates as I watch him leave. I didn't think there was anything else that could shake me. But I'd also hoped for common decency and personal safety.

My hands shake as I dump my plate and head to the elevator. Lily sends me a curious glance, but I wave her off. There's only one person I want to talk to now.

As soon as the elevator doors close, I sag against the wall and pull out my phone. "Zeph?" I say when he picks up. "Where's Mom?"

"Packing the car. We have to check out, but we'll be there before the game starts. Why?"

"Someone asked about Dad this morning."

There are shuffling sounds on his end. "A reporter?" he asks, voice clearer.

"No. I think he's a local." The elevator opens, and I turn toward my room.

"What do you mean?"

"One of those college jerks who sits behind the away-team's dugout and heckles the players about personal stuff. He must have done a lot of research to find out about Dad."

Zeph exhales. "I should've been there. Don't worry, Riv. I've got this. He won't bother you."

I stop at my door, leaning my forehead on it. "I wish we knew where Dad was."

"I know," he says softly.

Later at the field, I think the routine of warming up has settled my nerves. But when I startle because Zoe and Lily enter the next cage, Abbey watches me with concern.

I don't hit a University of Kansas player with a pitch until the fourth inning, which gives them a tie run. It wasn't my first mistake. My first mistake, on base with a walk, just scored that tie. Now the hecklers cheer knowing they have a go-ahead runner.

What is wrong with me? Hit by pitch, walks, wild pitches. If the muscle memory of pitching that remains leaves me entirely, I'll be stranded on the mound like a dirt clod.

Then the runner scores on a sacrifice bunt. Sarah claps her glove and shouts reassurance, but I sink further into my own head. We're down by one. By one.

I need a lifeline, an anchor, a miracle. I close my eyes and Coach O'Daniel, who's usually in my head, morphs into Dad with his dark hair and laughing eyes. He's sitting on a bucket at one of my early pitching lessons, trying not to flinch when I hit the beams again.

"Count the stages of your pitch to get the rhythm," he says. "Go slow and get the feel of it, like a dance."

Not caring if I look like a fool, I do that now. My arm and knee. Windmill and landing. Snap and finish. Again. Abbey gives me a questioning look, but I wave her off. She slides her helmet on and squats.

The batter pops up the pitch for the final out, and I almost melt with relief.

"It's all right." Coach Bosswood leans into the huddle by the dugout. "We can get that run back. Stay focused." She glares. "But I promise the first person to swing at that pitcher's rise ball again is going to sit next to Coach CJ all the way home. Is that clear?"

When we break the huddle, Bosswood rounds on me. "What happened to your spin?"

It takes everything I have to stand still. "I released it too late. I'm sorry."

"You left your elbow out. Pull it back in and stay tall." She tucks her clipboard under her arm. "I don't know why you're blessed to be six-foot tall, but you try to pitch like you're five-foot-five."

"Okay," I say, turning away.

"River." She moves in front of me again. "Get your head in the game. You're distracted. Now fix it."

I nod and glance at the scoreboard over my shoulder. If we have any hope of winning, we need to show up now and do something.

But Abbey dies on a fly ball and Rachel wades through jeers from the stands only to strike out. Then I'm up, and although a different batter may be a wiser choice with two outs, there's no one more determined.

The pitcher eyes me coolly when I step into the box. I half expect her to hit me, tit-for-tat. And, honestly, I'll take any opportunity to get on base. Instead, she sends a drop-curve away from the plate, and I check my swing. I hit the next one past third base with a quirky bounce, and barely beat the tag at first.

Coach CJ pats my helmet. "Thank goodness for those long feet of yours, Harte. That was close."

Mia is told to slap-bunt and I glance at second. It's mine. My legs tense, arms flex.

The pitcher releases the ball. Mia's perfect hit touches the dirt and I run. The third baseman rushes forward, scoops the ball. I drop into a slide.

And the second-baseman's glove cuffs my ankle a fraction before my cleat hits the base.

I stare at the sky as the Jayhawks clear the field. It takes a lot of effort to pull myself up. On autopilot, I follow Abbey back out a minute later to pitch.

"Are you all right?" Abbey narrows her eyes as she hands me the ball after we warm up.

"Yes." I dodge her gaze

Gesturing to the Jayhawks, she says, "I don't know what's going on, but they aren't the only opponent today. You're going to have to beat yourself to stay in this game. And I'm right there with you. Do you hear?

It's you and me."

I slip my glove on with steady focus. She's right. I can make it about more, but it's the two of us. And I consider it progress to be able to clear my mind of everything else and pitch the rest of the game.

But when we lose, the L for loss is recorded under my name like a scar. And I carry it as I leave the mound, hoping that I've learned my lesson—whatever that is.

Chapter 36

As I pack up after the game, the hopelessness of our situation overwhelms me. I lean my head against the wall and slap it twice, welcoming the sting. Across the field, the scoreboard clears the 2-1 loss.

"Pack it up." Coach Bosswood marches through the dugout. "Let's go."

Abbey sits to unbuckle her shin guards. I move to the bench beside her. "That's five, Abbey."

"I've been thinking." Her fingers nimbly unhook her equipment and stuff it in her bag. "We can get the last wins in the Super Regionals."

"But what if we can't?" Kim asks over her shoulder as she zips her backpack.

"We just do." Lily reaches grimly for her sunglasses.

"That's not an answer." Kim frowns.

"Here's an answer," Lily snaps, rounding on her. "Stop quitting. Maybe if you'd shown up to be the designated driver like you promised, things would be different."

Andy pales, glancing wide-eyed between the girls.

Dawz drops her backpack. "Whoa." She pushes between Lily and Kim. "That was last semester. You don't get to say things like that."

"Shut up, Dawz." Rachel moves behind Lily. "Let her talk."

Dawz stiffens. "Attacking each other won't help us play like a team."

"A team?" Lily's face is as red as her hair. "Maybe that's the problem. We're not a team. We've got too many people who are only out for themselves." She glares at Kim again. "People who put themselves first."

I stand up, intending to break up the knot of girls, but Zoe and Bree and others, drawn by the drama, begin talking all at once. Bosswood notices and starts across the dugout, but Sarah stops her. I don't know what she says, but Coach nods skeptically and holds up five fingers, as if she's giving us five minutes to figure this out.

Abbey presses between the girls in the center. Lily, Emma, and Rachel against Katie, Andy, and Dawz. Kim stands behind them mute, looking like someone slapped her.

"Break it up." Abbey grips Lily's arm.

Lily jerks free. "Back off, Abbey."

"Lily's right," Rachel says. "We've all seen it. Kim won't sacrifice for the team, but she'll be the first to whine about not winning enough games."

Abbey shoves Rachel back a step. "Stay out of this, Rachel."

"I'd like to see you make me." Rachel tries to shove back, but can't budge Abbey.

"Talk about someone who won't sacrifice for the team," Dawz says hotly, and Rachel's eyes widen as Dawz gets in her face. "What about you, Rachel? You don't try to get on base, you only swing for the fence. We needed you on, but it was all or nothing for you. I mean, we had the pitcher on base instead of you."

Rachel chest-bumps Dawz, her face dangerously tight. Zoe stares at me, but when I turn, she looks away.

"If it's so easy," Emma taunts Dawz. "Why weren't you on when we needed you?"

Lily throws her hands up. "No one gets on base every time. It's not the way the game works. But I'd take ten people who try instead of one who won't think of their teammates first."

Kim, red to her hairline, blinks against welling tears. "I'm sorry, okay?" Her voice is high and ragged. "I didn't mean to mess up."

"What about the rest of you?" Rachel eyes Dawz, Katie, and Andy, and jeers, "You going to a party tonight because that's what you do when things get hard?"

Both sides surge closer at that.

But I know exactly where they're headed. I whip my hand through the air, as if I could rip away the words. "You're tearing my heart out," I cry, my chin trembling with the force of it.

The girls turn in astonishment.

I bite my lip to steady it, but it doesn't help. "If you want someone to blame for losing this game," I say unevenly. "It's me. I did it. You saw. My head wasn't in the game. I let those hecklers get to me about my dad, and I couldn't find my way back."

"No." Zoe pushes through the crowd. "No."

"I couldn't..." My breath hitches. "I tried, but..."

"Cut it out." Zoe grabs my arms and shakes them. "If we beat ourselves up every time we fail, we might as well go home. And we've got a lot left to do." She turns to face the girls. "I will not let her take the blame for this because she doesn't let me take the blame for my losses. That's not who this team is."

My body shudders as I fight for control.

Sarah points at me in the silence. "The only person on this team to prove she'd sacrifice for any of us just tried to take the blame for a game with nine people on the field. Is that what you want?"

And then my chest tightens as I watch their gazes drop to their feet. Sarah's voice softens. "Do you know why we say, 'We've got your back'?"

Some shift. A few lift their heads to eye Sarah warily.

She continues, "It's because in ancient wars, the soldiers were armored on the front, but exposed on the back. To stay alive, they had to fight back-to-back. Someone may charge forward to meet threats, all tough and mean with their protection and weapons, but it was the ones at the soldier's back who covered the soft spots, who knew how vulnerable they really were. A team was crucial to stay alive."

Rachel shakes her head and stares into space. Lily flicks a glance at me. And I realize I may be to blame for this upheaval as well. No matter which decision I made that night, whether to pick the girls up or not, someone suffered.

"What you're doing now is small," Abbey says. "I don't mean the party or the suspensions. Those are big and real. But it's *small* to think we're going to all be perfect. That's what you believe when you're too young to know better."

Sarah shares a look with Abbey, and I wonder about the history there.

"What we need," Sarah says. "Is to move beyond blame and find a way to believe in each other that'll free us to do something great."

In front of me, Zoe's spine is long and straight—a little stiff—maybe from putting herself out there for me. Her shoulders and arms are round with muscle. But when you really look, there's a fragility to her that tugs at my heart. Because I know her self-doubt. It's just like mine.

I clear my throat. "You might not remember, but Zoe and I got off to a rocky start." She looks at me, all innocence, and I nearly roll my eyes. "But we've found a way to work together. What we're doing now to support each other is working. Maybe you could all do that, pick a person and make it your job to keep their spirit up. Softball is mental, and everyone has an off day."

Emma grimaces. Kim swipes a knuckle under her nose.

I should keep my mouth shut, let the silence work, but find I can't. Maybe this is how Ty feels. "How did we decide to win games for Coach O'Daniel?"

Lily meets my gaze. "Together."

"Yeah." I give her a lopsided smile. "You all invaded the smallest apartment in town and were unanimous about it." My voice softens. "And how did we promise to face this season, win or lose?"

Rachel crosses her arms. "Together."

There are sniffs and shuffles. Goosebumps rise on my skin when Zoe puts her arm around my waist. I reach over to draw Kim close, and she startles, then softens, letting me tuck her at my side. One by one, we join in a circle. It's hot and smelly, and my chin trembles. Teardrops stain the concrete. Then someone giggles and we're jostling each other and swaying. Sarah tells them to dry up the waterworks and pair off, and they do.

It's the first good thing to happen in a long time.

On Sunday afternoon, Coach Bosswood pitches me again. She won't look me in the eye, but I know it's a dare. Dare to repeat what happened yesterday. But we're too on fire to do anything but win eight to zero.

The next weekend, close to exhaustion, I go home.

Chapter 37

There's no comparison to sleeping in your own bed in your own home. I wake up feeling bruised, but ready to explore the farm with fresh eyes. Has it even noticed I've been gone? For me, every familiar sight and smell is a buffet for my starving heart.

I pause outside. I'd forgotten that you could taste the farm in the air—its fields and trees and earth. I squint up at the white curtains pulled aside at my window. It's incredible to be here and strange at the same time.

I wander into the barn. It feels lean, like it always does this time of year—dehydrated and spent. My Olympic softball team posters hang in the corner beside the blackboard where I listed my workouts. The buckets and equipment are dull with neglect, and the pitching screen has cobwebs. But I stop at a poster and study the athletes' faces with new understanding. Life as a college athlete has given me an appreciation for what they went through to compete at elite levels. Their sacrifices probably rivalled their scars.

Five dark spots disturb the dust on my blackboard. I frown and lean closer. They're fingerprints. In fact, almost a whole handprint is visible, as if someone had reached out for comfort. I lay my hand against the board—it's Mom's print, then. The thought of her standing here and yearning for me tugs at my heart. I know just how she feels.

When I find her cleaning feed buckets, she smiles. "Good morning. How did you sleep?"

"Great." I lean against the fence. "Can I help?"

"I'm almost done. Did you see the cinnamon rolls I made?"

"I ate two. Thanks for that."

She looks pleased. "What's new at school?"

I launch into stories and follow her inside to make hot tea while she washes her hands. Dad's pictures are everywhere, on the refrigerator door, on top of the refrigerator, on the side table in the family room, past the kitchen. The twins come in, leaving their boots at the back door, and I take out two more plates for rolls.

"Are you coming to Regionals?" I ask Kody after handing him a plate at the bar.

"We'll be there," he says, but his voice is cautious.

Slowly, I sink to a bar stool. "What's going on?"

"Nothing." He sighs. "You know we've sent letters to nongovernment agencies recently for help to find Dad?"

I look between my brothers. "How would I know if you haven't told me?"

"I'm telling you now." He picks up his fork and turns it in his fingers. "No replies yet."

I can almost feel Dad flinch in each picture around the room. The rolls sour in my stomach. Why are they changing how we've done things for four years? I have no problem adding to what we're doing, but we aren't stopping. I won't stand for it.

"So, what?" I cross my arms on the table. "That doesn't change any-thing. I'll go with you on the next trip. Maybe that'll help."

Mom leans against the cabinet, her mug cradled in both hands, and stares at Dad's picture on the refrigerator.

"No one's giving up," Kody says crossly. "And you've got school."

Zeph sets his fork down, his cinnamon roll half gone. "But we're not getting anywhere either."

"That's not true." I scowl. "We've got contacts now. You've followed up on a lot of rumors. You even helped find those hikers last year."

"River, I know this must seem sudden to you, but it's not for us," Zeph says. "We need to make some adjustments."

"You can't change anything," I say fiercely. "You've both shut me out of all of your plans just because I'm the baby. He's my dad too."

"We didn't shut you out," Kody says. "You were thirteen."

"I'm not thirteen anymore," I interrupt. "I'm almost the same age you were when he left."

"You're two years younger than we were," Kody shoots back.

"It doesn't matter," Zeph says loudly, putting up a hand to stop my furious answer. "You're going to get to help, Riv."

"Well." I adjust my volume. "Good."

"But when would you like to start?" he asks quietly. "Before region-als? Maybe after, but then there will be a Super Regional. What about before your team gets their sixty wins?"

I grit my teeth. "That's not fair."

"No. It's not. And that's the point. We're looking at all our options right now and we need you to be on board with that until you're free to join in."

Mom sets her mug down. I notice how pale she is and consider how all of this must sound to her. I duck my head. "Okay."

They go back out to work and leave me alone in the kitchen. I put the dishes away, rearrange pillows on the sofa, but when I find myself pacing, I pull out my phone. I need out of here. I need to see my best friend.

The drive into town is familiar, and I pull up to Jaiden's house just as she opens the door.

"Let me see," I say in a sing-song voice.

She rearranges the bundle of blanket in her arm to hold out her left hand. Even expecting it, the thin gold band surprises me.

"Not that." I smirk. "I want to see the boss."

Jaiden folds the blanket to reveal her miracle mini-me. Mesmerized, I keep my gaze on the baby and pull Jaiden close to lean my head against hers. "You did good," I whisper.

She guides me into her bedroom, where she keeps a watchful eye over my shoulder as I hold baby Claire. Jaiden sits cross-legged on the bed, so close her knee brushes my side. Claire's fine hair is soft as I kiss her forehead. She smells like spring.

"Yesterday was her first night to sleep six hours," Jaiden says proudly. "Scotty said we're lucky. His mom told him he didn't sleep all night for a year."

I giggle. "Free-spirit Scotty?"

She nudges my side. "My Scotty." We share a smile.

"I wish I could've been here when she was born. She's so perfect." Everything about my godchild fascinates me. Her delicate lashes, miniature fingernails, soft forehead.

"There wasn't room." Jaiden smooths the blanket and smiles. "With Mom and Scotty and the nurses, and finally the doctor, you couldn't have gotten closer than the lobby. And after she was born, we cried more than Claire did." She runs a hand over Claire's head, like she needs to feel her, to connect because it'd been a few minutes. Claire smiles in her sleep, and we both giggle.

"What made you decide to get married?" I ask.

She raises her finger until light flashes on her ring. "Scotty." Her face softens.

"Okay. I don't want to know."

"He convinced me." She laughs. "We were going to elope, but it didn't seem fair to our parents. So, we asked them to stand as our witnesses at the courthouse. It really was wonderful, Riv."

"I'm glad." I touch Claire's finger, and it curls around mine as she sleeps. "And he's starting his own business?"

"His dad loaned us the money to buy the mowers and equipment. Scotty already has five customers."

"I didn't know he liked to do landscaping and yard care."

"He loves it," she says. "Because you can see what you've accomplished as soon as you're done. He says that poetry runs through his head while he works. Being outside in the sun and rain makes him happy. He keeps a notebook and writes stuff down all the time. He'd like to publish a book of poetry sometime."

"I'll buy it," I say, running my thumb over Claire's knuckles.

"My parents are going to help us get our own place. We're going to pay them back because we want to do this on our own. But for the first couple of months, until the business gets bigger, I doubt we could make it without them. And, you know... they're doing it for Claire."

"Then they're pretty smart. She's got to be the closest thing to a princess I've ever seen."

Jaiden giggles. "How's your coach?" She rests her chin on my shoulder.

I almost give my pat answer, but stop. It's Jaiden, after all. "It doesn't look good. They don't know why he hasn't come out of the coma yet."

"Do you think you'll get his sixty wins? It's hard to imagine that larger-than-life guy from the state tournament not getting the record."

Claire squirms and sticks out her lower lip in a pout. I force the tension out of my muscles, but Jaiden reaches for her anyway.

"You're a really good mom, Jaiden." I watch Claire settle in the crook of her arm without waking.

There's a vulnerable, eager shine in her eyes before she ducks her head with a pleased smile. "She's easy to love."

I swallow and wait until my voice is steady. "Yeah. My goddaughter's the best." I tuck the blanket around one small foot. "What're you going to do next?"

Jaiden rocks slightly and pulls her long hair to one side so it won't tickle Claire's face. "I'm going to get a job," she says finally.

Neither of us say it, but it sits there between us, all the whispers we've shared, all the dreams we've had. Jaiden's a real adult now. No sense talking about what might've been.

Chapter 38

May — Ten wins needed for the record

Coach Bosswood doesn't seem surprised that our home stadium crowds have grown past capacity. By the first game of regionals, the area outside the fence looks like a summer party with people toting ball gloves and chairs, tailgate ice chests and large televisions. The campus bookstore sells out of Northbridge's softball t-shirts. I even see my homeless friend Ian make himself comfortable beyond the outfield—a party of one.

The University of Tennessee, the University of Central Arkansas, and Mississippi State arrive in town with their respective fans for the tournament. They fill the local restaurants and hotels. But despite the carnival air, concern for Coach O'Daniel lingers.

Inside the locker room before our first game, Bree braids Sarah's hair.

"Hey, would you braid mine, too?" I drop my bag and join them.

"Sure." She gestures to the gray carpet beside her while she works.

"Did you know our story is trending?" Sarah asks, peering sideways without moving her head as I sink next to her.

"Trending on what?" Bree asks.

"You name it." Sarah's head jerks as Bree grabs hair. She hands me her phone.

"How many comments?" I tilt it to see better.

Bree nudges me with her knee. "I heard Old Whit had to hire two guys to help clear away the get-well flowers and signs and softballs from the dugout fence so he could mow."

"Good softballs or old?" I look over my shoulder.

"Some are good." Bree shrugs and ties off the braid. Sarah runs a hand over her head as I lean forward so Bree can scoot behind me.

"Who leaves old balls?" Sarah frowns. "That doesn't make sense."

Bree rakes a brush through my hair, and I try not to whimper. She swipes it again.

"When's the last time you combed your hair, Harte?" Bree asks. "I know—it's not your fault that your hair is thick, and the wind ties the ends in knots. You poor, unfortunate soul, living with celebrity hair. Speaking of that..." She leans forward and points the brush at my face. "Can you walk through a restaurant now without someone wanting to buy your meal?"

"What? Because of my hair?"

"No. Keep up." She not-so-gently taps my shoulder with the brush and resumes working. "Because we're having a good season. I mean, I know we can't let anyone buy our food or the compliance office will call for a face-to-face, but fans really want to connect to us. To Coach. They want to contribute to his cause and wear his bracelet during his fifteen minutes of fame. They live through us to share the glory, you know?"

"Wait." Dawz looks up from threading her belt through the loops. "Can we accept Gatorade?"

"Not going there with you, Dawz." Bree narrows her eyes. "Anyway, the point is, if all of them think we're so tough, and great, and nothing will stop us from getting the record, then I start thinking they're right. We can do anything, as long as they're behind us."

"Yeah." Sarah stands up. "Our fans are the best."

"Woohoo." I lift my arms, then squawk as Bree yanks on my hair. Sarah laughs.

"Show some spirit, Bree," I whimper.

"I am. Thank you." Bree tugs again. "By making you look good for your admirers."

That gives me a nasty twinge of stage fright. I'm only eighteen. I'm not ready to be famous.

Andy shoves the door open, scowling over her shoulder at Emma behind her.

"... and they don't care—" Emma pauses. Andy whips around.

"Who doesn't care about what?" Sarah asks in her best upperclassman/lawyer voice.

Andy's gaze flicks to me and away. "Nothing." She ducks into her locker, and my senses rattle like the tail of a snake. It's Andy after all.

"What's up?" I narrow my eyes.

Emma starts to answer, but Andy shoves her. "Boy stuff," she says. "That's all."

More girls crowd into the locker room as Bree finishes the braid, but I scrutinize Andy's profile.

Lily leans around the corner, her face flushed. "Television crews." She points back toward the lobby windows, and the sudden noisy rush from the room wipes all thoughts from my mind. I'm bumped and pushed as everyone strains to see the marked vans across from the stadium.

"Ignore them." Sarah shoos us away. "You've got stuff to do and becoming a diva isn't one of them." But she stops to study the crews herself.

When we exit the lobby later, I swear Coach O'Daniel's eyes follow me from his portrait, as if he's on the verge of saying something I need to hear. Under his picture, a vase of blue-tinged carnations wait—ten total—secret code for the wins we need to earn.

I hold the door for Abbey and Dawz, who laugh as they try to go through at the same time. Mia slaps my butt as she passes, saying something about polite freshmen. I follow her out and tell myself not to look at them. I just don't know if I mean the cameras or the carnations.

Later, when pregame is over and announcements made, all twenty-three of us press into a circle so we can hear over the crowds. Sarah puts her arm over my shoulder, and I do the same to Lily.

"Look to your left and right," Sarah says. "These are your sisters. Your family. Who you fight for and take care of."

Andy bobs her head, staring at me with eye-black thick on her cheeks... so much stronger than she'd looked the morning after that awful party. Beside her, Dawz spits on the ground. And it's seriously intimidating... yet, there's no one I'd rather have at my back. And Zoe. How many hours have we spent practicing next to each other? She winks, and I want to laugh, but... still... nope. Don't want her with either of my brothers.

"Do you want to pray, Mia?" Sarah asks with a questioning glance.

Mia shakes her head. "I think Liz should do it."

With a tilt of my head, I see the sharp glance Liz gives her. My heart breaks a little at the sight of the wrap still tight on her right ankle. She's enveloped in the circle, but shifts her weight in pain.

Liz clears her throat and closes her eyes. She asks for protection, the ability to do our best, and the strength to accept whatever happens in a quiet, firm voice. She ends with, "God gets the glory, but Coach, this is for you."

There's a chorus of amens and color blooms on Liz's cheeks. As we break apart, though, loss etches the corners of her mouth and shadows her eyes. I look out at the field and wonder what it's like for her to be this close, yet excluded from the sweat of the game. And her injury isn't just a nuisance during the season either. It's part of her future. But I shove those emotions deep. You don't pity family. You support them.

We play nearly flawless softball and beat Central Arkansas, then sing the school song for our fans at the backstop. But when we're alone in the locker room later, either because of OCD or superstition, only Rachel numbers a new ribbon for our feather board, and only I attach it while the others watch with solemn reverence. Each bulky layer signifies a game we'll never forget. A struggle fought and won. To me, the board is even more satisfying than the State championship trophy.

#

In my tiny apartment that evening, Kody pours a glass of tea and asks, "Still single, Li'l River?"

I roll my eyes. Dang, brothers are annoying. Zeph laughs, but Mom sits on my sofa with a shake of her head.

Fletcher opens the door as he knocks. "What'd I miss?"

"Nothing." I take Kody's glass and hand it to Fletch, pleased at Kody's groan.

"Congrats." Fletch gives me a one-arm hug. "Heard about the win.

One down, two to go. Have you called Ty?"

Kody chuckles and my cheeks warm.

"His game isn't over yet," I say as I settle beside Mom.

"I can't believe Ty spent the summer with us and hid all that talent right under our noses," she says.

"So rude," I say wholeheartedly.

"Changing the subject." Kody shares a glance with Zeph. "Dad?"

Mom inhales, as if bracing herself, and I snuggle close, tucking my arm through hers. My brothers are solemn, and their resemblance to dad is almost painful.

"It looks like one of those non-governmental organizations might come through." Zeph leans forward. "I've got a guy who's going to take Dad's file to another committee. We might qualify for more resources."

Mom's hand closes over mine. "When will you know?" she asks.

"In a few weeks." Zeph leans to knock on the wood of my desk.

This is the best news we've had in forever. More resources—if Dad will hold on a bit longer. But the elation is short-lived when the twins share another look.

I've seen that grim expression on Dad's face before, too. What are they not saying?

#

The next day, despite the heat and a short game delay, we beat Mississippi State three to five.

A school reporter corners me for an interview in the midst of the post-win chaos.

"That was great softball. As a freshman, did you expect to pitch in the NCAA regional tournament?" The reporter tilts the mic toward me.

Liz falters as she drops empty cups into the nearby trash. The ankle wrap is visible again below her softball pants. Even so, it's obvious she pushes through the pain to help... the way she used to push through pain and fatigue to improve at pitching practice. She glances over her shoulder and stiffens when she catches me watching.

"This was way beyond my daydreams in August." I turn to the reporter. "But this entire year has been full of the unexpected. Our senior pitcher, Liz, should've been in this game. She earned the spot. Instead, she's recuperating from injuries. That girl is made of steel. Do you know the guts it takes to keep going from the sidelines of your senior year? Someone should interview her."

Liz flushes as the reporter glances at her. The rest of the team flows around us.

My voice softens. "She's a good example of how our team pulls together. Everyone does their part, or we wouldn't be one win away from Super Regionals." Liz's eyes fill, and I give her a small smile.

Coach Bosswood takes my place for the next interview. Her hair is perfect and clothes spotless, but I feel her gaze pierce my back as I leave.

The next morning, Bosswood appears in the training room doorway and points her chin at me on the treatment table. "You're pitching today. You ready?"

I come up on one elbow and do my best to sound confident. "Yes. I'm good."

Down the hall, someone, probably Emma, yells "Coach? Hey, Coach?"

"Tennessee'll be good and ready, too," she says.

"No problem, Coach."

She almost smiles.

"Coach? Hey, Coach?" It's definitely Emma's voice, and she's getting closer. Bosswood rolls her eyes and disappears as fast as she came.

The trainer keeps working, and I lay back again, drumming my fingers on the table.

"Why the frown? Sure you're okay?" she asks.

"Yeah, I'm sure." I still my fingers. "It's just, I assumed she'd rotate us, and Zoe would pitch against Tennessee."

The trainer lifts my leg to ninety degrees. "I guess she's trying to tell you something."

Then she leans into the stretch, and I whimper. Where did she learn to be such a masochist?

#

In the seventh inning of the Lady Vols game, I have a blister on my big toe and my shoulder is tight, but I leave the field satisfied with the hard work of a two to zero score. I drop my glove and lift a water bottle, enjoying a moment of peace in the commotion of the dugout.

Until someone bumps my arm.

I inspect the water spilled down my jersey, and glance up to find Zoe oblivious to what she's done. Her bat is squeezed between her knees as she bunny hops towards the stairs. That'd be bad enough, but her hands are busy pulling on her batting glove, so the bat cuffs things left and right with each hop. I grin and turn to see if anyone else thinks this is funny.

"Hey, batter," I call. "Whatcha doing?"

She looks back with bright eyes and gives me a thumbs-up, her other glove gripped between her teeth. Then she continues her hopping progress forward and hits the back of Rachel's knees, earning a scowl.

Emma turns, assessing Zoe critically. "She's a pitcher," she says, as if that explained it. And what's with the tone of voice?

Andy jabs her thumb toward me. "And she's DH-ing for a pitcher. Double-trouble." They shake their heads and return to the game, but Zoe and I share a grin.

I bump her fist. "Go get 'em, Pitch."

She whoops and dons her helmet on the way to the on-deck circle. The Lady Vols are behind, so some of their fans yell insults and jeers and senseless stupidity at Zoe. Actually, they don't even have to be behind to do that. I hate that it happens at all, but instead of getting mad, I picture them taking their poor sportsmanship and packing it under the bus with their luggage after they lose to us. Maybe then our entire team will bunny hop around the field just for fun. Stamping our ticket to a Super Regional could do that to us.

"River." Andy presses against my shoulder. "Are we supposed to do the Gatorade-shower-thing to the coach after the game?"

My eyebrows rise as I peek at perfect Coach Bosswood. "Don't ask me. Talk to Sarah."

"Sarah said no. Not regionals." She taps her fingers on the dugout rail. "It might be because she's scared to mess with Coach, but that's okay. After we get sixty wins, what could Bosswood do to us then?"

Obviously, I can think of a few things.

But when we win the game, instead of tossing Gatorade, we wash away the sweat of the day and celebrate all night in dresses and heels that bare our bruises—until nine o'clock when I fall asleep.

The next morning's headline reads "The Dream Is Alive." The article recaps our game against the University of Tennessee and lays out our next stop at Super Regional. I think the words nicely frame all our hard work, stress, and general lack of a life outside of softball.

In the hospital, though, Coach's family and doctors continue broadcasting the games for him, hoping it'll wake him up. Does he know he only needs seven more wins? Or that we'd be glad to come and bunny hop around his room, if he'd only open his eyes?

#

Someone nicknames us "Coach's Sweethearts." Coach O'Daniel would like that, I think. I don't know what Bosswood thinks, but she nods with her usual cool efficiency when we arrive for the school's charter bus to take us to the Super Regionals at Stillwater. We giggle and christen our bus wearing makeup and fingernail polish, and taking selfies, instead of whatever the football players usually do when they take it.

In some ways, it's just another tournament. The NCAA Super Regionals is a best two-out-of-three platform played over two days. But Coach O'Daniel is on our minds, and no other aspect of this tournament is like anything we've faced before.

There are media shoots, which make my hands sweat. And there are always people watching, directing, evaluating, and when they think we aren't listening, calling us a long shot and underdogs. None of them cared while we were stapling ribbons on our board during the season, but now that we're within seven games of earning Coach's record, they mention us. Even during interviews, we know behind the scenes we're being dismissed. As if it's a fluke that we're here at all.

That's why when "experts" gauge Coach O'Daniel's chances of recovery, we don't believe them. They don't know him like we do. And, when we pass cameras on the way to the field later, our attention is on beating Oklahoma State, no matter the professionally whispered odds against us.

But Mrs. O'Daniel sending a box of cookies to the dugout to wish us luck does influence us. We win two games in a row for her. Actually, it wasn't quite that easy, more like mortal combat with blood and bruises and blisters, but we get it done.

After we untangle from each other at the pitching mound, where for once I wasn't squished in the middle, we make our way down OSU's line to shake hands with the stunned Cowgirls.

Their pitcher stops me, gripping my hand instead of tapping it, her brown eyes serious. "Good luck at the world series," she says so sincerely that I'm dumbstruck.

"I hope y'all crush the record for your coach," the sweat-stained catcher behind her says, although I know, competitively, she'd love another chance to beat us.

Sweat beads our foreheads and, while we're on opposing sides, I know these athletes go back to school after a game to pass tests or finish labs or write papers, just like me. They take ice baths and nurse bruises. They've missed parties and celebrations and vacations, just like me. We truly are a sisterhood no matter the jerseys we wear, and it makes me proud of our sport.

On the way to the dugout, Emma grabs my elbow, interrupting my sentimental thoughts. "Gatorade shower?"

"Next time," I murmur.

As soon as we can, we gather to call the hospital. Mrs. O'Daniel says that nothing has changed for Coach, but she listened to the game with him and she's sure it helped.

Then our celebration is cut short when an ESPN reporter holds up a picture of all of us crowded in our locker room around our board of feathers.

"Have you seen this?" he asks with satisfaction at our shocked faces.

My heart sinks, and I search for Dawz. Her eyes are dark in her pale face, but she studies the photo of fifty-five bulky ribbons.

The reporter informs us that the picture will grace the back cover of the softball World Series program. Even worse, there are plans to use it in TV clips.

I feel violated, and it's obvious my teammates do too. Someone has stolen the triumphs of our sweat and tears and exposed them with a cruel heartlessness.

But we still have to endure the interview. Sarah, Abbey, Zoe, and I answer questions about whether the pressure is too much and what we think our chances of earning the record are. Despite reeling from the betrayal, we answer and smile, all the while protectively shielding Dawz. I can't imagine the trauma she feels at the intrusion and it infuriates me.

Then the reporter cues a video tribute to Coach O'Daniel. As it plays, my teammates draw even closer together, taking comfort from the contact. He looks so alive that my eyes fill with tears. There's no gray pallor, no tubes, no beeping.

We've done this. We've brought him this attention. No one will forget him now. Then they ask us what was so great about him.

"What *is* so great, you mean?" I correct. "He loves us. He makes time to talk to each of us. He really wants to know how we're doing. He made me want to be the best, not by being a bully, but by being such a great person that I don't want to let him down, no matter if it kills me."

"Up Against a Wall" is the headline for our television segment. I can't say it's exaggerated that much.

Chapter 39

My footsteps echo in the empty library tower as I drop my backpack by a bench and prowl from window to window. Emotions stalk me from behind like a predatory cat, tail twitching and eyes hot. When I can't escape, I finally slump on the bench, with arms wrapped around my knees, and let the late afternoon sunshine lay me bare.

I should be elated. My wildest dreams have come true. Just look what we've accomplished… in one crazy week, softball will be over.

The WCWS will be history.

Coach will or won't hold the record.

And my psychedelic freshman year will be reduced to black-and-white photos in a book.

The whirlwind, the trauma, the hope of an impossible task—all in the past—to be dealt with the best we can. I rest my chin on my knee. Will we have been enough?

Heavy footsteps echo up the stairs, and I tense. But Ty appears at the door, broad shouldered and real. "River, you aren't suicidal, are you?"

A year of loneliness and heartache seems to fade at the warm twinkle in his eyes. "Did you come to jump with me?"

"Not me. I'm scared of heights." He crosses the room and peers down from the window. "But I guess I could take one for the team."

I smile. "Did you need something?"

"Just you."

I roll my eyes, but he sits inches from my toes on the other end of the bench and leans back on his hands. An object slips from his pocket to clatter on the floor. When he picks it up, he doesn't put it back right away. He braces his elbows on his knees and studies the pink LED flashlight he'd purchased at the student union all those months ago.

"I can't believe you kept that."

He gives me a playful scowl. "It's my favorite." He points it at me. "I went in specifically to get this light, in this color, so no judging."

"You did not. Why do you need a flashlight?"

"Self-respecting dudes are always prepared."

"Whatever." But I smile.

Sunshine glints off the ends of his hair. "Okay. Maybe it was spontaneous, but the logic is sound." His eyes soften. "And it reminds me of you."

"I'm touched, truly." I nudge him with my toe. "But why do you need a reminder?"

Instead of answering, he rolls the flashlight in his palm and huffs a laugh. "Remember how it'd rained that day? I'd been watching from upstairs in the math building when you danced by with your hood up like the puddles were hot lava."

"How could you tell it was me?"

He shakes his head like that's a stupid question. "The first thing I wondered was what in the world you were up to now."

"No. You wanted to scare me to death." I mock frown.

He chuckles. "That's your own fault. You never look around. Always so focused." He rubs a finger under his nose. "Anyway, I wanted to see you."

My eyebrows rise. He glances up, and his intensity makes my stomach clench.

"Just like I've wanted to see you every day since we met."

When he finally looks away to return the light to his pocket, my heart stutters.

"Lucky you," I say breathlessly. "You came to the right farm, huh? And now we live next door to each other."

His smile plays with the corners of his mouth, but suddenly he fills the room. He leans close, locking gazes as he skims my face and tucks hair behind my ear.

"You know that's not what I mean," he whispers. I hold my breath.

He pulls back, careful to put space between us. I almost groan in protest. With casual grace, Ty stands to lean against the windowsill. Irresistibly drawn, I rise and mirror his stance on the other side.

"What's wrong?" I ask.

He hesitates. "Can I ask you something?"

"Sure."

His eyes grow serious. "Why didn't you want to slow dance with me at your prom?"

I blink. "But we did."

He crosses his arms, shoulder against the wall. "Half a song, then you bolted." His expression shutters. "I've always wondered what I did wrong."

I remember being in his arms. The way my head fit at his neck. How happy I'd been. The best night of my life until... until... My eyes widen. "I promise, it wasn't you."

His mouth twists. "Whatever." He straightens and tucks his hands in his pockets as if he might leave.

I touch his arm. When he looks at me, I squeeze gently. "It wasn't you." Even now, the intensity of that night makes me shudder, and I drop my hand. "Why are you asking now?"

His expression softens, then he purses his lips. "The next couple of years are so unpredictable," he says slowly, as if talking to himself.

"Well?" I smile uncertainly. "When is the future not unpredictable?"

His cheeks flush. He reaches for the bill of a hat before realizing he's not wearing one and drops his hand to the back of his neck.

"River, I'd like to ask you out." He flashes a side-long look. "But you're going to be busy with softball and school..."

I squint. "Is that a question?"

"It's just, there's a chance... it's possible... if things keep going the way they are." He builds up steam and lets it all out in one breath. "There's a good chance I'll be drafted into the pros in the next couple of years, and I don't know where I'll live, if I'll have free time, or whether I could afford to support us..."

"Ty." I throw up a hand. "Wait. Whoa, there. What're you talking about?"

He scowls. "I'm trying to tell you what I see when I think about the future."

It's all I can do to keep my face blank. I drop back to the bench on weak legs. I didn't see this coming. I mean, I know he's a practical person. And Lexi'd told me he was stubborn. Obviously, he's pig-headed and strong-willed, too—walked away from baseball, didn't he? Now, he's turned all that considerable force toward imagining a future with us together, but only a safe, well-planned future.

Then I smile. This is my dream, too. And, really, is he any match for me? He watches, a furrow between his brows, and a vulnerability in his eyes that melts my heart.

I lean back on my hands. "*The course of true love never did run smooth.*"

His jaw drops. "You're quoting Shakespeare?"

That response is even better than I'd hoped. "Has anyone read your palms?"

"No." He frowns, looking as bewildered as I'd felt a moment ago.

"And you don't have a crystal ball? Has God spoken to you?" He straightens and I lean forward before he can scowl again. "Then you really don't know how things will end, right? That's why you play the game."

The ghost of a smile battles with his frown, spurring me on. "So." I tilt my head. "Do you think we could share onion rings or something? I mean, everyone has to eat, right?"

He rocks back against the wall, crosses his arms, and studies me from under his lashes. "They used to stake pirates in a lagoon and let the tide take them as punishment for mutiny like this."

I pat the bench beside me. "Braveheart anyone?"

He chuckles despite himself. "Different genres."

"And who said you're the captain of this ship?" I gesture between us. "Equal partners."

"Except this is a hostile takeover." He taps his chest. "This was my idea."

"Are you sure?"

He glares, but the humor in his eyes ruins it. "Don't say I didn't warn you when things get crazy."

I smile and lean back again. "You know, you don't scare me. If I don't mind your pink flashlight, not much will bother me."

He pushes off the wall to sit beside me and wraps one hand around my neck. Just as his lips touch mine, an image flashes of him looming behind the backstop fence, dark sunglasses on, and arms crossed like a club bouncer—that pink flashlight in his pocket.

I think I fall in love.

Chapter 40

OKC - Bracket games – Five wins needed for the record

"Why Texas?" Lily's voice comes out of the dark. I lift my head from my hotel bed across the room to squint at her scrolling on her phone.

"Bad luck?" I punch my pillow and turn to face her.

She huffs a laugh. "They've been to the Series before. We haven't."

"And they beat us two-out-of-three this year. They're going to be cocky."

"Shows what they know." She turns off her phone, and the room goes dark. "I was thinking if it weren't for needing to break the record, the fact that we're in this tournament would be my biggest dream come true."

"Yeah. And the hype would make me more nervous if we didn't still need five wins."

It's quiet, and I assume she's fallen asleep. But just as I'm nodding off myself, she asks, "Do you think Coach will wake up? That he'll even care about the games?"

My eyes pop open. "I don't know." I sigh. "I'd like to think that we're helping him come back. That he can feel us pulling for him."

"Me, too." She turns over with a rustle. A minute later, she says softly, "I'm so lucky to be on this team."

The next morning, I realize I've underestimated my nerves. We gather around Coach Bosswood and Coach CJ in the dugout to hear the lineup over the crowds. Although Zoe will pitch, my palms sweat. To keep my mind off the millions who watch at home, I study Coach Bosswood for a hair out of place or a bead of sweat as she gives us a pep talk. Nothing.

"I can't make a play for you or pitch for you," she says in her brisk way. "Coach CJ can't bat for you. We can give you the information you need to do what you've been training for all year." She tucks her clipboard under her arm. "You know each other. To be successful, you're each going to have to use that knowledge and trust. At this level, if you out-think and out-hustle the other team, you'll stay in the game. If you want the ball more than anyone else, you'll play the game correctly. But if you're determined not to let down the teammate next to you, you'll win."

There are echoes of "Yeah" and "Let's do it" as the coaches leave. Taking the field together fortifies us in the way touching the dense feathers on our board has. The awareness of drones and cameras devouring our every move rolls harmlessly off us, like rain off a duck's back.

Except for the one dark, lifeless eye of the camera attached to a human outside the dugout that follows Zoe to the mound and then, weirdly, turns back to focus on me.

I try to ignore it and the fact that someone is commenting on me from a desk somewhere. Do I look confident? And relaxed? Are they comparing me to another pitcher, coldly going over our stats just to establish why we won't win when it's my turn to pitch? Ugh. I wish I was on the field. At least then, I'd have a routine to settle my nerves.

Zoe doesn't seem bothered. She looks good on the mound, calmly tugging at her glove. But when she glances at me, I realize the routine isn't enough. I give her a thumbs-up and yell, "You're ready, girl." Then bite my cheek to keep from glancing at the camera.

At the bottom of the first inning, Zoe jogs in with a satisfied smile. But, somehow, I know she'll want to talk. The part of me that had leaned on my brothers through all the grown-up stuff in our lives drives me to her side, only to find she really is looking for me. I miss her words at first, because realizing that I think like her is... disturbing.

Then Andy crowds my other side. Her visor is upside down, and she jumps and cheers, but I hear wisps of commentary on the pitches under her breath. She grins when she catches me looking, but underneath, I feel her yearning to be out there herself as if she'd cried it aloud. I blink, scan the field, and goosebumps creep over my arms. It's not just Zoe. When did I start feeling my teammates' emotions?

Before I can freak out, Zoe slaps my rear and bares her teeth. "Is something in my teeth?"

By the bottom of the seventh inning, the noise level is decibels above comfortable, and we're tied three to three.

For our last at bat, Mia slap bunts and races to first base. Loose strands of hair stick to the sweat on her neck. She turns and claps encouragingly for Sarah, ignoring the Texas first baseman hovering at her elbow with a grim expression.

Sarah's bunt spins in the dirt in front of home for a sacrifice out that moves Mia to second, where she can easily score. Despite being out, Sarah punches the air in triumph on the way back to the dugout. The crowd's "Go North" relays around the stadium.

One hit and we'll take the lead on this team that's beaten us twice this year. One good hit and we'll put them back on their bus. But Rachel strikes out and looks tempted to slam the bat into the ground.

Two outs. *Hold the Hope* swings on our wrists, a little worn.

Texas fans react as if they've already won. They jump and crow, and conveniently ignore that the score is tied. Katie and Emma start the wave to remind our crowd to remind Texas we're not going anywhere.

Then Dawz steps into the batter's box. One foot. Then the other. Her glare rises with her chin as her bat comes up. Everyone in the stadium seems to inhale. Like they know Bosswood told her to hit away.

And Dawz does like a good show.

Her form is perfect. She crushes the ball high and long as the day. Sunshine illuminates her white batting gloves punching the air now and again on her lope around the bases. Mia scores and turns to wait for her at home. Our dugout empties.

We'd needed something big, I think, as Dawz crosses the plate. Well, Texas, how about a two-run homer? Game. Over.

The cameras crowd in as we jump and laugh. They peer over our shoulders and between our jerseys, trying to capture the elation. As the tallest in our group, I see the way they circle us. I'm sweaty and flushed, and maybe I should try not to look like an unbridled colt on a television screen somewhere.

Nope. Don't even care.

#

We check the day's bracket for carnage as we leave the field. OU beat LSU. Florida State beat UCLA. The Wolverines...

Every day, teams are eliminated one by one, but Michigan hovers, seemingly impervious to the chaos. I turn from the board.

Outside the stadium, the WCWS trophy waits under glass, a photo-op for fans and the focus of every team. Except us. Our prize is back home fighting for his life.

I tug my backpack higher and trudge toward the gate. Still, I'd give anything to not face Michigan again. That early loss to them was my first, so obviously, I hated it. And, although none of the losses have been easy, I never want to feel like that first loss again. A residual of that feeling makes me dread playing them. It's not a logical fear. I mean, they don't have my pitching figured out. I've played a lot of games since then and gotten a lot better.

And if that's what it takes... fine. I clench my teeth.

Give me another shot at them.

#

That evening, the lobby sounds like Northbridge's Student Union. Fletcher and Emma debate over their ice cream, or maybe they're flirting. I can't tell which, because Ty jabs his spoon toward my peppermint ice cream and laughingly holds his own cup safely out of reach. But has he seen my wingspan in action?

Just as I take another bite, I notice Andy in the shadows of the breakfast nook and bound toward her.

"What're ya doing?" I hop in front of her, then freeze at her tear-stained face. "What's wrong?"

Emma is there instantly, and all humor leaves Fletcher and Ty as they near.

"Is this about Jace?" Emma asks.

"What?" I step back. The guys stiffen.

Andy's eyes widen. "I'm sorry, River."

"Andy!" I throw my hands wide. Heads swivel toward us, and I lower my voice. "I told you. I. Told. You."

She shrinks with each word. "I know. I didn't... he seemed nice. We liked each other."

Ty and Fletch pivot away, as if they've had enough. I step closer. "What happened?"

She holds up her phone reluctantly to reveal a photo of Jace and a smiling, petite girl under his arm. "He's upset about not getting as much playing time since..." She glances at Ty.

"...since I joined the team." Ty returns her stare grimly, then drops the rest of his ice cream in the trash. "That's what he's saying, right?"

Andy nods. "I felt sorry for him. But as soon as I leave town, he's with someone else."

Ty shakes his head. "He's the backup catcher now because he competed for the spot and lost. And I'm only on the team because he couldn't keep his trap shut." He gestures to the phone. "But he'll always be that guy."

"Is that all, Andy?" Fletch asks in his relaxed drawl, but the look in his eyes sends a chill through me. "Or do I need to have a talk with him?"

Emma nods encouragingly, but Andy's face pinks. "Tempting," she says and ducks her head against Emma's shoulder. "But no. Thank you, though."

The look that Emma gives Fletch above Andy's head almost melts my ice cream.

#

The next day, we beat Ala-freaking-bama. It's so momentous that I'm afraid to admit it out loud in case I pass out with happiness.

Not only did we beat a powerhouse team, but that win puts us squarely in the playoffs. More games... more opportunities. An impossibility just months ago. Now, we huddle at the bracket board, sweaty and sore, and stare at our name in the championship playoff box. It's not a typo or in pencil. It's ink.

Behind us, a bus gears up and leaves the curb with a whine and puff of exhaust. Fans swarm the official store for t-shirts and hats.

"Oklahoma or Michigan?" Sarah asks without taking her eyes from the board.

"Oklahoma scares me," Emma says.

"No kidding." Dawz squats to slip off a shoe. "Personally, I want to beat Michigan."

"Ten bucks it's Michigan," Mia says beside Dawz. Then her face puckers and everyone near Dawz scrambles away.

"Oh, my goodness! What's that smell?" Zoe holds a hand over her face. "You still haven't washed those socks?"

Dawz casually slides her sweat-stained foot back into her shoe. "I'm on a hitting roll."

Emma grimaces. "We realize those are... lucky... socks, Dawz. But this is not normal. Have you heard of Febreze?"

"It's probably good old athlete's foot by now." Bree takes another step back.

Rachel elbows closer. "You're not wearing those on the bus."

"The shoes or the socks?" Dawz ties the shoe and stands, hiking her backpack higher. "Cuz, I'm not taking either off."

Zoe and Rachel bracket her all the way to the bus, inventing deadly threats if she decides to expose any of us to that punishment again. But no one risks telling her to wash her lucky socks. Luck is luck.

I linger at the board. The championship series is another best two-out-of-three games. More importantly, they're the only games left for the year. There will be zero chances beyond them to get the record. And we need two wins. I close my eyes briefly. No problem.

The next night we crowd around the big screen in the hotel lobby to watch Michigan and OU tug the game back and forth. The smell of popcorn drifts through the room. Some of my teammates wander off with their families or pull out their phones. I lean closer to study the players. OU has unearthly talent and plays like one expertly honed unit, nearly impossible to beat. And Michigan...

As Michigan pulls out the upset win in the last inning, my heart races at what I've seen. They have a bond similar to the one that binds us—one thicker than blood. I sit back. How do you beat that?

Chapter 41

First Playoff game for win number 59

Michigan is going down. It feels like a morning to celebrate—it being Dad's birthday and all. No better day than today, just for him. I lift my pancakes off the conveyor belt in the breakfast room and drizzle syrup in a big "W." For "Wins" not "Wolverines."

"River Harte?" a man's strong accent is so surprising that I'm not sure he's talking to me. I turn with a quizzical frown.

"Have they found your dad's body yet?" he asks.

My syrupy pancakes slide toward the floor in slow motion until Lily grabs the edge of my plate. "Don't listen, River. He's trying to upset you."

Caught so unaware, I don't realize he's asking a question. At first, I think he's said that someone found dad's body.

"What'd he say?" I breathe, looking desperately at Lily.

"He's fishing. It's not real. It's okay." She rescues my hot tea.

Bosswood's chair scrapes as she pushes up from her table and intercepts the thick, scruffy-looking man.

"Let's go." Lily tugs on my shirt. "He doesn't matter."

Head down, I follow her to a table, my heart thumping. There are crumbs and sticky outlines, but I slide my plate over them. Lily sets my tea in front of me, and I slump into the chair. Why does this keep happening? Who is so heartless they'd dangle my dad's life in front of me? Heartless and cold and cruel and... Then I imagine what Kody would do if he were here, and I surge out of the chair, nearly tipping it over.

"I'm going to kick his—"

Emma grabs my arm, pulling me back. "Hey," she says. "Don't let them win." When I glare at her, she leans close. "If you get in trouble, they win. Be smart."

Haunting images flash through my mind of helicopter accidents I've researched in my dumber moments. Mangled metal, missing blades, blackened cockpits. Dad survived, but my imagination fills in the blanks of his reality. Bodies scattered. Empty helmets. Blood. Torture.

I sit, but my gulp of tea scalds my mouth. Dad survived his crash. Tears spring to my eyes. He's alive. He's surviving, no matter the unspeakable horrors. I wipe at the tears. I am not falling apart. Not on his birthday. Lily nudges a glass of water close.

"What's up, River?" Dawz asks solemnly from the next table.

I look over and freeze. They're all staring. Across the room, my teammates are riveted by my every move. The television echoes through the quiet dining room.

Lily touches my hand. "We know something happened to your dad, but we haven't heard the details. I mean, we google things too, like those jerks." She gestures over her shoulder. "Except we keep your secrets."

"We're here for you," Emma says. "You know that."

Coach Bosswood comes back, takes one look, and pointedly checks her watch. A couple of girls clear out, dumping their plates and disappearing down the hall. Coach studies my face as she passes, like I'm a particularly strange piece of art.

I need my teammates. More than they know. But who would understand what it's like to have someone missing? That I don't know if my dad is alive or not?

I take a bite of pancakes, but it's like cardboard in my throat. More girls leave, heads bent together. Lilly turns to talk to Dawz and says something about me being stronger than I look. I turn my phone face down, determined to stop freaking out. Mom and the twins don't need to know either. I can do this.

Coach stops at Zoe's chair and tells her she's pitching.

I miss my dad.

#

Michigan wins the coin toss, then beat us by one. It's not Zoe's fault. All of our bats were cold. We couldn't string together hits and left too many runners stranded. In a word: pathetic.

The sound of the celebrating Wolverines drifts to our dugout as we pack up.

Sarah's shoulders slump. Mia yanks her bag up and stalks out of the dugout without a word. All that's left are quiet sniffs, shuffling feet, and closing zippers.

"On the bus, ladies." Bosswood swings her messenger bag over her shoulder. "Don't stop to talk to your families. Just get on the bus." She marches out of the dugout like it's been a waste of a season.

#

When the bus pulls up to the hotel, Jaiden and baby Claire are visible in the lobby. I wince and shut my eyes, wondering why she would think that I wanted visitors tonight. I hang back as my teammates shuffle past, heads down, their dirt-streaked pants and stained socks sagging and worn. Jaiden studies each face, finally focusing on me.

"Hi," she says.

"What're you doing?" I ask as she follows me to a side niche.

"Coming to see you." The friendly light in her eyes dims, turning cautious at my tone. "What's wrong? You look awful."

I shrug irritably. "We lost, Jaiden. I think I'm entitled to feel awful."

"Bull." Jaiden hitches the strap of the baby bag without jostling Claire. "Feeling determined, I could understand. But defeated? That's just a pity party."

Wait. Let me count the ways that is an unfair thing to say by someone who should've had my back, no less. But she doesn't give me the chance. She reads my expression and turns with a disgusted shake of her head.

"Jaiden." I step around to face her again. "We lost today. Do you realize what'll happen if we don't win the last two games? It's..." I throw my hands up. "It'll be the end. Everything will be over. We'll fail."

She stops suddenly and jabs her finger at my collarbone. "No, River. If you lose, then you've fought a good fight. That's it. Life will go on."

I want to shove her hand away, but she's holding Claire. I grit my teeth. "You don't know what we've been through."

"Oh, get real, River." Jaiden rolls her eyes, but I see her grip tighten on Claire. One little fist rises from the blankets along with a whimper and I'm reminded that she hasn't exactly been on a picnic either. She lowers her voice, closing her hand protectively around the baby's. "You're so dramatic."

"Why'd you come?" I lower my own voice, staring at Claire's small profile, desperately missing my old friend—the one I could talk to about anything. "Obviously not because you care."

Unexpectedly, Jaiden's shoulders relax and she kisses Claire's little fingers. "I came to talk something over with you." She raises her head. "But forget it."

She pulls the blanket over Claire and turns to leave, making me feel small and ugly.

"Wait," I say before she reaches the doors. I take a breath and steady my voice. "What did you want?"

She pauses, head bent to Claire, then looks at me over her shoulder. "I wanted to tell you I'm going back to school in the fall, to the junior college at home."

"Oh." I swallow and nod stiffly. "I'm happy for you."

Jaiden faces me with that same bullish pose that she wore behind the plate so many times, except instead of her helmet on her hip, it's little Claire. "And tomorrow, I'm signing my letter of intent to play softball, so I'll have a scholarship to pay for school. I've decided to be a softball coach and teacher." She glares, daring me to be critical.

I nod. Neither of us moves. Why is everything always about Jaiden? She's so stubborn. If she walks away right now, would our friendship survive? What about all our growing-up years together? Were they pointless? Can we make it as adult friends? Will we end up polite Christmas card pen-pals and nothing more?

The differences between us are stark and painful. Me, stiff in a rumpled uniform with a bat bag over my shoulder, squared off against her, stiff with attitude and a baby in her arms. Ridiculous. Impossible.

So utterly us.

The longer I study her, the more the sight of that familiar mulish chin makes my lips twitch. She sees and sets her jaw, too pig-headed to give in. But I know all of her weaknesses.

"I feel sorry for your players," I say, and allow the smile to shine in my eyes.

She gives me a warning glare, and I can't resist—I snort. Her tough-girl face breaks, and we stand there grinning at each other. But too soon, the smiles fade. She lowers her gaze.

"I'm sorry, Riv." She raises her head, eyes soft. "I should've realized this wasn't a good time. I know what you're trying to do is unselfish. It's freaking noble." She sighs. "It matters."

I step closer and run my hand over Claire's smooth head, admiring her perfect eyebrows and plump cheeks. "It's not life or death," I say softly. "But it might inspire some little softball player someday." I shrug one shoulder. "It might inspire Coach to wake up. Maybe."

Jaiden reaches around to hug me, and we rest against each other. I whisper, "I think Claire will be proud of you for doing this." I can feel her nod against my shoulder.

After she leaves, I ride the elevator up alone, feeling better, like I used to after Jaiden talked to me in the circle. But I've known her and her expressions for a long time. I lean my head against the wall, staring at the ceiling. If that wasn't fear underneath her bravado, I'd eat my socks.

#

The next morning, the elevator opens to Bosswood's unsmiling face.

"River, you're on today." She looks up from her notepad as I pass to go to breakfast.

Despite the sleep crease across my cheek, I didn't sleep much. I pause, suddenly hopeful that she'll say more, needing something, I don't know, like a pat on the head, but she enters the elevator without another word. My shoulders sag, and I chew my fingernail as I follow Lily and Emma.

All night, snippets of the past year flashed through my mind—the hard work, the sacrifices, the sorrows—magnified by Jaiden's visit. My nerves are raw. What I wouldn't give to only be back playing for a high school championship. Instead, if we don't win today, we might as well not have played this year at all. The Hall of Fame won't care if we get close. Everyone will know we've failed. Coach Bosswood will hate me for the rest of her life.

The smell of bacon rises nauseatingly from a pan and I close the lid.

"Why can't she..." I say under my breath.

"What?" Lily asks, glancing back.

"Nothing." I pick up a breakfast plate and put it down again. "It's just... I don't need anything from her. I know who I am. But for once, I wish I could hear her say 'good job.' You know? Would it be that hard to say?" I freeze when Lily's gaze shifts over my shoulder. I close my eyes.

Coach Bosswood's face is tight when I turn. "I'd like a word with you."

I can't even swallow. I follow her out of the dining room with my guts trailing behind. Am I going to get benched? For being stupid? The girls are watching again. If I let them down, it doesn't matter what she thinks of me.

She stops in the hall and crosses her arms. "You have a problem, Harte?"

"No, Coach." I grit my teeth. The bumping of a rolling suitcase gets louder, and I step to the side to let the person pass, avoiding Coach's eyes.

"You looked like you had plenty on your mind." When I don't respond, she says, "We're all counting on you as the leader of the team. Are you up for that?"

Leader? My dumb expression seems to irritate her.

She glares down her nose. "What is the matter with you?"

Through the doorway, a few girls flick glances our way. Others openly gawk for the second day in a row. When have I ever tried to tell them what to do?

"I'm not a leader," I correct. "I'm just a freshman."

Coach Bosswood rears back. "Don't waste my time saying things like that." Her nostrils flare and her lips tighten as if she's counting to ten. Then she frowns, like I'm a puzzle and she's just found a piece. "Do you think O'Daniel recruited you by accident? He had a sixth sense about people, and he was never wrong. He believed in you and said you were a natural leader—which you are."

I look away and bite my lip. Deep down, I know my brothers don't trust me to search for dad. That's why, even if I do something for my teammates, no one should follow me. Then, if I fail, it won't hurt anyone else.

She sighs and her tone changes, sounding almost defensive. "River, he called me from your high school game. I did my research while he was watching. Remember your YouTube recruitment video?"

I nod.

"Do you know why I called him back and told him I wanted you?" She raises her brows, but... she's never wanted me on the team. Probably still doesn't.

"You had all the numbers and the skill, but I was looking for more.

The little bits in interviews and social media from your teammates and friends made me think you had it—that character-quality that can't be taught. This year you've done what I've asked without complaint, which I expected." She tucks her chin and pins me with her gaze. "You've also worked on your own time and pulled this team together with no concessions from me."

She straightens. I stare.

"I'm aware," she says. "That you picked those girls up from the party, knowing the risk to yourself, but you did it anyway because they needed you. I was very proud of you." She looks uncomfortable but keeps going. "That's what you've done this entire year. You've put this team first with emotional maturity that most freshmen don't have, and it's cost you. But that's why they, and I, trust you to take this game today. You won't be standing out there alone. We'll be with you. And you won't let Coach O'Daniel down, no matter what happens on the scoreboard."

A shiver runs down my spine and I swallow. Silverware tinkles in the dining room. Bursts of laughter and clinks of plates.

"Thanks, Coach."

"You've probably thought I was hard on you." She frowns. "But it's the way I was raised. No one needs freebies handed to them. You need to be prepared and you need to be tough. This team knows you're a great pitcher—"

I make a choked sound, and she stiffens. She has criticized my pitching nonstop, but she probably wouldn't appreciate being reminded. Her glare is back.

"I didn't accomplish anything that we didn't do together." I fling a hand toward the dining room. "We have the best team."

Her frown melts into a wry smile as she tucks her notepad under her arm. "And you think you're not a leader? Pull my other leg."

Somehow, I manage not to roll my eyes at her old-fashioned joke. We both sink back against the wall, shoulder to shoulder. Coach nods once and mutters under her breath. It sounds a lot like "that wasn't so bad." I guess we could've stayed like that all day, but after a minute she drums her fingers against her papers.

"Well, I should call O'Daniel." She glances over when I flinch. "I'm happy to pass along updates. Let him hear my voice. But it's not always fun." She snorts. "Yesterday sucked."

"You talk to him?" My voice rises.

"They give him earphones, and I tell him about practice, or a game, who's pitching, who's hitting well. That we're in the play-offs." She rolls one shoulder in thought. "Man, I wish he were here. I never expected to coach without him."

"I didn't know you..."

"Talking to him is supposed to help. I'd do anything for that guy, and he'd do anything for all of you." She straightens, smoothing invisible wrinkles from her shirt. "Maybe he'll wake in time for today's game and watch it on TV himself. So, get out there and show the Michigan Wolverines what you've got. O'Daniel will know."

And, in my heart, I hope it's true.

Chapter 42

For win number 59 - again

It's bittersweet to walk onto the field that's the home of the WCWS. The memories are overwhelming. Last year, I took it for granted when Coach O'Daniel came back into my life during a high school championship game. This year, I understand what I'm missing without him.

And there's Dad, always the ache in my chest. I scan the sold-out crowd for an older version of Kody and Zeph. If Dad were here, I think he'd be too excited to sit. A group of men collects on the breezeway to survey the field and swap stories. That's where Dad would be, beaming with the other dads. Thrilled to see his only daughter play. I let my focus blur and imagine him there until I almost believe it and warmth wraps around me.

Then I notice my teammates' furtive glances, like the kind they'd given me in the dining room before my meltdown, and I realize that standing stock still might send the wrong message. So, I fold the dream deep inside and stroll back through the dugout, giving a high five here, another there. My smile grows more genuine as the girls bump my shoulder, smack my palm, swat my rear. It makes it easier to breathe. If only the feeling could be bottled and sold as a miracle drug.

Then the game starts.

#

The seventh and final inning comes faster than seems possible. For the last time in this game, I drop the ball on the mound and run in.

"Good job," Liz says as I toss my glove on the bench. "Nice three up-three down."

I nod and check the scoreboard over my water bottle, hoping it's changed and we're not down by one. Andy and Mia make room for me on the fence.

"I hate her rise ball," Andy says.

"Because it's a good one," I say. "Just don't swing." Mia chuckles from my other side.

Sarah's first pitch is outside and low. She steps out, takes a practice swing, steps back in. Then the screwball jambs her, and she swings involuntarily. Rising to my toes, I yell for her to try again.

"It's coming," Mia mutters ominously.

I glance at her. Then my gaze shifts back to the pitcher because we know Mia's acute senses have unfailingly put her on base.

Sarah watches the rise ball all the way to the catcher's glove.

"Good call," I say over the crowd. Mia smiles.

"What's the count?" Andy asks, still clapping.

"Two balls. One strike." I clench the fence. We need someone on base.

Sarah's focus is tangible. She slams the next pitch with all her strength. The left fielder back peddles in line with the ball, but it rises. And rises. Then it's gone.

Fans beyond the fence scramble for the catch. Chaos breaks out around me. Tied is a long way from defeat.

Sarah slows to a fast jog. When she rounds third, her smile is wide and bright, and then she's home. Relief shoots through me. She really did it. We can work with a tie.

Michigan's catcher jogs to the circle for quick nods with the pitcher behind their gloves. Then Rachel adjusts her helmet, tugs up her right sleeve, and turns the bat twice in front of her face.

She hits the first pitch.

It's a hard, line drive, and Rachel runs so fast that it takes ten steps beyond first base to slow her momentum. She turns with a bellow as we jump and cheer.

Dawz misses her bunt. But Rachel is halfway to second. She drops into a slide, then pops up on base to beat the catcher's throw. I pound the fence rail, and Andy dances unashamedly. Half the stadium joins us.

The next pitch, Dawz swings hard, but it's a strike. The catcher tries to pick off Rachel, but she dives back under the swipe and grins when she rises, not bothering to brush dirt from her uniform.

Dawz points at Rachel and yells something lost in the noise, then steps back into the box, touches her bat to home plate, and pulls it up by her ear. She's so focused, I doubt she even hears the crowd.

Dawz bunts. A beautiful bunt in front of home. The ball spins in the dirt. The first baseman charges it. The catcher beats her, scoops it up, checks Rachel at second, then throws to first for Dawz. The right fielder rushes to cover the throw at first, and Rachel takes off from second.

The throw is wide. Dawz is safe. Rachel is running, running, running.

The Wolverines scramble for the ball. Rachel takes one look at Boss-wood's waving arm and doesn't slow as she rounds third for home.

Man, she can run.

Dawz heads for second, but all eyes are on Rachel. If she makes it home, we win.

She dives, arms out. The ump squats, eyes narrowed on the plate. The catcher snatches the ball and swipes at Rachel. The ump rears up...

And she's safe.

Rachel is dusty, and gasping, and radiant. We tumble out of the dugout to surround her.

Over my teammates' heads, I glimpse the disbelief on Michigan's faces. The careful space between them as they trickle off the field reminds me of strangers in an airport who've missed their plane.

Fans shoot pictures of our celebration. Big television cameras circle. A drone hovers above, orbiting our ecstatic huddle.

They never see the text that circulates between us later from someone at home.

A single carnation in a vase.

Chapter 43

The elation from winning doesn't last long. In fact, it flees the moment I take off my cleat after the game and spot a tear in my pitching toe rubber that wasn't there before. Snags and gouges are no big deal. But this looks deep. I glance around to be sure no one's watching, then lift the flap and peer under.

The damage makes my stomach hurt.

I replace the flap and apply pressure like it's a bleeding wound.

Dawz can never see this. These are my lucky cleats. The one-and-only pair I've worn all season. I can't afford to worry about damaging them, but I cannot play for the championship without them.

"Do your best," I tell them and gently tuck them into my backpack. I'm not supposed to pitch tomorrow, so if they will just last a few more days, they can retire.

Back at the hotel, we study films and plan the next game. Then some girls and their families play cards in the dining room or watch a movie in the lobby. My long-legged family spreads out in a quiet corner.

Ty sits so close that his thigh muscles shift against mine when he reaches for a water bottle. His throat bobs as he swallows in a fascinating way. And maybe it's because he's leaving soon for his own games, but the warm smell of him sends heat across my chest and up my neck.

He replaces the lid and leans forward, elbows on his knees. "Could someone tell me about Mr. Harte?"

I blink in surprise, but Kody crosses his ankle over his knee. "You already know."

"Evidently not," he says. "Lily said his situation still rattles River. Don't you think it'd be better to talk this over? She has another game to get through."

Zeph stiffens. "What're you talking about?"

"It's nothing." I pull away from Ty.

"You were rattled." Now he pins me with his gaze. "It got to you. I could tell from watching you on television."

"Leave her alone, man." Warning rumbles in Kody's voice.

"Okay." He shrugs and sits back. "What if it happens again? You're just going to leave her to handle it alone with the pressure she's under?"

Mom shakes her head. "Be careful how you judge us, Ty. You don't know everything. We've been cautious and held information close because Matt's life depended on it."

Ty nods, chastened, and avoids my gaze in the awkward silence.

Zeph sighs. "It's not a secret that Dad is in Costa Rica."

Ty nods again, but I watch as the cartographer in Zeph traces the country's outline on the armrest.

As if feeling his twin's struggle to find words, Kody says, "He was part of a humanitarian mission. We thought it was a small nonprofit fighting hunger and trafficking, but they were loaded up. Helicopters, doctors, engineers. After his helicopter went down and he disappeared, we learned that it was actually a war on drugs."

"Who told you?" Ty's forehead creases. "That his helicopter went down."

"The president of the NGO board. He lost most of his senior staff in the accident."

"Mr. Harte wasn't active duty, was he?" Ty asks.

"No. He couldn't have gone if he was. He was Coast Guard Reserves." I still have a plaque from his retirement hanging by my bed at home. Ironic that it had provided a false sense of security that he'd be safe at home from then on.

"So why doesn't the military have answers? They've tried to find him, right?"

I recognize Ty's questions because they echo our own.

"There are fewer sightings now," I say, but don't add that Dad has a marketable skill as a pilot. We can't know for sure, but with those skills, he could be a hot commodity.

"What's that look?" Ty asks.

"Nothing." I glance from him to Mom, then shrug. "It's just someone sent flowers before I left for school, and for a while, I hoped they were from Dad."

Zeph's fingers halt. Mom pales and leans toward me. "Oh, honey. I thought you said they were from a boy?"

Ty frowns, but he clearly recalls the flowers being delivered. I don't want to hurt Mom. And it doesn't make sense. But Dad could've sent them, right?

I lift a shoulder. "Who else could it have been?"

"Daisies?" Kody asks warily.

My breath catches. "Yes. How'd you...?"

He winces. "Did you get the flowers from the co-op?"

Mom frowns. "What?"

"The guys at the co-op asked if it was okay to send her flowers last summer." He glances at me apologetically. "They've all watched her grow up and were so excited for her. I told them she liked daisies."

I wrap my arms around my stomach. "The card wasn't signed. I thought maybe…"

"I'm sorry." Kody scrubs his forehead. "What a mess."

Zeph reaches over to squeeze my shoulder. "You're the youngest. We know this has been hard on you. But we're proud of you, you know. Just like Dad would be."

Mom's eyes are misty above her gentle smile. "You've handled it well, sweetie."

Kody runs a hand through his hair. "That makes me think, though. Keeping Dad's abduction quiet has done no good, as far as we know. Maybe we should stir things up. Maybe media attention would be helpful?" When no one speaks, he adds, "It's just a thought."

"Because we're not giving up," I say.

"No." Zeph shares a look with Kody. "No one is giving up. But realistically, it could be years before we find him. It may not be all neat and tidy just because we'd like it to be."

My eyes sting, but I lift my chin. The day he missed our call, and we knew something was wrong, is seared in my memory. "I'll look for him for the rest of my life."

"We'll look for him," Kody corrects.

Ty twines his fingers through mine and squeezes.

Chapter 44

The next day, it's nearly impossible to hear over the sold-out crowd, even in our team huddle by the dugout. I limp about, consciously baby-ing my cleats, until the second person asks me what's wrong, and I quit. The cleats are fine, I tell myself. They still have what it takes to win a championship.

In the huddle, Abbey rubs her hands together. "This is it."

Sarah grins. "Are we ready?"

We grab each other, whooping and yelling, tightening the circle so forcefully that our heads almost bump. We sway side-to-side, slow at first, then quick and fierce. I clench Lily's jersey with sweat-slicked fists. Mia's fingers dig into my ribcage as she does the same. Our cleats wedge together.

I've always thought it overly dramatic when a group brags about them all bleeding if one was cut. But tucked this close to my teammates, I get it now, this side effect of months of sharing blood, sweat, and tears. It builds a space in the middle of us, a tender place where our hearts beat for each other. It makes me feel invincible. Good luck to anyone on the outside today.

The stadium buzzes with anticipation. From the bleachers, the field looks small but, from down here, it's huge and full of potential. From down here, the perfect seams of white chalk on the red dirt remind me of Coach Bosswood.

Michigan is the home team and takes the field. As Mia gears up to bat, I watch their pitcher warm up. She has great spin and movement, a killer combination, even though she only clocks at sixty-six miles per hour. Her pitches got them to the championship, after all.

I shift toward my teammates. I've seen them at the plate for months—in every circumstance—and learned to trust their skills and instincts. A killer combination of our own that's gotten us to the championship, too. Then I wince as our first three batters strike out.

Zoe goes to work and strikes out three in her turn. After that, the game moves briskly, just not in a straight line. More of a revolving door, with seasoned batters on both teams entering, only to be chewed up and tossed out. There are no messy plays to slow the innings—three up and three down, over and over and over.

But anticipation for that first run tries my patience. By the fourth inning, my fingernails are ragged. Then the Wolverines' second baseman makes an error and Rachel scores.

In the sixth, they tie us. One to one.

That anemic score, one to one, taunts us from the Jumbotron at the beginning of the seventh inning. A whole game has passed with only that single run to show for it. It mocks how hard we've fought through this game, this tournament, this entire year. Then Mia gets on base.

We have two outs when Dawz hits the ball so hard I lose it against the sky before it clears the fence. Mia scores and waits as a triumphant

Dawz rounds the bases. Then we swallow them up and slap their helmets with relief, like we've held our breath since last October and can now breathe.

Three to one. A winning run and a spare. When our third out comes, it's not sad. It's just one step closer to our goal. We're going to win.

Zoe and the defense take the field for the last time.

The idea that started in my tiny apartment has led us to this moment, to this impossible goal. But look at us... three more outs and we'll clench the best gift we could ever give Coach. If he'd only wake up.

But the Wolverines aren't here for their looks. They prove why they've been ranked number one all season and score.

"Harte." Our grad assistant cranes her neck and waves her clipboard toward the practice area. "Warm up."

"Lily?" I turn, but she's already snapping on her equipment. I glance out at Zoe.

Lily catches my look. "She'll know it's just a safeguard, like you would if it were you out there. She's got this."

I nod, but as Lily and I warm up, there's a loud cheer. We reach the fence in time to see the Wolverines' score their tying run. Lily hands me the ball and turns toward the lane again.

"We'll come back," she says. "We're the comeback kids."

"Then it'll be bye-bye-pumpkin-pie to the Wolverines," I say, and she giggles.

When the crowd erupts again, we keep throwing, grimly determined. Then, with cold clarity, we hear Zoe walk a batter. The Wolverines' winning run is on base.

I'm called to the field. As I enter, Zoe hands Coach Bosswood the ball and, head bowed, begins the long walk to the dugout. I know what that feels like. Like carrying the weight of a thousand dreams. Like bleeding beneath see-through skin. But what had been polite applause turns into something more.

Zoe's steps slow at a loud whoop, then another. She looks up in surprise as all over the stadium, fans rise, a great wave of people she's never met personally. Her face flushes as our team files out of the dugout to join in. Zoe catches my eye, though how she sees through the unshed tears is beyond me, and a genuine smile spreads over her face. She tilts her head, as if telling me to go get the Wolverines, and I nod.

The ump leans past Coach Bosswood on the mound so I can hear. "Seventh inning," he reminds me. "Tied three to three. You've got one out, Pitcher, and one runner on base. Okay?" He waits for my nod, then leaves.

Coach Bosswood steps close. "We need two outs, River. You good?"

"Yes." I meet her gaze.

"All right. Let's finish this."

And then, with the winning run already on base, I pitch. The batter watches my fastball for a strike. Fouls my second pitch. Whiffs my third, and she's out.

Abbey gives me a discreet thumbs-up. Two outs. One on base. I catch the throw-around and rub the ball against my thigh as twenty-one prepares to bat.

Behind me, Bree yells, "Two outs, ladies. Stay sharp."

Out of the corner of my eye, I see the Wolverines' first base coach tap his runner's helmet. She lunges out, arms cocked. Twenty-one steps into the box and grounds her cleats. She pops up my rise ball. Sarah calls it and catches it. Third out.

Dawz runs to high five Sarah. I leave the ball on the mound and follow them in, but I can't let down. Mentally, I've got to be ready for an extra inning.

Mia swats my rear as she passes. "Way to go."

In the dugout, Zoe hands me a towel. "Good job holding them."

"Come here." I pull her to the fence. "Tell me everything." While the Wolverines play defense, Zoe points out each player and what I should watch for as I pitch.

We're still tied in the ninth inning. "You okay?" Bosswood asks as I tuck my shirt. The dugout empties around us.

"Great." I check my glove.

"Nine innings." She glances over my shoulder at the lighted stands. "This'll be the game talked about for years."

It seems like a weird thing to say. Then I recall who her family is and turn toward the bleachers across the field. I don't know where her dad is sitting, but I imagine that no matter how this ends today, Coach's family dinners will serve a course of this game forever.

Which reminds me of all the meals I won't share with my own dad. All the discussions we won't have. At least not yet. But I shake it off. I won't dwell there today. These athletes on the field who're counting on me—who need me—deserve my full attention.

And in my hurry to join them, I trip.

My right cleat jams the concrete and my arms cartwheel. Only Coach's quick reflexes saves me from a face plant. I stand up slowly.

Her gaze travels down to my cleat, and I know what she sees. I felt the flap give. Her eyes rise to mine.

"Only you, River." The resignation on her face would've been comical, but there's no time. I have to take the field. "Can you pitch with that?"

I take a tentative step. The flap flops. "Yes."

She shakes her head. "They're done." She surveys the dugout, then squints at me. "What size do you wear?"

"Nine and a half."

She reaches down, pulls off her right turf shoe, black, like mine, but instead of metal cleats, hers has rubber nubs. "Here. Trade me." When I stare, she snaps, "Now, River."

I undo the double knot and slip my cleat off as the home ump gives his chest protector a decisive tug and marches toward our dugout. Her shoe is hot as I tug it on and cinch it tight.

The ump gets closer.

I finish the double knot and grab my glove as he leans into the dugout. The jog to the mound feels as uneven as driving with a flat tire, but I tell myself it doesn't matter. My power comes from pushing off with my right foot. The metal cleat is still on my left where I need it to stick the landing. That's lucky. Right?

It still feels weird.

Then Dawz pauses mid-throw. Her bemused gaze runs down my body to my feet, and her mouth slackens. Superstition is written all over her face when she looks up. It'd be even worse if she knew that my ripped cleat will be the first un-perfect thing Coach has ever worn in a game. Double whammy.

I give her a confident thumbs up. "Magic shoe," I say, just like Kody would've if he were here. "It's good luck."

I wave Abbey off when she starts to run toward me. If this were a marathon instead of a game, we'd be rounding the bend of the last six miles and telling ourselves not to quit. With shoes or without.

The sky is starless above the bright field lights. Tiny bugs flit in the cool air like falling ash. They all disappear when I drop the resin bag and step onto the rubber. In three pitches I've forgotten the shoe.

The first two batters are easy outs. I wipe my cheek against my shoulder as the ump examines his clicker and adjusts his face guard. The Wolverines' catcher twirls her bat and steps up to the plate.

She pulls the bat up. I adjust my grip and pitch.

She hammers the ball, the crack echoing across the stadium. Mia races across centerfield.

The infield shifts as the batter nears first. The ball looks like it's going over, and my stomach drops.

Mia zig-zags back—a game of chicken with the brick-and-mortar behind her.

At the last second, she leaps. Twists in midair, body crashing into the wall, and snatches the ball from the air above.

She lands in a superhero lunge, and the crowd erupts.

Mia runs in, and I wrap her in a bear hug. "That was a monster catch. You're such a beast."

She laughs, cheeks flushed. "I knew I could get it."

Katie switches cleats with me and Coach takes hers back. But I watch Coach walk away, knowing we've forged a special bond. I've walked in her shoe, after all.

But, after all of the excitement, the tenth inning passes with no runs. Then the eleventh. And the twelfth. At thirteen innings, I wonder if the commentators are going hoarse in the media booth. I wonder how long this can go on. I wonder if it's going to be lucky thirteen or unlucky.

Then a stadium official gestures to the home-plate ump and he breaks away. I watch, puzzled and a little punchy from adrenaline. The ump calls time out.

Bree and Callie, batting helmets in their hands, drift toward each other on deck. The fans slowly shift their focus to the ump and the growing commotion behind one of the cameramen. We tentatively trickle out of the dugout to see what's going on. The Wolverines do the same. Both coaches approach the home ump, obviously calculating whether this interruption will benefit the other team.

The crowd murmurs uneasily when the ESPN reporter, who's been on and off the field with a microphone all evening, hurries out.

She's crying.

Dismay ripples through the bleachers. When the president of Northbridge University, who'd been in the crowd, follows her onto the field, my heart drops. The reporter hands him a microphone, and he clears his throat. The stadium becomes eerily quiet.

"I." He stops and tilts the mic away. He blinks rapidly, eyes lifted toward heaven, before his chest rises with a deep breath, and his jaw muscles twitch.

Instinctively, we bunch together, holding hands to combine our strength.

Finally, he lifts the mic again. "I've just received a phone call."

Chapter 45

"Coach O'Daniel is awake."

His words echo through the speakers and drop on the silent stadium. I feel the deep thud of them, then my eyes fill with tears. A roar like I've never heard thunders through the stadium. We reach for each other, like prisoners released from a firing squad. My arms are around Lily and Abbey as the exuberance becomes too much, and we're jumping and laughing and crying.

It takes forever to get back to the game.

The officials finally regain control and remind us where we are. Although we're still at the top of the thirteenth inning, to us, it's a new day. A fresh game. A bluer night sky.

Bree hits a double. Callie tries so hard to kill it that she strikes out, but Kim strides to the batter's box, and electricity snaps with her every move. Behind her, Mia adjusts her batting glove and picks up her helmet to head to the on-deck circle.

Coach Bosswood calls time.

"Andy's batting," she announces. And while her death-stroke still falls over Mia, she walks out to tell the ump.

The blow takes my breath. Mia's hand pauses in midair. She's our sure-thing, our best on-base percentage slapper, our sweet Mia.

Andy is a freshman.

Our dugout falls silent. Andy's a championship playoff novice. She's brought her big bat out five times this year. Okay, two of those were home runs, but if Kim gets on base and moves Bree to third, we'll have runners at the corners when it's Andy's turn. That's a game changer. Would Coach O'Daniel make this call if he were here?

The girls give Mia a wide berth, too confused to know what to say, and too tough to whine. It's not that we don't like Andy, but can she handle the pressure?

And in that solitary space, Mia looks at the helmet she'd started to put on, and her face pales. Past the dugout gate, she watches Coach talk to the ump. A hand touches my arm, and I turn. Andy.

In slow motion, I look back at Mia. Sweat glistens on her forehead and grass stains her knees. She's a senior in the biggest game of her life, holding her batting helmet for the last time. She's got to be heartbroken. Then she turns, and whatever was going through her mind shifts. Dropping her helmet, she wraps her arms around Andy.

"I'm sorry, Mia." Andy's voice is strained.

"No. Cut it out." Mia leans back and grips Andy's arms, pinning her with a confident gaze. "It's all you, girl. Keep your head in there and swing. You've got this."

Andy studies Mia, sees the conviction there, and her face relaxes. Her constant anxiety of the past months slips away. This moment is what all the waiting and work has been for, after all—her first big-event appearance.

"All right." Andy takes the helmet Mia hands her with steady hands. Her ribbon bounces as she marches up the steps.

I pull Mia up to the fence. "You freaking hero."

"Hope is launching yourself toward failure and missing. That's what we've been doing. It doesn't matter which one of us is jumping," she says softly.

For a second, she rests her head against my shoulder, then she straightens. The rest of the team folds around her, and someone starts a cheer. Mia's pressed so tightly to my side that I feel her deep, indrawn breath. It takes all my strength not to chew my nails as Andy warms up.

Katie and Emma urge the fans into a frenzy. Little girls in jerseys sit tall in their seats with their gloves like I used to, ready to catch a foul ball if someone will just hit one to them. All around, fans lean to see better.

Kim knocks the ball over the shortstop's head and makes it to first, moving Bree to third. The catcher jogs out to talk to the pitcher.

"What're they saying?" Lily asks.

"Probably not the same things you say." I smile.

The catcher returns home. Andy takes a final practice swing, nods at the signs from Bosswood, adjusts her helmet, flips her ponytail, and steps into the box. Our dugout is a mass of blue jerseys and up-side-down visors. Then Andy fouls her first pitch.

Young girls crane their necks to watch the ball's path with envy. Mia cups her mouth and yells encouragement.

Andy fouls the next pitch and the next. Hope fills my chest.

A wild pitch hits the plate.

"What's the count?" Emma asks.

I don't look at the JumboTron. "One ball, two strikes."

Andy pulls up her bat again. Mia mutters something, then pushes off the fence. She strides through the rest of the team and jogs up the steps until nothing stands between her and Andy.

Bosswood folds her arms at third base. Coach CJ adjusts his hat beside first, then leans to say something to Kim. She nods and lunges, ready to run.

I can't hear my heartbeat above the noise in the stadium, but it pounds against my ribs. The pitcher snaps the ball...

Time slows.

Andy uncoils. Drives through the ball. Mouth twisting to the side as she connects.

Then she drops her bat... and runs.

Kim pauses halfway to second to see if the ball is caught in left field, but it climbs higher and higher.

At third, Bree points one foot home, impatient to go as soon as it's safe. Someone elbows my ribs.

Mia's bent, analyzing the trajectory like the center fielder that she is. Suddenly, she explodes, punching the air.

And Andy's ball clears the fence.

The stadium goes wild. It vibrates with feet-stomping, hand-clapping triumph.

Bree and Kim cross home and turn to wait. Coach Bosswood's grin is blinding as she waves Andy past third. Andy opens her arms, bright as pure sunshine, and races home. She tags the base, then disappears into our jubilant embrace.

Pancaked in the middle, Mia wraps Andy in a hug and lifts her off the ground.

I close my eyes, a sob catching in my throat. Andy almost quit this year. If she had, she'd never have had this moment. This triumph. She'd never have pulled out of the ashes.

By the time we finish celebrating, the scoreboard shows six runs to three. We're not finished, though. Michigan is home team. They'll bat last. We need more runs.

The pitcher is stoic as she faces Sarah, but I know what she's feeling. How she's reeling. She wants to come through for her team. Instead, she walks Sarah.

The fans cheer, but the Wolverines' coach calls time and brings in a new pitcher with fresh energy. Bosswood waits with Rachel, watching the pitcher warm up.

Then Rachel steps in and hits the first pitch.

The shortstop scoops the ball, tags second—forcing Sarah out—and leaps, firing to first.

It's so... it's so quick. A double play.

Rachel's out.

I can't quite believe we're done until their defense clears the field.

Then I grab my glove and swear to myself this ends now. No more innings. No more fear.

Chapter 46

Game 60. Two outs. No one on base.

Number twenty-seven swings her bat in short, sharp arcs that thump her back, as if visualizing how she'll smash whatever I send her.

"Come on," I beg under my breath.

But in a move that's all too familiar, she holds up a hand, and her coach calls time. The girl on deck lowers her bat and glowers at me, but she's not my problem yet.

The coach whips white tape around two of twenty-seven's fingers as a breeze lifts the loose hairs from my face.

Abby jogs to my side. "Doing good, girl."

"You too." I tuck the softball in my glove as other infielders join us on the mound. Bosswood looks deceptively calm on the sidelines, but... I'd seen her rattled earlier. Family or not, this game is personal.

"Does twenty-seven have broken fingers? Look at the way he's taping them," Sarah says.

I snort. "You tell us. You've probably played with broken fingers and broken toes, haven't you?"

She shrugs with a smug smile. "And your point is?"

"Point one, she leaves her bat open." Bree leans past me to Dawz. "Be ready. She might pull a grounder."

They talk each other up, knowing just what to say after all this time.

"She'll be looking for a ripe pitch." Dawz swats my rear. "Just send her your junk. We've got you covered."

"I bet Coach O'Daniel is listening," Abbey says, and we all sober, shifting our feet. "Even with a comeback team like Michigan, he'd put his money on us."

"Yeah." Sarah smiles. "Maybe he'll think we ran this out to thirteen innings just to give him time to wake up and catch the end. Let's make it worth the wait."

The batter grabs her bat, and Sarah steps closer. "This is our game. We've got this as long as we're together. Go North!" She breaks the huddle.

Abbey pauses and covers her mouth with her glove. "Let's have fun, Riv."

"Absolutely." I tap her glove. She grins and jogs home as I smooth the pitching lane like always, the small ruts gritty under my cleat.

I pause to look up at the dark sky. "I've got this, Coach," I say quietly.

I glance at the place where I'd sat with Dad all those years ago, filled now with a young team in matching jerseys. I don't know the day or year I'll see my dad again, but what he taught me, I can't lose. That part of him is always with me. I think he'd be happy about that.

And it'd be nice to know where Coach O'Daniel had been seated last year before changing my world, but me? I'm back here, where I'm meant to be.

My dugout is unruly, clapping and yelling, and the crowd is a chaos of cheers. Music vibrates in my bones. I take a lung full of air tinged with grass and sweat that always reminds me of softball. And hope—my old friend—stirs in my chest.

Sarah swipes her foot across the dirt at first, then nods at me.

Dawz, a "make my day" look on her face, pulls her glove on and punches the palm, ready as she always is.

Bree waves her index and pinkie fingers at the outfield for the two outs, then turns and grins.

Callie yells, "It's all you, Seven. You've got this!"

Abbey gives me a thumbs up.

Then twenty-seven steps up to the plate, and I take a deep breath and pitch.

It smacks Abbey's glove. Strike one.

The batter swings at a fastball inside for strike two. An 0-2 count. Just like a million other times, no balls and two strikes. Except elation rises and lashes through my body. *Too soon.* The game isn't over. I struggle to tamp it down and stay in control. My hand trembles.

Abbey asks for a change-up.

Twenty-seven drops her bat head and waits for the ball. It's low and off the plate, but she reaches across and pulls through, sending it bouncing over the infielders.

"Move, girl," I breathe as Rachel reacts from the outfield. "Come on. You've got this..."

She barrels in from the right, eyes glued to the ball.

Twenty-seven sprints for first.

Rachel closes in and dives, glove outstretched. She slams into the ground. Her chin bounces off the turf, but she never loses focus. She traps the ball in her glove, and in one move, slides up into a lunge and side-arms it to Sarah.

Twenty-seven is nearly to first. My shoulders hike up, my hands rise, my whole body one unending inhale even as I move to back up the throw.

Sarah drops into the splits and snags the ball out of the air.

Twenty-seven pounds through the bag.

And the ump, in the most important play of the game... closes his fist. She's out.

In the roar that follows, twenty-seven slips off her helmet and trudges to the dugout.

Sarah jumps up and keeps jumping. Our teammates burst onto the field. The trainer and manager hug by the benches.

But with a heavy sob, my bones dissolve. It's been too hard. Too much pressure. And my body has had enough, like ice in a frying pan. One minute I'm solid, and the next I'm a syrup of silver heat.

Abbey scoops me up and holds every oozing part of me. We trip when she jumps because I have nothing left to hold me up, but I don't feel the dirt when I land on my back. There's navy sky over her shoulder, and I think I pat her arm. She tenses as the first girls fall on us. Her breath huffs. But I'm lucky. I don't feel the weight of twenty-two girls piled on, and I don't have to get up for a very long time.

Looking down at me from inches away, Andy's eyes grow big, her smile white in her red face. "Gatorade bath!" she wheezes.

Chapter 47

Ever wonder what twenty-three girls sound like when they're trying to be quiet in a hospital? A rockslide, uphill—feet thundering up the stairs punctuated by giggles and gasps as, unsurprisingly, it becomes a race. Wind through trees—heavy breathing as dry-fit-covered shoulders jostle through the narrow third-floor stairwell door. White water in rapids—forty-six sliding feet on the linoleum.

Every head at the nurses' desk turns as we shuffle down the hall. They return our variations of hello and hi, smiles, and more than a few waves.

Coach Bosswood slants her head out of Coach O'Daniel's door—his new normal, not-ICU door that he's had for three days—and rolls her eyes.

"You heard us?" Rachel asks.

"We were trying to be quiet," Emma stage-whispers.

"Who's out there?" a man across the hall asks, leaning over to see. "Sounds like an invasion."

Above the renewed snickers and whispers, Mrs. O'Daniel calls from the room, "Tell them to come in."

Suddenly, my heart thumps in my ears, and it's not from running stairs.

We bottleneck at the entrance, and by the time I get inside, the only space remaining is just left of the doorjamb. I have to lean to the side to catch a glimpse of Coach reclining in bed. His blue eyes touch each of us, linger for a moment, acknowledge, then move to the next girl. You could hear a pin drop.

Mia and Sarah squeeze through, carrying the large trophy between them.

"This is for you, Coach," Sarah says.

He lifts his hand. My eyes water as Mrs. O'Daniel reaches out to guide his fingers to the trophy, letting them rest there. He sighs, and his eyes crinkle at the corners, but I don't know if he can see through his curtain of tears.

I helped put this look on his face.

All the rewards I could ever want for this year are in this room. Zoe clutches my elbow. Lily sniffs. Rachel puts her arm around Dawz's shaking shoulders.

Coach Bosswood clears her throat and wipes her cheek. "Anything else you'd like them to do, Coach?" She smiles at his upturned face. "They're kind of on a roll."

We giggle and shift. Coach's laugh is rusty and breathy. Mrs. O'Daniel kisses the top of his head, lingering there before leaning back and smiling down into his face.

Emma raises her hand. "I volunteer to push your wheelchair around the hospital."

Those closest turn on her with hushed protests.

Bosswood narrows her eyes, and you can tell she still remembers the Gatorade bath.

"Personally," Mrs. O'Daniel says, and all movement stops. She keeps her hand over Coach's. "I think with all of you around to encourage him, it will be no time before he's up and around, talking up a storm and telling all of us what to do again."

At that, Coach's mustache spreads like bird wings over his smile.

Chapter 48

I swear that, since I've been home, the sun is brighter and the air fresher. In the evening, farm noises lull me into the deepest sleep with my stomach full of Mom's cooking.

My welcome home party on Saturday, Jaiden and little Claire, bring their smiles as gifts. We talk for hours as we roll a ball back and forth across the grass and tickle Claire's pudgy pink feet with dandelions.

Like magic, when his princess rubs her eyes, Scotty drives up in his not-so-new car. Jaiden's face shines when she kisses him, and I cover little Claire's eyes, making them both laugh. Scotty's smile lingers as he secures the baby in her car seat. I'm a puddle of hearts by the time he backs out.

"Are you ready?" Jaiden asks, still watching his retreating car.

"You're going to have to get a new glove."

She snorts and pulls my arm toward the barn. "You still have something to prove?"

I almost say yes, out of habit. But do I?

I must take too long to answer because Jaiden stiffens with an uncertain smile. "I was joking."

The year apart hangs between us, uneven and a little treacherous. "I know, but it's a good question. I don't think I do."

"Of course you don't," she says, letting go of me. "You were your own worst critic. Everyone could see you were driven, but only a few of us knew it was because of insecurity rather than ego."

"Jaiden." I gape at her. "I wasn't insecure."

She waves that away. "No one blamed you. You were just so young when your dad left."

I shrug impatiently and return to the original question. "I still want to play softball, and it's still important, but I'm not playing to impress Dad like I was."

We reach Jaiden's bag. She unzips it and pulls out her catching gear.

I grab my glove and a bucket of balls... and pause, cocking my head to the side. "Do you feel you've got something to prove?"

She glances up, then finishes snapping her chest protector. "Because of Claire?"

"And because of sitting out a year."

She gives the protector a good tug and bends to get her glove. "I don't think of it like that. It's more that I can't fail. One piece leads to another, you know? Softball pays for school because Scotty and I can't afford it otherwise without taking out loans. And the sooner I get an education, the sooner I can start working and contribute to the family."

"You sound like Ty." I pick up her helmet and hold it out.

We're throwing the ball and working out the kinks when the mailperson's car slows at our mailbox, then speeds up again.

"Speaking of Ty." Jaiden raises her brows, that old knowing look back. "What's the deal? Are you trying a long-distance relationship?"

"Shhh," I hiss. "If my brothers find out, I'll never hear the end."

"Hear the end of what?" She cocks her head and throws the ball. "Say it, River."

"What? Why?"

Her glance over my shoulder warns me.

"Because," Kody's deep voice answers, "I need to get gas if I'm going to run over to Northbridge for a little chit-chat."

I spin to face him. Brothers can push a high school sister around, but not a college sophomore. I rip my glove off and stalk toward him.

He raises his palms with a smile. "Just kidding, big shot." Then his humor dims, and his eye twitches. "I have something to tell you."

"What?" I frown.

Instead of words, Kody hands me a key chain with two rings, but only one key. The green metal four-leaf clover is cool in my hand, and I tilt it to see my name engraved through the middle. First a lucky bat. Then a lucky hat. Now a lucky key chain?

Before I can ask about it, Mom calls my name. Her normally composed voice is high and urgent, and Kody and I take off running. The sun blinds me at the edge of the barn, then I see her wave a white envelope in the air and slow to a walk. It can't be too bad if it's just mail.

Zeph appears from the garden. "What's wrong?"

"This is so great," Mom actually squeals. "Here, honey. You got a letter."

Kody and I share a look of relief as she practically shoves the envelope into my hand. But when I turn it over, I almost drop it. There's a red, white, and blue USA softball emblem. My heart races as I tear it open and read a few lines.

"It's about the Junior Women's National team." My voice trails off.

Mom tugs the paper from my limp fingers and skims it. "They're having open tryouts from which they invite a few athletes to try out for a spot in the Selection Camp. Those athletes then compete for one of the seventeen spots on the national roster."

"The Olympic roster? That's amazing, Riv." Kody clamps a hand on my shoulder and shakes it enthusiastically. But I catch the look between my brothers and Mom.

I recognize that look, and my smile dies. I've seen it too often.

"But?" I bite my lip when he can't hold my gaze.

He pulls his hand away and rubs his neck. Zeph and Mom fidget, so I know Kody was supposed to have told me already. He's not usually my reticent brother.

"No 'but.'" He shakes his head. "This is a dream come true for you." He swallows. "It's just... I've got news, too." He braces himself anxiously. "I have a job offer in Texas."

As that sinks in, I'm surprised at the pain. At how blindsided I feel. How could he leave? Forget about Dad? Abandon our plans. Abandon me.

I pivot, my instinct to run, run, run... then I see Jaiden.

She stands by the barn with sympathy-filled eyes. Her shin and chest protectors are a dull black in the sun, but she opens her arms a little like she's offering me a hug. No judgment—I can do whatever I feel I have to.

I freeze. For the first time, I face the emotions, let them swamp over me, and try not to get washed away. My heart rate slows, and I swallow. I turn back to Kody.

"I'm—" I clear my throat. "I'm happy for you."

Relief fills his face. Mom has tears in her eyes as he wraps me in a hug.

"Thanks, Li'l River." He protectively cups the top of my head while he holds me close. "And I'm super proud of you, too."

I lean into his hug. When Kody releases me, I notice how pale Zeph is behind his smile. It breaks my heart that I've been so self-absorbed that I didn't see how tired my brothers were. They've searched for Dad, run the farm, and taken care of me for years. Some sister I am.

"You guys deserve to get on with your lives," I say. "It's about time that I do the hunting for Dad."

All three gasp and start protesting. Mom waves her hand impatiently and pushes aside my brothers. She winds her fingers through mine.

"Is that what you thought?" she asks. "That if any of us left or moved on, it meant we gave up on Dad? Silly girl. We're all in this for the long haul. Together."

Kody reaches down and pulls the forgotten key chain from my clenched fist. He holds up the little key, pinched between thumb and finger. "This is your new key for our map room. You get to help plan the next trip." He circles it around, indicating everyone. "But we're all going." Then he singles out the empty keyring with his other hand. "And this is for the key to my new place in Texas. Come any time."

A slow smile warms my face. I guess I could use a magic key chain after all.

Author's Note

I was a softball mom for a lot of years before I became a writer. It's a world all its own. It moves at a different speed, has its own language, and its own gravity. The community shares a love of the game and of the girls who play, and they share sacrifices (time, money, sleep, comfort—take your pick—and why is it always windier on a softball field?)

I started this book as a new empty nester while attending all of my daughter's college softball games. But the idea came from someone in my writing club. The friend told me to write a softball story, and she'd read it. That was 2013.

This book has been my hard-knocks education. I wrote in hotels, beside chlorine-fumed pools, and in the car. It would've been disheartening to know it wouldn't be published until years later, but not surprising that I'd make every mistake possible on the way. It forced me to grow, and I didn't give up. I love this book for that.

The title was originally *Signs*. I thought it was clever since every team has a secret language and, at the same time, we humans always watch for signs that we're on the right path. But the soul of this book came after I observed how often we show interest in the athlete and the sport, but overlook the young person behind the jersey.

The softball players I knew were dedicated athletes, but they were also complicated humans, dealing with many areas of life at the same time. The mental toughness it took to focus on the game, no matter what else was going on, amazed me. So, I wrote about it. I hope it does them justice.

Thank you for reading this book. I appreciate your time. If you're interested, it'd mean a lot if you would leave a review online, then let me know. I'd love to see what you thought.

Acknowledgments

I'd like to thank the people who supported and encouraged me while I wrote this book.

To my critique groups, thank you for reading and re-reading this manuscript three pages at a time. It is finished! But, without your encouragement, I never would've gotten here.

Thank you to editor and writing mentor William Bernhardt, editor Alicia Dean, and developmental editor Jennifer Rees, who made the book so much better, and to the many more who looked at early drafts and told me to study story structure.

To the artists: Thank you first of all to photographer Ali Kirtley for the amazing headshots and your skill of expertly drawing out the best shots while making the process so fun! To my professional cover designer and formatter, Annemieke Beemster Leverenz, you captured all the emotion, and you did it with such enthusiasm and skill—thank you. I love this cover. And to photographer Dawn Muncy, who still had senior picture archives of my daughter in her uniform, thank you for taking us out and creating just the right photo for the cover. It couldn't be better. We did it!

And to all those who had my back on this journey—from my writing club to everyone at Gym, you've been so encouraging! To my family, family-in-law, and friends, you made me feel like I was doing something special. Thank you for keeping me going.

My husband—favorite coach and fountain of information—you didn't laugh *too* much that time I tried to play softball, but you did brainstorm softball plays and situations when I needed it. Thank you for putting up with the quiet days when I was lost in my story.

Thanks to my baseball catcher son, who once pointed to where he would hit the ball, then negotiated a night of movies with his friends if he was successful. You gave me a lot of inspiration and always make life full and interesting.

But, my softball pitcher daughter, I wouldn't have written this if not for you, with your ribbons and blisters, hours of practice, your joy, and even your tears. Your passion for life and bubbly way of living opened this whole world for me. Thank you for letting me share it.

Finally, to my Heavenly Father, thank you for working this out in your own way.

Just for you, Reader ...

Dawz burst out laughing and gestured to the computer screen. "Just for you, Reader? Who are you? Dear Abby?" Her grin grew at Rachel's glare.

"It's called being polite," Rachel said tightly, but deleted the words with staccato stabs of her finger. "Trying." Stab. "To." Stab. "Help Paula." Stab. Stab.

"I get it." Dawz raised her hand. "I'm with you, even if she did make us run triangles, over and over."

Rachel rolled her eyes. "She also let you keep your lucky socks. I wouldn't have given in so easily."

"Liar." Dawz shoved her arm. "We were on a streak."

The door opened and Lily appeared, taking in both guilty faces and the computer between them. She stepped into the room. "Does River know you're using her computer?"

"Not so loud, Lily," Dawz whisper shouted. "We're almost done."

Lily eyed the empty screen suspiciously. "What are you almost done with?"

Rachel's fingers hovered over the keyboard. "Paula needs help." She glanced over her shoulder. "She doesn't know how to ask if the readers would leave a review."

"Seriously?" Lily shut the door and moved behind Rachel. "Why not say, '*We'd love to know what you thought, leave a review here.*' Then have a clickable link."

Dawz threw up her hands. "Can we say please? I mean, how rude."

Lily's face flushed ominously. "Say please, then. But honestly, if the readers get this far, they've finished the book. They just don't know how much it helps to have reviews."

Rachel began typing. "And who wouldn't like us? Hmmm? We're all so nice. So interesting. Everyone probably wishes they were on our team."

Lily and Dawz leaned closer, reading over Rachel's shoulder.

You, leave a review. And, you, leave a review. And, you, leave a review... Please.

Lily and Dawz shared a look, then shrugged. Rachel always did have a way of saying things.

www.ingramcontent.com/pod-product-compliance
Lightning Source LLC
Chambersburg PA
CBHW070604300726
48975CB00006B/1706